CURSE OF THE BASTARDS

BRIAN KEENE
STEVEN L. SHREWSBURY

TPB ISBN 978-1-955765-03-9

Adobe PDF 978-1-955765-04-6

EPUB 978-1-955765-05-3

Cover art © Matt Forsyth.

Jacket design by Justin Stewart.

Published by Apex Publications, LLC, PO Box 24773, Lexington, KY 40523

Visit us at www.apexbookcompany.com.

For Steven's mother
Esther Elizabeth Shrewsbury
Who died as she lived ...
A warrior

THE SAGA OF ROGAN, OR, WHAT HAS GONE BEFORE

From the Book of the Yidde-oni

Rogan, born in a savage age before the great flood, was sliced from his mother's belly by his father, Jarek. Raised into barbarism among the fabled Keltos folk in the Caucaus Mountains, Rogan accepted violence as a simple way of life.

Roaming the lands north of the Black Sea, Rogan grew strong among his rugged kin. He soon wearied of a life disrupting the obsidian trade from the east, and raiding the great cities of Chanoch, Urak, and Jericho. So, Rogan journeyed west, crossing the land bridge at Bosporus.

Eventually, he became a mercenary for King Akhensobek, ruler of Kemet. Rogan led the king's armies until a tryst with the royal daughter aroused Akhensobek's ire. As punishment, Rogan was walled up alive inside the great idol of the reclining cat god, Bastet. After a miraculous escape, Rogan slew the king and his 150 children and returned to the primal kingdoms of the north.

Cutting a bloody swath through the lesser realms of Lascaux, Agudea, and Gordes, Rogan became a leader in the revolutionary forces of General Thyssen in Albion. The two men became great friends and comrades at arms. Thyssen wished to oust Silex, the cruel ruler of the realm of Albion. The revolution ended when Rogan seized the crown from Silex's decapitated head and placed it on his own.

Rogan's rule of Albion ran stern but fair. Thyssen was given command of Albion's military might. Border clashes with native Prytens and their savage Queen Tancorix kept them busy for decades. Rogan wed Thyssen's sister, Desna, and sired an heir, Rohain. Several more children followed, and Rogan came to know contentment, however fleetingly. After the death of Queen Desna in childbirth, however, he grew weary of palace life and abdicated his throne to Rohain.

Accompanied by his nephew Javan, the youngest son of General Thyssen, and his bodyguards, Rogan journeyed across the western ocean, discovering fabled lands and great cultures far to the south in the new world, beyond the edges of scholar's maps. There, Rogan set about adventuring again with the aid of fresh friends from the mysterious realm of Olmek-Tikal.

Attacked on the sea by raiders from his former kingdom, Rogan fights with Karza—a warrior who claims to be his son. Karza tells Rogan that his brother Karac, supposedly another of Rogan's bastard sons, has toppled Rohain from the throne of Albion. Rogan kills Karza, with some assistance from Javan. In the great ensuing fight, wrought with monsters and the magic of Damballah, only Rogan and Javan survive, shipwrecked. They are soon befriended by the Kennebeck folk, natives of the land, and their shaman, Akibeel. Javan becomes romantically involved with a young warrior named Zenata.

To return to his kingdom, Rogan agrees to help Akibeel, whose folk are threatened by a dire time-traveling wizard on a mountain, who brings forth a member of the Thirteen, Meeble, to that reality. While Javan and the Kennebeck battle the monsters and minions of the wizard, Rogan engages Meeble in hand-to-hand combat, successfully pushing him through a portal and back into the Labyrinth.

When Captain Xuxan, an old friend from Olmek-Tikal, finds

them, Rogan—now joined by Akibeel and his Kennebeck warriors —vows to go back to his overturned kingdom and spill light and blood on the shadows that grip it. The despotic tyrant Karac rules with an iron fist, aided and abetted by two powerful wizards, Papa Bon Deux and Maman Ezili, both of whom serve the dark god Damballah. All seems lost.

Rogan and his band are forced to ally with old enemies, including Andraste, Queen of the Prytens, who claims to be his illegitimate daughter. Together, they raise an army and bring forth a great war with the use of neighboring lands. They battle a demonic monstrosity called the Helvectia—a creature summoned by Papa Bon Deux and Maman Ezili. Eventually, they turn the tide, defeating Karac and turning his wizard's magick back on them, successfully routing the invaders. But it is a bitter victory, and most of Rogan's loved ones are killed, including Rohain, whose body is revealed to be possessed by Karza's vengeful spirit.

In the end, Rogan turns the crown over to his old friend Thyssen and leaves the kingdom in the hands of his youngest daughter, Algeniz, and her devoted companion Jasper-thal. Then, Rogan, Javan, and their surviving crew depart back to the ocean, intent on never returning.

As the months go by, they cross the world and the group splinters, returning to their own homelands. Rogan and Javan find themselves back near the Caucaus Mountains. The two make money by leading a ruthless company of mercenaries. Contracted to help in a battle against the forces near the great city-state of Nodd, Rogan, Javan, and their group arrived too late for the fight ... and Rogan seemingly encounters a ghost from the past.

When wasteful war shall statues overturn,
    And broils root out the work of masonry,
    Nor Mars his sword nor wars quick fire shall burn
    The living record of your memory.

— SHAKESPEARE, SONNET LV

CHAPTER 1

I AIN'T SUPERSTITIOUS

Twelve-year-old Rogan stood at the top of a valley, surrounded by the rest of the barbarian hordes, watching as far below soldiers prepared to rip the wings off a thrashing fallen angel.

One of his fellow tribe members grunted, "How the hell can they do that?"

"The angels are shapeshifters," Ivor, the Oracle of Wodan, answered. "This one is wearing human flesh, and thus, it is vulnerable. Otherwise, those soldiers would be decimated."

"It must have stolen the flesh of a giant, then. He's a big fucker."

Though Rogan didn't comment, he snorted in agreement. The fallen angel probably stood ten feet tall, but it wasn't so fearsome bleeding on the valley floor, its left leg sliced off at the knee by two soldiers from the axe corps of the opposing army, its long wings roped to the bridles of mammoths, an arrow lodged in its left eye, and two spears stuck into its groin. When the ropes went tight, the angel's right wing tore loose, popping out of its back by the roots. The mammoth on that side stomped down on the appendage. Slowly, the mammoth on the left began to drag the being away. The dying angel howled, leaving a trail of black blood in its wake. The soldiers in the valley laughed and cheered.

"Which fallen one is that?" Rogan asked quietly.

The Oracle of Wodan cleared his throat. "They say it is Samual, but demons lie."

"That so, Ivor?" Rogan's father, Jarek, laughed. "Men lie, too. Especially when they've been caught screwing the wrong person."

Ivor gestured over to the right side of the valley where the mammoth trudged on with the detached wing. Floating above it was a figure bearing the overall shape of a man but sporting scales, plates, fins, and many reptilian qualities. "Angels screw the wrong things, too, Jarek. You see Pergamus hanging in the air over there? He didn't screw any women, just the saurian beasts of the field. That is why we have such things as that to deal with."

Ivor then pointed to their left. All heads followed along. From over the valley's far ridge arose a large beast, reddish in the sunlight. It flapped its massive, leathery wings and roared.

One of the youths near Rogan screamed and then was whacked on his hindquarters by his father with the pommel of a spear.

"Damn things." Ivor sighed, gazing down at the army in the valley. "Now we shall see how good their magick works."

Rogan felt a hand slap the back of his head.

"Breathe, boy," Jarek grunted.

Rogan hadn't realized that he'd been holding his breath. No matter how much his father beat toughness into him, the natural reaction to seeing a dragon couldn't be stopped. In this case, he felt his bladder near to bursting but hated to ponder what the punishment would be if he pissed on the leg of the Oracle of Wodan.

"Jarek," Ivor said, "see the priests down there?"

"I see them." Rogan's father nodded. His long tresses of auburn hair fluttered in the wind. "Would that they were all dead."

"See what they do?"

"Waving their hands about and chanting. Isn't that what priests always do?"

"Other than not get laid?" another barbarian chimed in.

Undeterred by the horde's laughter, Ivor said, "See what they draw out to send at the dragon?"

The broken body of the fallen angel Samual ceased leaking black blood and began to emit something else. Mist rose out of the wounds like long ethereal eels. As the barbarians watched, the mist formed into humanoid shapes. The soldiers in the valley, while visibly awed, held their ground. The dragon hovered as if confused by these new arrivals.

"What are they?" Jarek asked.

Ivor folded his arms. "The escaping souls of all the flesh the angel used to walk around on earth."

"People?" Jarek gripped the hilt of his sheathed sword.

"Yes. And a lot of them, given the size of that cage of flesh the demon wrapped itself in."

Rogan frowned. "But the souls don't fight. They just confuse the dragon."

Ivor smiled. "Sometimes, young Rogan, that is enough."

The soldiers in the valley made good use of the delay and shot several projectiles from bows at the dragon. These were not arrows or bolts, and not meant to pierce the creature's hide but to wrap it. Within seconds, the beast sported eight lines of heavy rope that tumbled down to the earth. Soldiers rushed forth and quickly secured the lines to mammoths and horses. The dragon bucked and sent a few men aloft. One of the horses went airborne as well. The dragon twisted about, long neck extending, and bit the animal's head off.

Rogan realized that he was holding his breath again. He let it out before his father noticed.

The mammoths trumpeted and turned, urged on by their taskmasters. The dragon was jerked out of the sky and crashed to the ground. As it struggled to rise, one of the mammoths galloped away, torquing the rope around the dragon's left wing. The rope snapped off, but the wing twisted, folding in the middle, ruined. Like an army of ants, the soldiers in the valley ran forward and stabbed their lances into the beast's limp wing. Soon they had the monster pinned.

Jarek shook his head. "They are dead men."

Though it looked that way to Rogan as well, the taskmasters of the mammoths turned their great beasts and they thundered onward, stomping onto and into the dragon. The monster sank its slavering jaws into the leg of one of the hairy elephants, but the massive tonnage of the other mammoths pulped it, reducing the dragon to a wet, red carcass that steamed in the sunlight.

The barbarians around Rogan broke into applause.

Ivor grinned. "One would think they've done that before, aye?"

"Look there." Jarek pointed at the floating Pergamus. "They've pissed off that dragon's daddy."

The devil in the sky glowed orange. Rogan's hands shook, tightening his grip around his lance and sword pommel for comfort. He looked away from the angel and searched the sky. Rogan didn't see their god, Wodan. He didn't count on it, either.

Ivor eyed Rogan. "Are you about to pray, boy?"

Rogan nodded. "To the All Father, Wodan."

"The All Father doesn't care for words. What are the words of a trembling cunt on the wind to him? You would do well to remember that, Rogan."

"We just stopped to see what happened, Ivor," Jarek reminded him. "The guides were off due to bad dreams. We should move on. That well-formed army down there and their priests? None of our affair."

Nostrils flaring, eyes now aimed up at Pergamus, Ivor replied, "I wonder."

"What?" Jarek cracked his knuckles. "We need to get the tribe back on the route home."

Ivor frowned as the halo of orange light about Pergamus grew brighter still. "Damn, we are not here by accident."

"What do you mean?"

The glow left Pergamus and floated toward the barbarian horde like a fast-moving cloud. As it settled on them, all talk ceased. They stiffened, spasming, and their eyes rolled white. Then, they became of one mind and knew their purpose. Like puppets on strings, all of Rogan's tribesmen, his father, and their wizard charged into the valley with weapons drawn and smashed into the surprised soldiers.

Then came the blood. And the screams.

ROGAN SHOOK HIS HEAD, BLINKING. HIS HAIR, ONCE AUBURN like Jarek's, was now white and gray. That twelve-year-old version of him who had once fought here was just a ghost—a phantom of the past. So were his father, Ivor, and the rest of his kindred. And though today there were hundreds of mercenaries and warriors present in the valley, none of them were his tribesmen.

And yet, it occurred to him, he still had kin.

Lowering his spyglass, he glanced at his nephew, Javan. The youth—a keen archer if somewhat sharp of tongue—crouched beside him. Javan squinted in the sunlight, peering down into the valley, watching men burning at the stake while soldiers killed other soldiers.

He turned to Rogan. "Sire, have you been here before?"

"Yeah, long ago."

"Has it changed much?"

Trembling, Rogan checked the skies. No demons, no dragons. No Wodan, either.

"Not a lot really." He stretched. "The ground is still covered in blood."

"Forgive me, Uncle, but ..."

"Spit it out, boy."

Javan raised an eyebrow. "You seem ... uneasy."

"Oh? And what clued you in on that?"

"Well, for one thing, your hands are shaking. Your hands never shake."

Scowling, Rogan raised the spyglass back to his eye, tightening his grip around the viewer.

"Are you filled with trepidation at this location, sire?"

"Not especially. I just fought here before, as a kid, younger than you."

"That must be some tale."

Rogan changed the subject. "The ropes on that wizard burning at the stake just gave out. Looks like he's stepping off the wood-pile. Business is about to pick up down there."

"He still lives?"

Rogan shrugged. "For now. I reckon he's pretty well fucked, though. He's surrounded."

The battlefield stretched for nearly a square mile, and the valley's basin was littered with the dead and dying. Rogan and his troops were positioned on a ridge at the northern tip of the valley, which provided cover. They had hung back behind Rogan and Javan, but overhearing Rogan's comment regarding the wizard, they now crept stealthily forward.

A stout man with a beard to his belly took a knee beside Rogan. "We're all going to be pretty much fucked if we are caught up here watching this battle."

Rogan continued staring through the spyglass. "Very observant, Thaxter."

Javan wiped sweat from his naked face with his forearm. "A battle we were invited to and showed up late to attend."

Thaxter put his metal helm over his bent knee. "Looks like we made the right choice being late, aye?"

Rogan nodded. "Well, them whores in Irem are good."

The motley crew snickered.

Rogan shook his head and turned his attention back to the scene below. "Don't distract me."

The stake and the pyre beneath it were fully engulfed in flame, but the figure who had escaped the inferno was merely singed, smoke rising from his clothing and hair. Roughly two dozen fighters clad in chain mail armor and sporting short swords spread out around him, closing the distance slowly. The wizard opened his mouth, emitting a shower of glowing pinpricks that reminded Rogan of fireflies. The lights formed into small globes in the air then began to grow. The crescent of armed men paused at the display of sorcery but did not cede their position. Archers moved in behind their flanks and set their sandals, preparing to draw back their strings and fire arrows at the strange globes. But no thrum of bowstrings followed. Instead, there was only an ear-splitting squeal. The siren came from the hovering balls of light, loud enough to get the attention of all those on the battlefield. Even the stout pikemen, who were making great sport of their fleeing enemies, paused as the shriek grew louder. A soldier who had been struggling to free his boots, which were bound together by the bolo of a lucky shot from the slinger brigade, stopped his efforts. The opponent who had been about to spear him from behind turned instead, seeking the source of the cacophony.

From above, Rogan and the others watched as the globes suddenly shot forward, slamming into the archers' chests and disappearing inside their bodies. The impact left no wounds or marks. Their armor and undergarments remained whole. Many on both the battlefield and the ridge drew a breath, awaiting the manifestation of magick. However, none of the archers burst into flames or fell over dead.

Thaxter laughed. "Guess that wizard's spell failed."

Suddenly, each of the archers dropped their bows and clutched their crotches. They staggered, a few going to their knees, others falling over in full. Blood flowed through their clasped fingers. Rogan's eyes widened as he saw a green tentacle wriggle from one unfortunate victim's bloody groin and thrash against his thigh.

"Wodan …" Jaw tightening, Rogan offered Thaxter the scope. "Want a better look?"

"No." Thaxter stood and shook his head. "Judging by your expression? No, I'm good. If it can make you turn white as cow's milk, then I don't need to see it close up."

Looking through the viewer again, Rogan saw the men with

swords start to back away from the wizard. Again, the warlock raised his smoking arms and began to chant. Before he could complete the incantation, a great white draft horse, bigger than any Rogan had ever seen, thundered onto the scene. On its back rode a man adorned in blue plated armor and equal in size to Rogan himself. His helmet concealed his visage, but when he turned, Rogan caught a glimpse of his face. Gasping, he lumbered to his feet.

"It can't be," he muttered.

"Ah," Javan said, "their leader arrives to deal with the wizard himself."

Thaxter nodded. "That would be General Tolin, all right."

Rogan clutched the scope in one hand. His other hand balled into a fist. He stood, gaping, and shook his head.

"What troubles you, sire?" Javan asked.

"I ..." Rogan swallowed. "By Wodan's ass crack, La Gaul ... my ..."

Javan shook his head. "That is Tolin La Gaul, sire. Not Gorias La Gaul."

Blinking, Rogan crouched and peered through the spyglass again. "He wears armor like that of Gorias. The blue plated armor from a skinned wyrmling dragon."

One of their troopers, a blond youth, only slightly older than Javan, muttered, "Who is Gorias La Gaul?"

Rogan growled, teeth exposed.

"Gently, Sorvac," Javan cautioned, "lest my uncle rips your throat out with his teeth. Gorias was one of the greatest heroes of renown. A famed fighter and a childhood idol of Rogan's."

Thaxter nodded. "How can you have never heard of him, boy?"

The youth shrugged.

"Seven hundred years old!" Thaxter's tone was incredulous. "Badass of all badasses! What did they teach you while you were still clinging to your mother's tit? Gorias La Gaul wore armor made from the skin of a baby dragon and fought with swords made of angels' wings."

Sorvac rolled his eyes. "He had dragon skin armor and swords made from angel's wings?"

"That is what the ballads say," Javan replied.

Sorvac threw back his head and laughed. "What bollocks ..."

Rogan didn't even turn his head as he reached out with his free hand and grabbed Sorvac's crotch. The youth howled as Rogan used him as leverage to pull himself upright. He then dropped the viewer, reached out with his other hand, and seized him by the throat. The old barbarian's fingers nearly encircled Sorvac's neck. Furious, he lifted the youth off his feet and glared into his eyes.

"Don't ... kill ... me ..." Sorvac wheezed.

"I ought to squeeze your nuts until they burst so that you don't infect the world."

Sorvac's eyes widened as Rogan squeezed harder. Then, grimacing, the barbarian flung him to the ground. Sorvac landed on his back, the air whooshing from his lungs.

Rogan towered over him, pointing. "Next time you try and use that little prick of yours, remember that Gorias La Gaul fought and fucked his way across this planet before your grandmother was sucking cocks in Shynar."

Coughing, his eyes welling with tears, Sorvac writhed on the grass.

Rogan studied the rest of the mercenary horde. "Anyone else in this company have anything to add?"

The assembled troops looked at the sky, their feet, and the valley below. As Sorvac crawled away, Javan, Thaxter, and Rogan turned their attention back to General Tolin. The big man on the field barked orders, and a battalion of pikemen left their sport of nailing the runners to the sand and returned to their leader. The wizard watched them approach as well, still spitting pinpricks of light from his mouth.

"He's supposed to be Gorias's son," Thaxter said. "A bad seed."

"It is said that he sports the soul of a dragon in that body," Javan replied, "and the spirit of Tolin is long gone."

Thaxter frowned. "How does something like that happen?"

Javan shrugged. "Wizards and witches ... can't abide them."

General Tolin halted his horse in front of the wizard, seemingly unafraid of the dark magic. The wizard, his attention now focused on his foe, continued summoning more globes.

"Tolin will be struck down," one of the mercenaries whispered.

"No," Rogan said. "He's offering himself as a distraction. Watch."

One of the pikemen, a tree trunk of a man that almost mirrored Thaxter in size, moved away from his fellows and circled behind the wizard, whose attention was still on Tolin. The soldier brought about his heavy pike, a weapon thicker than a weaver's beam and sporting a spearhead akin to a forged helmet. Without hesitation, he thrust the massive spearhead into the sorcerer's midsection. The wizard's mouth opened wider but now sprayed blood instead of light.

"Old witchy man looks kinda surprised," Rogan said.

The pikeman raised the wizard off the ground and strode back toward the burning pyre, arms bulging and legs straining. The wizard struggled like a moth on a pin. Tolin watched impassively as the soldier drove the wizard's head into the fire. The sorcerer's hair was quickly ablaze. The flames spread to his eyebrows, beard, and clothes. Tolin gave another command, and the pikeman thrashed the body back and forth, breaking one of the wizard's legs, then an arm, and his neck, and then burying his face into the fire. He pushed his weapon in further so there would be no escape.

"He knew the right way," Rogan sighed. "Never put a wizard to the flames with his tongue still in his mouth. He probably conjured or chanted the ropes off."

Sighing, Thaxter reached for a flask at his belt. "Well, that day's work is over. We missed out on the pay ..."

Javan shook his head. "We'd be dead or slaves if we had joined that fray. Tolin's army crushed them."

"Thank our stiff cocks then." Rogan stowed his spyglass. "The whorehouse last night saved us."

Down in the valley, General Tolin turned his steed and pointed up at the ridge.

"Sire," Javan said, "we've been spotted. Perhaps we should depart, lest they turn their forces toward us instead of home."

"Best thing you've said all day," Rogan replied. "When we took this job, nobody said anything about Tolin La Gaul being the leader on the other side."

Javan mounted his horse. The other mercenaries followed suit. Rogan grinned, looking down at Sorvac, who still clutched his groin.

"We came all this way for a war, and we're going to ride away with our swords in our hands—except for Sorvac, who's riding away with his cock in his hand."

"We should make haste, Uncle."

"Not back to the whorehouse," Thaxter groused. "I need sleep."

"There is a town several miles off," Javan replied. "Ellivsulo, it is called. Or Immowtoau in the other tongue of this land."

Rogan swung up into his saddle.

Thaxter took a swig from his flask. "So, what's in that town?"

"It is the last place Gorias La Gaul lived," Javan said. "The last place he had a stable life before he went off on his final years of adventure. Much like someone else."

The youth glanced pointedly at Rogan, but the old warrior ignored him.

"I think they even have memorials there. A bronze statue of his countenance."

"Fair enough." Thaxter turned. "Well, boss? You want to visit?"

"What?" Rogan asked.

Thaxter reined his horse about. "It's as good a place as any. Your nephew is right. We shouldn't tarry here any longer, lest they decide to come up here and add us to the wizard's pyre."

Rogan shrugged. "Yes, let's get away from all this. That wizard's cooking head has stunk up the entire valley."

Sorvac, climbing carefully into his saddle, muttered, "It sort of smells like ham."

Rogan scowled at him and the others held their breath. Sorvac averted his eyes, unable to meet the grizzled leader's gaze. Javan opened his mouth to speak, but before he could, Rogan burst into laughter. Then he prodded his horse and led them away.

"Curse you, Sorvac." Grinning, Rogan patted his stomach. "Now I'm hungry for pork!"

He led them away from the valley. The company rode single file, and, one by one, they took a final glimpse of Tolin and his army.

They were unaware that a third force—a group clustered in a nearby copse of trees—watched them as well.

* * *

"Fallon, why are they executing those men?"

The young girl turned quickly and fell to her knee. Head bowed, eyes shut, she whispered, "My lord."

"Rise, Fallon." The towering figure stayed hidden in the shadowy brick opening which led into the great fortress. A huge black dog sat on its haunches next to him, panting. "Have I ever given you reason to fear me?"

Slowly, the girl stood but kept her head bowed. "I've served in your house all my days, Lord Nosmada."

Chuckling, Nosmada looked over the parapet. "Why are they executing those men? General Tolin's army hasn't returned yet."

"Those are the men that tried to sell General Tolin bad bones."

"Death for bad bones?" Nosmada took a step closer, set his boots flat, and yet remained hidden in the shadows.

"Yes, Lord. They tried to pass off the bones of elephants and large lizards as those of ..."

"Dragons?" Nosmada's tone was weary. "Ah well, we all have our hobbies and devotions, no?"

Fallon did not respond and glanced back down at her sandals.

Nosmada reached down and scratched the dog's ears. "My maid, Buchana, wears the bracelets you weave. You are a talented girl."

"Thank you, Lord."

"She will be retiring soon. Perhaps you would rather serve me inside when she does."

Fallon's eye widened. "I've always been a messenger and served in the stables."

"But that time is past," Nosmada replied. "You are growing up. You know there is nothing to fear from me. You shall not be molested as you would in some places of this world."

"I'm honored, my lord."

"I like you. I don't like many." He cleared his throat. "Today, though, you are still a messenger. So, go down there and tell that Captain Bradlee that he is not an executioner and if he cuts the head off just one more of those men, I'll feed him to the leeches." Nosmada stepped out into the light and stood beside her at the parapet. "Tell him if one more drop of blood hits the sands, I'll personally hold him down as the leeches drain him dry."

"Yes, my lord."

"And if he gives you any talkback, tell him I'll make it last for a week." Nosmada bent down a little, patted the mutt on the head, and then stood up again. "He'll believe you."

Bowing, Fallon hurried off to deliver the message.

Alone on the wall, Nosmada looked down on the inner court-yard. His shadow fell over those gathered below, and a collective gasp rippled through the throng as they glanced up. His name was whispered in surprise. The long tresses of his hair swung back and forth. Sunlight washed over his scarred forehead. Then, the people below knelt and bowed. Without acknowledging them, Nosmada turned his back on the crowd and went inside. The dog padded along at his side, nails clicking on the stone floor.

The two descended into the bowels of his fortress, several stories beneath the earth. The way was lit only by sputtering torch-light, and the walls were damp and covered with slime and mold.

The only sounds were the slow drip of water and their footfalls. Eventually, they reached a wide, high-roofed chamber where two guards stood by a locked iron door. A pair of chairs sat on either side of the door. Nosmada suspected the two men had been seated until they heard him coming. They snapped to attention and saluted.

"M-my lord," the guard on the left stammered.

"At ease." Nosmada waved his hand. "Captain Bradlee will be bringing down a half dozen bodies to the neighboring chamber. Bring me three empty leeches."

The other guard bowed before hurrying further down the subterranean corridor.

Nosmada opened the iron door and entered a great room. The dog obediently followed. Oil lanterns turned up high adorned the walls, revealing a series of tables sectioned off in sevens, all equipped with straps and metal restraints. The only other furnishing was a single large chair.

Sighing, Nosmada turned back to the remaining guard. "Bring me some water."

"Right away, my lord."

The chair creaked as Nosmada sat. The dog circled and then lay down next to him. The beast closed its eyes but opened one when the guard hurried back in carrying a pitcher of water.

"My thanks," Nosmada said.

Nodding, the guard placed the pitcher on the table and retreated from the room to take a position by the open door.

Nosmada drank, nearly emptying the pitcher before Bradlee and his men arrived. They filed into the room, leading a trio of chained captives. Both the prisoners and the guards seemed nervous.

"Captain Bradlee." Nosmada did not rise. He reached down and patted the dog's head.

Bradlee removed his cap and bowed. "Lord, I received your message. We did not execute them. We brought them here alive, as you wished."

"And you did not spill another drop of their blood?"

Despite the damp chilliness of the subterranean chamber, a bead of sweat ran down Bradlee's pale face. He nodded.

"How considerate." Nosmada slowly rose, as did the dog. "Tie them to the tables."

The prisoners moaned and whimpered and strained against their bonds as they were led to the tables and fastened into place. One of them pleaded, promising loyalty and all of his daughters if he could go free. Nosmada ignored his cries.

"Thank you for bringing them promptly, Bradlee."

"I figured they would be fresher this way, my lord."

Nosmada laughed once, and then his expression turned serious. "I'm not a vampire, Captain. The taste isn't the point."

"I ... see, my lord."

"Anyway ... well done. You follow orders almost as good as Charla here."

Bradlee looked at the mutt, who scratched behind her right ear.

"Then again," Nosmada continued, "she's a dog. A good bitch should obey a few things one commands, no?"

"Yes, my lord."

"You are sweating like a whore on the day of judgment."

"It is a long walk down here."

"Hm. It is. I'm far older than any of you and yet ..." His head turned as another pair appeared in the doorway—a brutish, scarred man clad in a kilt, a chainmail vest, and a dented helmet, and a tiny, slender woman of advanced age. She raised her left hand and turned her wrist, then stepped to one side. Bradlee's men grew even more restless.

"Ah," Nosmada exclaimed. "I see that Schlack and Zillian have brought me the leeches."

Bradlee glanced back at his men, and then at the floor. "Then, you have little need of us, sire."

"Oh, I have need of *you*, Captain."

Schlack stepped into the room, smiling. Nosmada fought hard to suppress his own urge to smile, as well.

The crone, Zillian, moved forward toward the series of tables, and three more willowy figures filled the doorway. Each of the nearly skeletal forms entered the chamber in halting steps, their clawed feet making clicking sounds on the stone floor. As they shuffled into the torchlight, the assembled men shuddered, and the captives screamed. The threesome were leeches. Each stood six feet in height and possessed arms and legs like humans, but that was where the similarities ended. Their leathery, obsidian skin made them look like a trio of hairless bats, and their flat heads sat sunken into their shoulders. Their faces were equipped with narrow, puckered mouths, but no nostrils or ears and only pinprick eyes. The creatures appeared nearly emaciated, their ribs standing out starkly beneath their hides. The stench roiling off them filled the room, making Nosmada's eyes water.

One of the captives whispered prayers, his breath hitching. Another sobbed, quivering against the restraints. The third wet himself, urine dribbling onto the floor. None of the guards snickered at this violation. Indeed, they pointedly stared at other parts of the chamber, doing their best to avoid setting eyes on the creatures.

Nosmada nodded at Zillian. The old woman made an odd clicking sound and gestured, and the leeches shuffled toward the captives, looming over the tables. Drool dripped from their mouths in long, glistening ropes, splattering the faces of the helpless prisoners.

Bradlee scampered backward as the nearest creature brushed by him. Nosmada reached out and grabbed him by the shoulder, stopping his retreat.

"Release him," he ordered.

"W-what?"

"Did I stutter, Captain? Release the prisoner."

Frowning with confusion, Bradlee glanced from Nosmada to the leech to Zillian. The old woman tittered, flashing a mouth filled with gaps between her black nubs of teeth. Swallowing, Bradlee reached down with trembling hands and untied the terrified captive. The restraints clattered to the floor. The prisoner gaped at the figures looming above him.

"Hold him down, Bradlee," Nosmada commanded.

"Sire?"

"Hold him down."

Again, Bradlee swallowed hard. He wiped the sweat from his brow and placed his hands on the prisoner's chest, shoving him down. The man struggled to break free, but Zillian clicked her tongue and the leech fell upon the captive. Its narrow mouth opened and four long, needle-like fangs protruded. A second later, those teeth were buried deep in the victim's neck. The man thrashed, swinging his legs and arms. He broke free of Bradlee's grip, but the leech's body weight held him in place. The creature pressed upon him like a lover, and the prisoner stiffened.

Then came the slurping sounds.

"That's it," Nosmada whispered.

"Damn ..." Bradlee choked as he watched the leech convulse and suck. Its torso swelled as the prisoner's began to shrink.

Arms folded over his chest, Nosmada grinned at Bradlee. "Shaking so? My, my, such courage. Don't piss on my floor."

Gagging, Bradlee covered his mouth with his hand and stared in horror. The leech had drained almost all of the blood from the prisoner.

"Now." Nosmada pointed at the screaming man on the next table. "Again, Captain Bradlee."

Bradlee gaped. His mouth worked silently.

"Do it," Nosmada said, "or the prisoner takes your place, and you, his."

Bradlee repeated the action of loosening the captive's bonds, then holding him down while the leech fed.

Nosmada nodded with approval. "I'm impressed. You haven't pissed yourself yet."

The process was repeated with the third prisoner. When all of the helpless captives had been drained, the now fat leeches waddled over to Zillian. The old woman clicked and cooed and stroked their misshapen heads. Then she led the engorged creatures out the door and down the hall.

Nosmada addressed Bradlee's men. "All of you assembled here, do you understand today's lesson?"

The group mumbled nervously, none of them meeting his eye.

"Do you understand why I had your captain attend the process personally, rather than simply leaving those prisoners tied and bound?"

More murmuring followed. Several of the troops shifted uncomfortably from foot to foot.

Nosmada spun around and pointed at Bradlee. "Don't ever fuck with my plans again, Captain. I've looked God in the face. What worth do you think your life has?"

"I understand, my lord."

"Do you? Do you really? I just ask obedience, Bradlee. Not gold, not sex, just obedience."

Bradlee took a knee and bowed his head. "Yes, Lord."

From somewhere deeper in the bowels of the fortress echoed the grind of a large, heavy door opening, and then a hiss like a thousand serpents. Abruptly, the sounds stopped.

Head held high, Nosmada stalked out into the corridor. Charla padded along behind, nails tapping on the floor. Schlack followed, as well, grinning. Once in the hall, the two flanked their master.

"I notice you offered him your back," Schlack observed.

"Then you also noticed that he doesn't have the courage to strike me down."

"Bah." Schlack spat on the stones. "He has no balls."

"What news?" Nosmada asked.

"General Tolin will return any time."

"Speaking of balls."

Schlack's eyebrows rose. "Indeed."

GENERAL TOLIN LA GAUL DIDN'T RIDE IN THE FORWARD column of his army. He'd seen many braggart leaders take that position and end up with an arrow in their hearts. Not that any weapon used thereabouts could penetrate his dragon skin armor, but he always chose intelligent caution rather than ego-driven ways.

A thin cavalryman with ginger hair and a beard rode up beside him and snapped a salute. "General."

"Colonel Shazeal." Tolin acknowledged him by raising his chin.

Their horses fell into cadence alongside each other. For a moment, neither man spoke.

"What troubles you, Shazeal?" Tolin asked. "Are you vexed that we didn't pursue those watching us over the ridge?"

Eyes forward, Shazeal replied, "It is always better to get all of our enemies gone at once, especially since the bulk of the army was deployed to crush that force of fools."

"They may not have been enemies. You always look on the bad side of all things, no?"

"Just want to be careful, sir."

"I try to be careful enough for all of us."

"Appreciated, sir."

"But?"

"Well, Yitzak Dar seemed to think ..."

Tolin sighed. "Taking the words of a wizard over my judgment?"

"No, sir, but ..."

"Wizards." Tolin spat to his left. "They are a necessary tool, at times. Nothing more."

Eyes on the columns ahead, Shazeal replied, "Not an admirer? I thought you and Yitzak Dar were good friends."

"Friends?" Tolin frowned. "I just told you that wizards are a necessary tool. Is a carpenter friends with his hammer? Is a stable boy friends with his pitchfork?"

"I suppose not."

"Can one ever be a true friend of a wizard? They tend to eat everything around them."

"True enough," Shazeal agreed.

Tolin smiled. "And speaking as one who uses the flesh given to him, let me say, that's my fucking job."

Both men laughed, but their humor was cut short as a horse with an almost orange hue and a blond mane thundered up behind them. The rider bounced along, side saddle, dressed in a long silken cloak.

"Speak of the devil," Shazeal muttered. He reigned his horse and hung back a bit.

"General Tolin," Yitzak Dar panted, breathless, as the distinctive horse settled in beside La Gaul's great black stallion.

"Where have you been?" Tolin scowled. "I expected you long before now."

"General?" The wizard's long face shifted expressions.

"Usually, I hear about every fear you can conjure up after a battle. You seem to delight in it. But you needn't try to frighten me into more flesh sacrifices for your magicks, wizard. I always spare you some. No need for you to lobby so hard."

"Sir, I tell you my fears because you are the one to best facilitate my magicks."

"Is that so?"

Dar nodded solemnly.

"Well," Tolin asked, "what is it this time?"

Grimacing, the wizard looked back to the end of the column. "I felt someone back there. A dirty, bloody presence like one I hadn't experienced in decades."

"In the valley, during the battle?"

"No, in the hills beyond. They were watching us."

"I caught a glimpse of a company of mercenaries," Tolin confirmed. "Maybe those were your dirty, bloody presence?"

"Perhaps." Dar nodded again. "I'm utterly confused, as the presence I felt is surely one I thought long dead and far away from here."

"Who do you mean?"

"A warrior I once knew, when he was very young."

"Who?" Tolin's tone grew impatient.

"It was Rogan, the barbarian who became king."

Tolin turned slowly in his saddle. "Are you really mad? It is said that he perished in the overthrow of Albion a while back?"

"No," Dar replied. "I'd heard those rumors, as well as the rumors that he abdicated, then recently returned, and then left once again. I just didn't believe them until now."

"Rogan." Tolin shook his head. "Next you will tell me Gilgamesh was with him."

"Not hardly."

"Even though I don't frequent taverns, I've heard the tales over suppers and tales from stable hands. I know about Rogan. But what of him? You think he was hiding in the rushes with a great force to slay me ... or you?"

"I'm not sure what he was doing there ... but he *was* there."

"Why did he not attack?"

"Our force rivaled his. He's no fool."

"So I have heard," Tolin mused. "But tell me ... if this was Rogan, then he is just an old man by now. Why worry about him?"

"Perhaps he can be a worry for us, for the land in which we ride, for our master."

Tolin shook his head as the city loomed. "What shall he do? Lay siege to Nosmada's great city? That is impossible, even for a man in his prime."

Ahead, they saw the curtain walls of earthen works set in rings about the great city, spread so far out that there were whole farms planted between them. As the armored column neared the first checkpoint, the idea that any army could assail this place, much less reach the inner-city walls, seemed ridiculous.

"Yitzak," Tolin said, "worry not about old, impotent warriors. Set your mind to things that could really harm Nosmada."

A glow rose over the city, but the sun was on the opposite side of the sky. All of the riders glanced upward, shielding their eyes against the light.

"Great God," Dar muttered.

"Hardly," Tolin replied. "But I agree. The sight of a fallen angel is staggering, no matter how many times you've seen one."

"And still having wings ..." Dar gaped with wonder.

"Tough to fly without them," Tolin said. "I miss it so."

Dar turned to the general. "Someday."

"Someday," Tolin repeated.

The glow dropped beyond the city walls and into the fortress.

Tolin glanced at the wizard again as the column moved forward. "Why do you fear this Rogan? He has no parlay with demons or the angelic horde."

Dar's voice was barely a whisper. "He is why I am the way I am."

"I thought your transition of gender was due to your magicks? I hear many an alchemist loses ..."

"Gender is not determined by what one has between their legs, General. It is something deeper inside a person. Regardless, I'm not talking about my gender. Rogan didn't turn me into a woman. I was already that. He turned me into a eunuch." Dar paused, gripping the reins tightly. "And I refuse to underestimate the one who gelded me."

Tolin's jaw tightened. "I can see that. Well, roll some bones when we return and see what his intentions are."

The wizard's expression brightened. "Then that means ...?"

"Yes, I will allocate flesh and bone for you to do this."

"You are most kind." Dar bowed her head.

"No," Tolin replied, "no, I'm not, but you have my curiosity up. So few good warriors exist. It might be amusing to know what Rogan is here for."

As the army moved on, horns trumpeted their arrival. Amidst the cacophony, Tolin spotted another rider traveling toward them. No soldier tried to stop this inbound youth. After a moment, Tolin recognized him.

"Anka, last son of teamster Prime Hayde. I wonder what he brings to me?"

The young man's sweaty obsidian skin glistened in the sun. Stocky and clad only in trousers, Anka dug his bare heels into the sides of the horse and gripped a saddlebag under his left arm.

"General," he shouted, his accent unlike any in the column.

Tolin raised his arm, and Anka struggled to salute as he dropped the reins.

"What brings you out here now, Anka? I'm heading inside."

Anka took position on the side opposite Dar and thrust the saddlebag toward the general. "I was excited to bring this to you."

Eyebrow raised, Tolin reached out and took it. "If this is full of snakes, I'll rip off your nuts and give them to Dar."

Anka grinned at the jest, but the wizard did not.

Tolin opened the bag, and his eyes widened.

"I have done well?" Anka asked.

Tolin reached in the bag and pulled out several objects.

Yitzak sighed. "Rocks?"

"No." Tolin held up a handful. "An unwise man might see them as long flints or spearheads. Anka here knows what they are, however."

Anka nodded. "Dragon teeth. Real ones, no filed-down fake ones these fools try to dupe us with."

"Well done, Anka." Tolin dropped the teeth back into the bag and closed it. "Well done indeed."

Anka bowed his head. "Tonight, sir?"

Tolin closed his eyes. "Yes, you can have the pick of Castellan Tremas' harem. I will see to it. You deserve it."

Bowing lower on the horse, Anka said, "Thank you, sir. Anyone you want killed? I owe you more."

Tolin opened his eyes and looked at the city. "We shall see."

CHAPTER 2

IF I HAD POSSESSION OVER JUDGMENT DAY

The town of Ellivsulo had proven to be a disappointment.

Rogan sat on a bench outside Gorias La Gaul's last abode and watched as smoke from a nearby tavern rolled past. The cloud irritated his lungs, and he coughed. Frowning, Rogan silently cursed his body for getting older. Closing his eyes, he let his mind drift to the battlefields of his youth, full of flaming arrows, and to his days as a pirate when loads of blazing pitch filled the air. Never once had a razed and burning village caused his breath to hitch, and yet now, the simple smoke of roasting venison was enough to make him hack.

"Can't live forever," he muttered.

He heard the clop of hooves stopping nearby, but he kept his eyes shut, not caring who it might be. The populace of the village had already proved meager at best and cowards at worst. There was no trouble here.

"Rogan."

The aged barbarian opened his eyes at the sound of Thaxter's voice and nodded a greeting. The big man climbed from the saddle and belched. Two other fighters flanked him on steeds of their own.

"Well?" Rogan asked.

"It's all done," Thaxter replied. "Horses stabled and the men fucking and drinking."

"Good."

"Good? Nothing too good about it, Rogan. You haven't seen the whores here. We'd have better luck in the stables."

"Somehow, I'm sure you'll make do."

Thaxter surveyed the small dwelling. "So, this is the place, huh?"

Rogan nodded.

"Good-sized door," Thaxter observed. "He was supposed to be a big fucker, that La Gaul."

"It would make me angrier than a broke-dick dog if he were a dwarf."

"Still ..." Thaxter rubbed his chin. "You'd think there would be more to it than this. More to the whole town, really. Their museum didn't have Gorias's armor on display. That bronze statue your nephew raved about was half-hidden by weeds and covered with bird shit and tarnish. And most of these townspeople didn't know which house was his."

"One of them did," Rogan grumbled.

Thaxter laughed. "When you asked him where the home of Gorias La Gaul was, and he answered, '*That old fucker's house? Who cares? What did he ever do?*' ... I don't know that I've ever seen you so mad."

"His memory improved after I pinned him to that tree and used the pliers on him."

"Yeah."

Rogan stood up. His knees popped.

"What's troubling you?" Thaxter asked.

Rogan gestured at the house, and then at the rest of the village. "As a boy, Gorias La Gaul was my hero. You know the tales. He fought and fucked his way across the world. He slew the last dragon ever."

"And died," Thaxter said, "at the hands of some cult leader who claimed to have arisen as that same dragon reborn."

"I've heard that ballad, too. But that's all that remains. Ballads. Stories repeated by old men whose best days are behind them. The young don't know. Sorvac, earlier today ... I could almost excuse his impudence and blame it on his youth. After all, if Javan weren't my nephew and hadn't heard me tell the old stories ... if he hadn't been educated before journeying with me ... he'd have probably been as ignorant as Sorvac."

"Where is your nephew, anyway?"

Rogan shrugged. "Mooning over a girl named Zenata."

"A whore?"

Rogan's eyes narrowed. "A warrior. One I'd match against any in our company."

"I apologize. Were they a couple?"

"She traveled with us for a while. Fought alongside us. The boy misses her."

"Where is she now?"

Instead of answering, Rogan turned back to the house again. "Gorias saved this world. Now all that's left are this shack, drunken songs, and words on the lips of old warriors like us. Is that all I will be someday soon, as well?"

"They already sing ballads about you." Thaxter walked over and stood by Rogan's side. "And after death? Well, I'd say most men would rather be forgotten."

"It isn't like I want a parade," Rogan barked.

Thaxter flinched, taking a step backward.

Rogan's expression softened. "I don't know what I am saying."

"Guess we all feel it as age rolls on," Thaxter replied. "Gorias lived seven hundred years. Imagine that? Maybe he saw death as a blessing."

"I'm glad our kind didn't get that ability," Rogan agreed. "When I was Javan's age? Sure. I longed for that sort of lifespan. But now? Death sounds better than my body turning against me."

They stood in silence for a few moments, reflecting. The two fighters who had accompanied Thaxter prodded their horses and rode off. Finally, Thaxter spoke again.

"I ever tell you how my dad passed?"

"No."

"He died screwing a whore half his age. No kidding. He came and went at the same time."

Rogan's laughter boomed across the village. "Were there tears at his funeral?"

Thaxter grinned. "Not a damned one."

"The gods must have loved your father to let him die that way."

"Or maybe they hated the whore he was with. She couldn't give it away after that. Everyone thought she was cursed."

As the two men laughed, Javan rode up to them.

"Sire?"

"There you are," Rogan said. "What has you so bothered?"

"I believe that Confederate army we spotted earlier is being led by the daughter of Gorias La Gaul."

Rogan's eyes widened. "How the hell do you know that?"

Javan shrugged. "That's what her banner reads."

"Things are working out, Rogan," Thaxter said.

"How so?"

"At least she'll remember him."

"Where are they now?" Rogan asked Javan.

"Approaching the village, sire."

"You think they want trouble?"

Javan shrugged. "A moderately wise man once told me to assume an arriving force always means trouble."

Rogan frowned. "That guy must have been drunk."

"Quite likely you were at the time, sire."

Thaxter laughed loud enough to spook Javan's horse. The youth quickly reigned in the animal, soothing it.

"How much do they outnumber us?" Rogan asked.

"I'd say three to one."

"Terrific." Thaxter groaned. "All the times you pissed in Wodan's supper dish, now hell has come to pay. I should have thought twice before taking up with your bunch."

"Is your memory fading?" Rogan glared at him. "It was either join us or swing from the gallows. If you're unhappy, I can see that happens before the end of day."

"My memory is just fine, Rogan. But speaking of swinging, let's see if your swinging-dick reputation brings us good or ill with this force."

"Nay." Rogan shook his head. "I should remain anonymous until we know more about them."

Javan nodded in agreement. Thaxter and Rogan pulled themselves up onto their mounts.

The trio rode to the outskirts of the village and watched the force approach. The main group stopped at the top of a hill overlooking the settlement while a smaller group of four rode forward. One of them was concealed beneath heavy robes.

The man in the lead put his hand up as he stopped, chin out, his long, braided black and gray beard bobbing slightly. "Ho, you men! We bring tidings from our leader on yon hilltop."

"And who is your leader?" Thaxter asked.

The emissary gestured to the hilltop. Rogan, Javan, and Thaxter focused on a tall woman, sliding off her mount. A man groveled at her feet. Her crimson hair glowed in the sunlight as she drew a short sword and proceeded to slap the cringing man with the flat of her blade. He clawed at her knee-high boots, but she kicked him away, smacking him harder.

Thaxter snorted. "That is your leader?"

"Yes," the man answered. "The daughter of Gorias La Gaul favors us with her leadership."

"She has a short temper," Rogan said.

The graying man looked to the hill and then back to them. "Her temper is quite long. Discipline is strictly enforced in our group."

"Wanted us to know who she is pretty bad, huh?" Rogan pointed at the larger force. "I can see why. You look like a bunch of mutts."

"Have a care, mercenary. You are standing in Gorias La Gaul's final homestead."

"You see, Thaxter? Someone recognizes the historic value of this place!" Grinning, Rogan turned back to the man. "Are you the tour guide?"

The emissary sucked in air and puffed out his chest. "I am Brok Yoshee. You should know my name. I have slain men across this world and slew the great Chimera Hurtzin of southern Kemet. I bow my knee to no man."

"Oh, I can see that," Rogan quipped. "You bow your knee to a woman instead."

"Indeed, I do. I serve her, the one that is chosen from God above to slay his own nemesis."

"All right," Thaxter said. "We respect your sacrifice and all, but what do you want with us? You're preening like a rooster. Why the display?"

Before Brok could answer, Javan interrupted. "What Thaxter means to say," the youth explained, "is that you surmised correctly. We are a mercenary company, not residents of this humble village. We were to join an army to face those in Nodd, but we arrived too late. We have no fight with you."

"Then you're here to plunder?"

Javan glanced at Rogan and Thaxter, and then back to the horsemen. "This village doesn't offer much in the way of that. A good vineyard and a still, but that's about all."

Brok looked at the youth to his left, a warrior of barely twenty summers but strapped with muscle and weapons. A patch covered his right eye. "What say you, Kenoth?"

"They look ready to fight and not just plunder." Kenoth's one eye narrowed. "Would you throw in with us? We can always use more swords."

"What is in it for us?" Thaxter asked. "You have the numbers, but maybe we work better as a small force."

Kenoth shrugged. "That is perhaps the truth. But we need men of steel—seasoned warriors like you and the old man there. Who are you, sir?"

Rogan shrugged. "You said it yourself, boy. I'm just an old

warrior. Perhaps I shall tell your leader my name if she ever quits spanking that soldier on yon hill."

They all looked again. The tall red-haired woman was still abusing the soldier, who now jittered in the mud in the grips of a seizure. At last, she stopped beating him and looked down at them.

"Brok Yoshee was it?" Rogan asked.

"Aye."

"I'd love to meet her before we agree to throw in. You know ... just to make sure my company is right for your group."

The emissary grinned, showing yellowed teeth. "She will be here soon."

Rogan nodded, and the group fell silent. He surveyed Brok and decided the man was not worth thinking twice about. More wind than iron in his veins, judging by how he carried himself. The one-eyed Kenoth might have some fight in him, though. Rogan turned his attention to the two riders flanking them. One was an enormous corpulent man seated on a huge draft horse. Either the rider or the mount reeked of spoiled cheese. The other was adorned in heavy robes. Rogan waited until he could cast a furtive glance beneath the hood and fought to keep his composure when he did. The thin rider sported green skin, had a maw like that of a toad ... and crimson eyes striped like a snake's.

Shuddering, Rogan leaned in his saddle toward Javan and Thaxter, nodding at them to do the same.

"What is it, sire?" Javan asked.

"I don't trust these pricks offhand," Rogan whispered.

"Yeah?" Thaxter's expression hardened. "Why not?"

"Well, for one thing, it was me who slew the Chimera Hurtzin of lower Kemet. That fucker is taking credit for my kill. So, watch that lying asshole."

Thaxter blinked.

"Secondly," Rogan continued, "that skinny one, dressed in robes? That's not a human. Be wary."

"Good advice, Uncle," Javan replied. "Here they come."

The daughter of Gorias La Gaul mounted up and rode their way. Her procession followed behind.

NOSMADA STOOD IN THE SHADOWED CORRIDOR, WATCHING Schlack steward the leeches into another chamber when Zillian approached. The withered woman stopped, staring at him attentively.

"What is it?" Nosmada asked.

"There is a visitor to see you." Her eyes flicked to the ceiling as if the person in question were there. Then she focused on Nosmada again. "It is Nisroch."

"Really?" Nosmada's eyebrows arched in surprise. "Why? What does that angel want with me?"

Zillian shrugged. "If I understood why he has come unto you, I'd tell you. Perhaps he brings you a dinner invitation."

Nosmada roared with laughter. "Oh, Zillian. You are one of the few people who can get away with speaking to me in that manner."

"The heavenly host get bored sometimes, just as men do. Some of them lay with women. Some teach men to make swords. Others impart the ways of magick. Nisroch has been known to pass on a good recipe or two."

"I've spoken to him before," Nosmada said, "but he never gave me wisdom on how to improve my meals."

Zillian shrugged. "Regardless, he awaits you above."

"Where is he?"

"In the south garden."

"I'll see to him."

"General Tolin will report to you as well."

Nosmada smirked. "He's not in the garden as well, I assume?"

"No."

"Good. I loathe a crowd."

Zillion held up a withered hand. "Oh!"

"Yes?"

"There are a few novice wizards up above, near the garden door."

Nosmada blinked. "And?"

"They seek to slay you."

"Do they now?"

She nodded. "I thought you should know."

"Thank you."

The chamber door opened, and Schlack stepped into the corridor. A deafening hiss filled the hall before he clamped the door shut again. Breathing hard, he nodded at them both.

"Zillian says more assassins await me above," Nosmada told him.

Schlack's eyes widened. "Want I should go up before you, sire?"

"No." Nosmada shook his head. "I will be fine. Finish up down here."

Nosmada ascended the stone steps. Charla plodded along after him. After several minutes, they reached the top. Nosmada stepped outside, letting the sun wash over him, and took a deep breath. Charla wandered away, lifted a leg, and peed on a bush.

A guard, clad in light chain mail and clutching a spear, snapped to attention. "My lord."

"At ease." Nosmada smiled. "Being outside is so much better than being in those coffins of stone. Pure soil and sky."

"Sir," the guard agreed.

Whistling, Nosmada headed toward the garden. When Charla hurried after him, he commanded the dog to stay. Charla pouted, then returned to sniffing the grounds.

"Keep an eye on my dog," Nosmada ordered.

"Yes, sir," the guard replied.

Nosmada resumed whistling and headed off again.

The acre-wide garden sat in the shadow of the biggest building in the city and was fenced in by clay stacks of bricks. These barriers cut a quaint appearance as they were overshadowed by a thick hedge. The garden had but one entrance, and the bronze gates, which were attached to stone pillars carved into the shapes of winged men, stood open, revealing a rocky footpath.

Nosmada stopped at the gate. Ahead of him, in the center of the garden, stood three broad trees. This was curious since only two trees grew in the garden. Smiling, he inhaled, smelling honeysuckle, tulips, mint ... and human sweat.

"Scared little mice," he called. "Come on out and face me like men. Your stink gives you away."

Out of the bushes to his right sprang two youths, probably not fourteen summers old. Each wore the light linen robe of a gardener. Nosmada grinned at their subterfuge. The taller of the two held up his hands over his head. Green light swirled in his palms.

"You, Lord Nosmada! I sentence you—"

"Shut up," the other teen snapped. "Just do it!"

As the first boy gave his partner a sour look, two more figures emerged from the staked rows of beans—a youth with a shaved head and tattoos on his scalp and a short-haired girl dressed as a servant from the stables.

Hands to his hips, Nosmada smiled at the assassin with the green light shining in his palms. "You were saying?"

Jaw stern, the teen shouted, "For taking the lives and blood of our master Zalznog, I sentence you to ..."

Nosmada's smile broadened. "You talk too much."

"W-what?" His palms glowed brighter.

"At this age," Nosmada said, "you cannot even see the forest for the trees."

The third tree—the one that had appeared in the garden overnight—moved.

The girl in stable clothes snapped her head to the side, mouth wide, screaming as she retreated to the beans. Roots erupted from the earth, snaking toward her, and she scampered backward, falling at Nosmada's feet. He spat on her as she groveled for mercy.

The bald youth's escape was cut short by a massive tree limb that smashed his head to pulp. Brains and blood splattered the ground as his body fell.

The other two assassins turned toward the tree. The second teen's hands now glowed green as well. The boys released their magicks, but at the tree, rather than at Nosmada. Orbs of green light sparked against rough bark, but it had no impact on their attacker. Branches wrapped around their waists and jerked them off their feet. The two assassins struggled, legs flailing helplessly as they beat their fists against the wood.

Then, the tree began to change shape. For a moment, it appeared as a gray-skinned, slender being possessing black, orb-like eyes. Then it shifted again, turning into a towering humanoid male, who sported six wings from his back. Only his arms retained the form of tree limbs.

"Greetings, Nisroch." Nosmada bowed slightly. "You honor me with your presence."

"You want these two alive?" The angel's voice was deep and sonorous and sounded as if more than one person were speaking in unison.

The girl screamed again, grasping at Nosmada's feet and begging for mercy.

Nosmada knelt and stretched out a hand. "Rise, my child."

Sobbing, she let him help her up.

Nosmada gently brushed the tears from her cheeks. "Your dead master Zalznog was flawed. But then again, all wizards are flawed, no?" He raised his fingertips, wet with the girl's tears, to the scar on his forehead. Then he looked up at the angel. "Well, some of us have flaws, wouldn't you agree, Nisroch?"

"If I had a flaw, I'd be sentenced to the abyss or cast out like the Morningstar."

"Or doomed to wander the Labyrinth between worlds like Amun." Nosmada turned his attention back to the girl. "Your master was weak for women and wine—a heartsick man spurned in his youth. He used magick to gain revenge on the world. He thought bedding the Nephilim harem to be nothing more than a joke. But I'm not laughing."

"Let us go," one of the struggling assassins shrieked. "Please!"

"Their screeching is unpleasant," the angel grumbled. "And I would have words with you, Nosmada."

"My apologies, great Nisroch. If you could render them unconscious for me, I would be grateful. I will bleed them later."

The angel slammed the two youths' heads together and then dropped their limp forms to the ground. The girl scrambled, running for the gate. Suddenly, Schlack appeared in the opening and grabbed the girl in a bear hug.

"Good timing," Nosmada said.

"Thank you, Lord," Schlack replied. "I had just finished below."

Nosmada nodded at the girl. "You know what to do with her."

Nodding, Schlack dragged the screaming captive away. As her cries faded, the angel's arms changed from tree limbs to a more humanoid shape. It flexed its fingers and stepped over the limp bodies.

"Where is their master?"

"His blood is below," Nosmada answered. "His flesh was used in General Tolin's project. His soul? You would know better than I."

"I pay little attention to that." Nisroch gestured with a sweep of his arm. "Tidy operation you have here in Nodd."

Nosmada stepped toward a hoe leaning against a sapling and grabbed it. "Although I am grateful, compliments I do not seek."

"Regardless, the cherubs by the gate are a nice touch. This garden ... is this what it looked like?"

"Eden?" Nosmada walked to the rows of beans. "You've been there, surely? Before it was sealed and access was lost?"

"No. I was never inside."

Nisroch watched him weed the beans and glanced back at the trees. "I am told it is still guarded. A giant sword holds sway over all."

"I have heard that as well." Nosmada prodded the soil with his hoe. "So ... why have you graced me with your presence, great Nisroch?"

"I've come to offer two warnings."

Not looking up from his labor, Nosmada said, "Go ahead."

"What you are planning—I don't think it will work. The very idea sounds like mischief birthed in the heart of Hell."

"I see." Nosmada used his boot to clear some weeds away. "Thank you for your thoughts, but my plans are only for me. And your second warning?"

"Someone is coming to kill you."

"Me? You know as well as I do the folly in that. I am marked."

"Nevertheless, someone is indeed coming to kill you."

Nosmada didn't respond.

"You feel safe here in your fortress on this land?" Nisroch asked. "Are you truly so strong that you fear no one? Do you feel strong here in this replica garden with that prize hanging from the tree?"

Nosmada looked up, sweat running down his forehead. "Angels and demons land in my garden. Little novice pricks plot my death."

"Despite the famed curse attached to such an act," the angel replied.

"Exactly! In answer to your question, no, I do not think I can hide here. But after so many centuries, I don't really fear death. I am tired of wandering. Tired of fighting. Tired..."

Nisroch nodded and his upper wings unfurled.

Nosmada frowned. "Is there something else on your mind, great one?"

"There is a fear ... a rumor in some circles, that this world is going to end."

"I see." Nosmada looked back to his bean rows. "If that's so, then I wish God would hurry the fuck up with it."

"Not God. A great deluge, put into motion by one of the Thirteen."

"Which one?"

"Leviathan."

Nosmada grunted. "He resides in the Great Deep."

"He would flood this world with the waters of the Great Deep."

"And God would allow this to transpire?"

Soft footsteps echoed on the garden path. Nosmada looked up as Fallon approached, carrying a tray with a mug and a large clay pitcher perched atop it. When the young girl didn't react to Nisroch's presence, Nosmada turned back to the angel, only to see that he had vanished—not flown off, just disappeared.

"Melodramatic sod," Nosmada muttered, "using the doors between worlds rather than his wings."

Fallon stopped before him. "My lord?"

"Yes?"

"I brought you a honey beer. Buchana said you enjoy it as your garden."

Dropping the hoe, Nosmada filled the mug and nodded at the girl. He drank deeply and smacked his lips together.

"Buchana usually tasted it for me first."

"I'm sorry, lord."

"Don't be." He offered her the mug and held it to her lips. Still holding the tray, the girl took a mouthful of the beer and swallowed.

"See?" Nosmada winked. "Now, if you poisoned it, we die together ..."

Fallon smiled and so did Nosmada.

Neither died.

Her eyes focused on the tree to the left.

"You say nothing," Nosmada observed, "but you hear something."

Head bowed, Fallon nodded. "What is it, lord?"

"That, Fallon, is the sound of a suffering god. It is weeping."

"Wizards are such an indispensable evil." General Tolin pulled on the heavy gauntlets and eyed Yitzak Dar's acolytes—four willowy youths of indeterminate sexuality. They chanted and tossed herbs and powders into a flaming brazier as Tolin stepped through the grand crypt chamber.

Tolin paused inside the large chamber and eyed the massive body before him. The chants echoed, muted by the stone walls. He adjusted the heavy gloves again, making sure they were secure, and then approached the carcass. The bag from Anka was tucked under his arm. When he reached the gaping maw, he fished in the bag and withdrew several teeth. He held up each one, examined it in the torchlight, and then inserted them into the corpse's jaw. After the third time, he cursed and tossed a fourth tooth across the room.

"Shark tooth," Tolin muttered. "Anka needs to do better."

Tolin carried on, finding only one more shark tooth until the bag was empty. When he was finished, he stood back, carefully choosing his footing so as not to step on one of the creature's wings, and studied the carcass as one would admire a sculpture or painting. After a few moments, he stooped and tried to pick up a long bone. Finding it too heavy, he barked for help. Although the chanting didn't cease, two acolytes scurried into the room.

"Help me with this," Tolin ordered.

Nodding, they helped him heft the bone from the floor and maneuver it into place on the skeleton. Tolin shoved it with a grunt, and a loud pop echoed through the crypt.

"Go on," he growled. "Back to your duties, or it will be your skin that I use next."

The acolytes rushed from the room. Tolin removed the gauntlets and ran his hand over the hide, feeling the textures change depending on what type of flesh he touched—different races and genders of humans as well as various animals and reptiles. Yitzak Dar had promised that when it was finished, the dragon's skin would revert to the flesh of its kind.

"Soon," Tolin whispered. "Very soon."

He left the crypt and saw Dar and Castellan Tremas approaching. A tall, thin, graying man in elegant robes, Tremas walked with his hands behind his back, eyes front, not staring at the acolytes.

"Do my children do their duty to your satisfaction, General?" the wizard asked.

"You don't hear me complaining, do you, Dar?"

"And the body remains fresh, and not rotting?"

"Again, I have no complaint."

"This pleases me to hear."

"It would please me to hear if you have determined the identity of the hilltop spy."

"Not yet, General."

"Then go and roll your bones, wizard." He thrust the gauntlets into her hands. "Find out if that was indeed Rogan watching us from afar. Let me know. I must go meet with Nosmada."

Dar bowed. Tremas did not. Tolin trudged past them, then paused to look back when the wizard called out to him.

"I forgot to ask," Dar said, "you haven't seen our master's dog have you?"

"Charla?" Tolin shook his head. "Why?"

Dar smiled. "No matter. We'll let you on your way. I'll send word of what I divine regarding our mysterious visitors."

The two walked away. Tolin watched them go.

"A politician and a wizard," he whispered. "I'd sooner trust one of those acolytes."

He stalked through the courtyards and alleys, making his way to the garden of Nosmada. Not lingering at the gates, he walked down the path, stones crunching beneath his boots.

He found Nosmada digging in the earth with an iron spade. The huge man wore only trousers, and his chest shone with sweat. The raised scar on his forehead stood out. Tolin had expected to find the dog with him, but Nosmada was alone. An empty pitcher and mug sat on the ground nearby.

"My lord." Tolin saluted.

"Don't ever have to water weeds," Nosmada sighed. "They just volunteer to grow."

Tolin stood rigid but said nothing.

Nosmada again thrust his spade into the dirt. "Not so with vegetables. Without watering and nurturing, they die, choked out by the weeds. Vegetables have to be coddled. Ironic?"

"The same could be said of people."

"Oh, General..." Nosmada slowly straightened and stared down at the towering Tolin. "Your hatred of humanity rivals many a devil I could name."

"Demons, devils, bad spirits... nothing more than spoiled brats. They always insist that they deserve so much."

"And humans don't?"

"At least humans don't dick around so much in their desires. They just go after them. For the most part, they don't set up elaborate plots and foolish means. They simply act—sometimes without thought. But action requires courage, and that's something demons lack."

"Well," Nosmada replied, "I shan't debate the high points of devils or people. How goes your project?"

Tolin's expression brightened. "Closer."

"Good! We shall both be through with all this soon enough, aye?"

"I long for it, sir."

"Meanwhile," Nosmada said, gesturing, "the trees bear no fruit."

"I see."

"Your lack of curiosity wounds me."

"I doubt that, sir."

Nosmada laughed. "I thank you for your victory today, General. Is there something else?"

"Yes. Yitzak Dar suspects that in addition to the forces we engaged today, there was another group of warriors out in the wilderness. A mercenary company."

"Why is that a concern? Is it a large band?"

"No, but it is possible they are being led by Rogan the Great of Keltos."

"The King of the Bastards?" Nosmada blinked. "I'd heard he was dead."

"Not the first time that rumor has been circulated about him."

"True enough. Well ... let me know if he knocks on our city gates, would you?"

"You wish to speak to Rogan, if he truly lives?"

"Not really, no. I hope he dies." Nosmada walked over and sat beneath the tree on the left of the garden. "But if he indeed reaches the curtain wall, do let me know."

Tolin gave a single nod but did not turn away.

"Is there something else, General?"

"I ..." Tolin closed his eyes, sighed, and then opened them again. "There is deviltry afoot, but I cannot square it away just yet. I shall. It is naught to concern you with."

Nosmada leaned his head against the tree. "I have full confidence you will take care of it, Tolin."

"Of course."

"On your way to the harem?"

Tolin's jaw tightened. "I am."

"Time is drawing very close."

"Yes sir."

With that, he saluted Nosmada and left the garden.

He traveled beyond the courtyard and entered the main citadel. He stopped at a cross-street and smiled as he saw Anka approaching. Clean and wearing a fresh kilt, the bare-chested soldier saluted his general.

Tolin returned the salute. "Imagine finding you near the harems."

They walked together, both slowing as the brighter lights filtered down from above.

"Yes, sir, I don't take a gift lightly."

Tolin opened a door, and they entered an opulent building. "You will drool over the décor here."

Anka looked about them. "I don't trust my footing on these shiny floors, sir."

"Don't slip and bust your ass. That'll make mounting one of the prized flowers here difficult."

"But not impossible."

"True. Just be wary if you run into Tremas or any of those other fucks."

"Will you be staying?"

"No. I'm checking on the other harem. Why? Is there a debate in the ranks on whether I can still get it up?"

"No, sir," Anka replied. "I'd just rather not encounter Tremas or the wizard alone."

"They'll ignore you, lad. They care only about gold. But I really am going to the other harem."

"Sir, I didn't suggest you weren't."

"But you wondered. I can read it in your expression. You're wondering if one with the soul of a dragon can still desire a woman."

Anka remained silent.

"You are a man of courage, Anka. Go ahead and ask me."

Swallowing hard, the soldier nodded. "Do you, sir?"

"Of course I do. You think dragons are celibate?"

Both men laughed.

"Though not today," Tolin said.

They passed through three series of guarded double doors, each one constructed of polished wood. Ladies in silken gowns bowed to them, offering them fruits and nuts as they passed.

"Pomegranates." Tolin winced. "I wouldn't feed them to cadaver dogs."

Two enormous eunuchs unlocked a fourth series of doors, and they passed through them into a vast space full of steaming baths, plush cushions, couches, and slaves fanning the assemblage. Though all of the women were dressed in the silky wraps of highborn harem girls, each reclined and waddled in the advanced stages of pregnancy.

Anka stopped, grabbing Tolin's elbow.

"Easy, boy," Tolin growled. "These are not for you."

Anka hissed a whisper, "I'd heard of these ones, but—"

"Shut your ass," Tolin snapped.

They moved on and were nearly out of the chamber when two of the harem caught sight of them.

"When will this be over?" one cried. "Please, General Tolin! Tell us!"

"We beg of you, General," another wailed. "Let it be done."

"Soon, my dears. You have my word." Tolin looked over at one of the attendants, an elderly woman carrying a decanter. "Give them wine, and fast."

The older lady filled three goblets full of cherry-red liquid and quickly handed them to the weeping women.

As Tolin and Anka hurried along, the younger soldier leaned close to him.

"Sir, is it wise to feed those women wine given the state they are in?"

"It doesn't make a damn bit of difference."

The next doors opened, and they entered a room filled with nubile, giggling young women running about nude.

Tolin slapped Anka hard on the shoulder. "Still feel up to it?"

Anka nodded, his eyes wide.

CHAPTER 3

TROUBLE IN MIND

Rogan watched as the woman's great white stallion thundered toward them. Behind her rode a force that outnumbered his company ten to one. More troops mustered on the hillside, staring down at them.

"That horse …" He turned to Brok. "A descendant of Traveler, the famed steed of Gorias himself?"

"It's not a descendant. That is Traveler."

Rogan grunted.

"I've heard those tales," Thaxter said. "Seven hundred years and Gorias rode the same horse all that time."

"I'm sure he changed mounts," Javan whispered.

"Right?" Thaxter shifted in his saddle. "I mean, I can buy a fella living that long, but his horse? That's fucking silly. Just a story."

"I've heard a story about that horse, too," Rogan said. "Remind me to relate it over wine or whiskey."

As she neared them, La Gaul's daughter spun the horse about, her red hair whipping around. She glanced at her men and then glared at Rogan, Javan, and Thaxter. Her forces halted behind her, stirring up a cloud of dust.

"Roan La Gaul, is it?" Rogan dismounted from his horse and stood, hands on his waist belt, his expression serene.

Thaxter turned to Javan and whispered, "Ever see eyes that green, lad? I think I'm in love."

"No, you are not." Roan's voice was deep but not masculine.

Blushing, Thaxter fell silent.

Roan focused again on Rogan. "You are their leader?"

"I am."

"And bold, to dismount so and stand there without a care."

"I'm not as bold as I once was," Rogan replied, "and even if I was, I wouldn't come out swinging to a stranger. As my nephew says, with age comes wisdom."

"Wisdom ... or a limp cock?"

"I have no complaints."

She studied him for a moment. "You're a seasoned warrior. That much I can tell. What is your name? You already know who I am."

"I know who they say you are, and who your banner claims you are, but I don't know if that's true. As for me ... what if I told you I was Rogan of far-off Albion?"

"Rogan wasn't from Albion." Roan smirked. "He was from the Caucasus Mountains, technically born in Larak."

Rogan smiled. "You know your tales, little lady."

"Bah!" She swung her long leg over the saddle, bounded to the ground, and stalked toward him. "I'm not either of those things. You're a good six and a half feet tall, and I'm staring you in the eye. And the last man to call me a lady got his skull split."

Rogan shrugged. "Regardless, you know your history."

"Rogan had the same origin story as my father."

"Except that your father hailed from Thule," Rogan replied.

Roan's smirk returned. "I guess wisdom does indeed come with age."

"Enough," Rogan growled. "That was about as polite as I get. You're Roan La Gaul, daughter of Gorias La Gaul, and you and your happy band of assholes are roaming around, looking for a fight. How's my wisdom?"

"Well, you've proven you're not senile at the very least."

"I'm wise enough to recognize an army when I spot it. But you were not here to engage the forces from over yonder, were you?"

"Not exactly, but my desires are my own. I don't know if sharing them with a braggart who claims to be Rogan the Great is wise."

"No, that would not be wise." Rogan pointed to the assembled forces on the hilltop. "Quite a group you got there. Not turning many away, are you?"

Roan brushed her wind-tossed red locks from her eyes. "An army needs bodies."

"No," Rogan countered. "An army needs soldiers."

Roan opened her mouth to respond but was interrupted by a screech from within the ranks of her army. She turned, eyebrow raised.

Javan and Thaxter, still on horseback, glanced at each other. Their hands crept to their weapons.

Rogan stood calmly, hands still on his waist belt, and waited.

A short woman clad in sandals and a faded dark dress stumbled out of the assemblage and ran toward them. Her gray hair was in disarray and shot through with a few black strands, and her pale skin was bruised and wrinkled. Her eyes, black and flaring, looked to the sky, and her mouth opened wide, revealing a set of shockingly white teeth. She screamed again and fell to her knees in the road.

"The All Father vexes me! Leave me be. I cannot save you." She grabbed handfuls of dirt and continued to shout at the sky. Then she balled up one fist and struck herself in her left eye. "I see, All Father! I see ... him."

Frowning, Rogan turned to Thaxter. "Tonight, after the wine runs thin? She's all yours."

"Piss off," Thaxter replied.

The crone dropped her fistfuls of dirt and pointed at Rogan, cackling. Then her hands began to work, clawing and flexing in the air.

Javan swung out of his saddle and stood alongside Rogan. "Sire, she appears to be a witch."

"I can see that."

"Not in the figurative sense, Uncle. I'd say by the way her fingers flash the symbols and pointed at you, well ..."

"She's a real practitioner?"

Javan nodded, hands on his sword hilt.

Rogan looked at Roan. "Leash up your witch, young lady, before I let my nephew kill her."

The old woman began to spasm and jitter, and fell to the ground, flecks of foam flying from her cracked lips.

"Not enough wine in the world," Thaxter quipped.

"The King of the Bastards," the witch wailed. "The scourge of Asmodeous himself ... the All Father needs you ..."

Roan knelt beside the old woman and gently lifted her head by the chin. "Hyden, what do you see? Who is this man before us?"

"The son of Jarek." Dirt fell from the crone's eye. "The Bastard King ... slayer of the Chimera ..."

Roan stared at Rogan, her eyes wide with wonder.

He shrugged. "Gonna take the word of an old witch? I'm just another pretty face with a raging cock."

Roan helped Hyden to her feet. "What say you of the rest? What beguiles you?"

"The All Father screams for them, for all of the barbarian bastards."

"What does he say?"

"Kill me," Hyden whispered. "Kill me ..."

"That doesn't sound like Wodan at all," Javan said.

"Agreed." Rogan folded his massive arms across his scarred chest. "Wodan would say kill everyone else."

Hyden's expression cleared and her demeanor grew suddenly calm. "Shows what you know, dirty-assed savages."

"Hey," Thaxter yelled, "I'll have you know I wiped this morning."

"But only this morning," Rogan quipped.

He stepped toward Roan and Hyden. The old woman shrank away from him, but Rogan held out his hands.

"Easy, witch. I mean you no harm. I'm only curious. Why would the All Father speak to you, here of all places? Why would you even know of him here?"

"He haunts not only my dreams," Hyden groaned, "but my waking thoughts as well."

"But why? Why you?"

"You misunderstand, barbarian. It's not for me he comes. It's for you."

"Well, isn't that something." Rogan shook his head, grinning. "My god speaks through you and says for me to kill him? That's rich."

"How are your dreams, Bastard King?"

Rogan's smile faded. "I don't dream."

"You lie."

Rogan's hand went to the hilt of his sword. "Your crone had better mind her tongue, Roan."

"Is she right?"

"I am," Hyden replied. "Wodan calls to you, doesn't he?"

"No." Rogan turned away from them.

"He does," Hyden insisted. "What does he say? What does he show you?"

Ignoring her, Rogan turned again to Roan. "The day is dying. Shall we all eat together and get drunk?"

Brok, who had remained silent since his mistress's arrival, now stepped forward. "You have wine?"

Thaxter pointed back at the village. "These little pricks have a hell of a vineyard. I'm sure they won't mind giving us some of their stores."

Rogan nodded. "What say you, Roan? Shall we discuss over wine why I should hire my company out to you?"

Roan's eyes narrowed. "By all means, Bastard King, get drunk and ignore your god."

He leaned in close and winked. "I don't have to be drunk to ignore a god."

"Then you're a fool."

"A fool is someone who believes that every bad dream he has is the words of a god."

Hyden laughed. "But he's spoken to you before, hasn't he? And near here?"

Ignoring her again, Rogan turned his back on them. "Javan? Have those cured hams prepared. I'm hungry enough to eat a witch, tits and all."

Hyden fell back down into the dirt and started to laugh.

She was still laughing as the company rode by her.

DARKNESS FELL ON THE GREAT CITADEL OF NODD. THE MOON and stars shone down coldly on the garden of Nosmada, where Fallon knelt before one of the two big trees. Tears wet her cheeks as she gazed upward. There, suspended among the broad branches, swung a body on a noose—placed high enough that the leafy canopy concealed it unless a person was standing directly beneath the tree. Even then, one would have to squint to find it. And yet, the girl had spotted it easily enough.

Slowly, she rose from her position and took a few halting breaths. She paused when she heard a similar panting behind her. Fallon turned and saw Charla, Lord Nosmada's dog, watching her, pink tongue lolling.

"C-Charla," Fallon whispered. "Good doggy ..."

"Child," the deep voice of Lord Nosmada filled the garden. "What are you doing here alone?"

Fallon cried out and stumbled backward. As she hurriedly scanned the garden, she spotted a shadowed figure back by the lattice works entangled in vines.

"You are wondering how you missed me when you came in, hmm?"

Fallon nodded.

Nosmada stepped out of the shadows and walked toward her. "I didn't want to be seen."

"You make that sound so easy, my lord."

"It is easy, for one such as I. But you still haven't answered my question, Fallon. Why are you here?"

Lips quivering, she glanced upward at the hanged man.

"So, I was correct." Nosmada smiled. "He speaks to you. He talks in your head, not your ears?"

"Yes."

"He has no choice," Nosmada replied. "His mouth is sewn shut."

Fallon gasped. "That's ..."

"Horrible?" Nosmada shrugged. "Trust me, listening to him is worse. If you had heard the things he had to say ages ago, you would've ripped off your own ears."

Again, she looked up at the hanging man, and then back to her master. Nearby, the dog nosed through a plot of pumpkins.

"Does he speak with his mouth in your dreams?"

Fallon nodded. "Yes, Lord."

"He sounds majestic, doesn't he? Magnificent? Benevolent?"

She nodded again.

"Well, he is none of those things. Perhaps they are what he dreams he is, hmm?"

"But he told me ..."

"What?" Nosmada's voice grew louder. "That he is a prisoner? That he suffers on the tree for his folk? That he is an imprisoned god who desires release?"

She nodded a third time.

Nosmada reached out, snatched Fallon's wrist, and pulled her close. "Were there great tales of adventure, of his sons, wives, and friends? Of monsters, devils, and the battle for this plane of existence?"

"Yes, my lord!" She began to cry again.

"Did he tell you of his six-legged horse?"

"No."

"He will." Nosmada pulled her hand up to his lips. His breath brushed her fingertips. "Can I tell you something about him?"

"Yes," Fallon sobbed. "Please ..."

"He lies."

Nosmada released her, but Fallon didn't yank her hand back. Instead, she let it fall. Then she knelt in the garden, head low.

"Please don't kill me," she begged.

Nosmada sighed. "Get up, Fallon."

Still weeping, she did as commanded. She blinked tears away, steadying herself.

"I'm not going to kill you," Nosmada promised. "I give you my word. But that one up there? He'll be the death of many."

He pulled the girl close, wrapping his arms around her and crushing her against his chest.

"Who is he," Fallon mumbled, "really?"

Nosmada rested his bearded chin on her head. "He's not who he says he is, nor who he dreams to be. Indeed, I often wonder if he even recalls his real name anymore."

"He's forgotten?"

"He's lied so much, he believes his own lies. Perhaps the lies we tell ourselves are more comforting than reality."

Fallon took another shuddering breath. "Do we all lie to ourselves?"

"Certainly. Right now, you're telling yourself over and over that you'll never come near this garden again if I let you walk out alive. And yet, you lie. He's set his mind and spirit on you, so you cannot resist. You'll return again and again."

"My lord," she sobbed. "I don't want to disobey you."

"You fear death?"

"Yes."

"I understand." He closed his eyes and held her fast. "Fear of death scares me, too."

"W-what?"

"Of course. What lies beyond for a man like me? Seasons in the abyss?"

"You believe it is there? The abyss?"

He petted her hair. "Yes."

"Have you seen it?"

"No, but I've heard about it from ... entities that know."

Fallon relaxed in his embrace. "Angels and demons?"

"Yes."

"But aren't all demons liars, my lord?"

"Yes," Nosmada chuckled. "They most certainly are. Nevertheless, they know fear the same as you or I do. And when they are afraid, they tell the truth—one such truth is that death is not the end for any of us. Something lies beyond."

Fallon pointed up at the hanged man. "How did he come to be here if his story is not true? Why do you keep him here?"

"You ask so many questions." Sighing, Nosmada released the servant girl. "I will answer just one. Fair enough?"

"Yes, my lord."

"Very well. I keep him up there so that he can't infect the rest of the world with his evil. However, even indisposed as he is, he can infect dreams. But that's all he can do."

"I thought there was another reason, my lord."

"You doubt I keep him imprisoned up there out of the goodness of my heart?"

Fallon didn't reply.

"You are a wise lass, dear Fallon." Nosmada laughed. "Very well. Most men or women do things for selfish reasons. No matter how much they talk about the betterment of humanity, they are full of excrement. People do things for their own selfish benefit and then polish the manure off the reasons to glean acceptance from the world."

"But, my lord, you never care for acceptance. You are the master of Nodd and the grandson of God himself." Gasping, Fallon covered her mouth with her hand. "My apologies, my lord. I did not mean to speak that aloud. I'm sorry, I really am."

"Why be sorry? You simply repeat what others say about me. Mind you, I noticed you didn't ask me if it was true."

"I used up my question already tonight, my lord. You said that you'd only answer one."

Again, Nosmada laughed. "I like you, child. Really, I do. I'll see that you are not given to the leeches."

"Thank you, my lord."

"As for this one here? I keep him hanging around because it pleases me to do so, and part of him helps make me strong."

Nosmada reached into his coat and withdrew a small flask. He swirled it about, showing her that it contained a copious red substance. Winking, he pulled the cork out with his teeth, and then drank the liquid down.

Fallon clutched her stomach in revulsion.

"Besides ..." Nosmada licked the crimson from his lips. "He's delicious."

Fallon turned, dropped to her knees, and threw up.

"Oh, Fallon." Nosmada shook his head. "If you're going to do that, at least aim for the cabbage patch. They could use the fertilizer."

The girl tried to respond, but her words were garbled as she retched again.

Charla waddled over, sniffing at the steaming vomit. Sighing, Nosmada was about to reprimand the dog and call her away when a bright light illuminated the sky. He looked up and saw that it came from the twin towers of Yitzak Dar.

Fallon heaved again.

"Now what do you suppose that wizard is up to?" Nosmada asked.

Charla responded with a low whine.

TOLIN RECLINED ON A CUSHIONED BENCH BEFORE THE DORMANT fireplace, and then glanced out at the balcony and to the stars beyond.

"General?"

Tolin looked up and smiled. "Hello, Spence."

Clad in a silken wrap, Madam Spence stood over him, hands to her ample hips. Her purple-painted lips glistened in the firelight.

"Take your armor off and relax, sir."

"I am relaxed."

Spence smiled. "What's on your mind?"

"When you walk... that thing you do with your hips? Were you taught to walk like that or is it just natural?"

She laughed. "My mother taught me. She taught all the girls in our family."

"That is some family."

She sat down next to him. "We were trained to be courtesans at a young age. If one cannot be a good wife or be given away for marriage or property, sometimes this is the only vocation."

"Like sons," Tolin agreed. "One inherits the estate, one might be kept as a spare, but another son must be a solider. Or, god forbid, another is born, and he becomes a priest."

"Or a concubine," Spence teased.

"Whoredom doesn't seem as common for men." He scowled in disgust. "Humanity is worse than dogs."

Her smile remained, unshaken by his words. "It's cold outside tonight."

He gave her a quizzical look.

"It's warm in here, and there's food in the other room. I'll sleep on cushions tonight and not on the ground. I'll pass water in a pot and not up against a tree. This life isn't so bad, General."

Tolin grunted.

"Take off your armor," she urged again, "and I can take care of your tension."

"Bring me some wine and I'll think that over."

Nodding, she stood up. "The mind cannot always be full of dragons and war, General."

"So very true. At least regarding dragons and war. Freedom and vengeance, however, are tough to shake off."

Tolin watched Spence cross the room and slip through a door. Before the door could swing shut again, a familiar figure passed through.

"Anka?" Tolin frowned. "Why are you here? Had your fill already?"

The warrior drank from a wineskin as he walked over to the balcony. "Oh, my mind isn't quite with it. Yet."

"At your age?"

Anka stared out into the darkness. "Maybe it was seeing all of those pregnant women, knowing that they'd gotten that way by sleeping with the angels. Or maybe it was just this clean environment."

"I made no such excuses in my youth. The angels were fucking human women back then, too."

"Yes, but you are an exceptional man, General." Anka swigged more wine. "I find that for myself—gods!" Anka gripped the balcony railing, staring wide-eyed at the citadel's skyline.

"What is it?"

"The towers are full of light. I'll bet that Yitzak Dar is conjuring something wicked." He held up one hand, palm extended into the darkness. "Even the wind feels different."

Tolin arose just as Spence returned. In one hand, she carried a decanter with two cups on her thumb. In the other was a tiny piece of parchment.

"Word?" Tolin asked, nodding at the paper.

Nodding, she handed him the tiny scroll. Then she sat down the cups and poured two glasses of wine. She offered one to each of them.

"I still have this." Anka raised his wineskin. "Help yourself, my lady."

Smiling, Spence curtsied. "Thank you."

Tolin eyed her as she sipped. Then she offered him one. Reassured that the wine wasn't poisoned, he turned his attention to the scroll, unrolling it and reading the fine scrawl.

Anka stepped away from the balcony and crossed the room. "What is it, sir?"

"More bones," Tolin replied. "A big shipment is on the way from far beyond."

"That's good, right?"

Tolin toasted him with the wine cup and Anka raised the wineskin. Just then, a loud screech echoed across the city. A sound like thunder rippled up from the ground. The building shook beneath their feet, swaying back and forth. Wine spilled across Tolin's hand, and Spence cried out in alarm. Then, everything fell still again. In the aftermath, the three stood staring at each other.

"Sirs?" Spence's expression was fearful.

Far below, people began to scream in the streets.

"Damn it!" Frowning, Tolin handed Spence his cup.

Anka snapped to attention. "Orders, sir?"

"Soldier, you stay here and concentrate on your reward. Chances like this don't come along often. I shall go deal with it."

"What do you think is happening?" Spence asked.

"I don't care. Whatever it is, I won't have the city terrorized."

With that, Tolin stomped out of the plush room. He headed through the interchanges, exiting the building.

Once in the street, he mounted his horse and made his way through the chaos. Panicked citizens had filed out of their homes, fearing an earthquake. Fights erupted in the tavern district, but a company of soldiers was breaking through the crowd to quell the violence. Nodding, Tolin spurred his horse ahead, shouting at people to move lest he run them down. He noted with satisfaction that while his troops had immediately jumped into action, the men of the city guard—who did not answer to him—seemed just as confused and frightened as the other civilians.

As he drew nearer to the twin towers of Yitzak Dar, he spotted the Captain of the Guard guiding his horse in the same direction.

"Bradlee," Tolin grumbled. "I was just thinking about you. I saw some of your men back there."

"Aye, and I saw some of yours, too, General Tolin. They seem to forget their duties."

"Maybe if your own forces did their jobs better, my soldiers wouldn't have to cover for them."

The two men reached the shadow of the twin towers. This area was clear of passersby. Not even Dar's acolytes were present. A great stillness seemed to permeate the stones.

Bradlee reigned his horse to a halt. "I don't want to fight with you, General. We serve the same master."

Tolin slid from his horse without responding and stared up at the looming towers.

Bradlee shuddered. "What is he up to now?"

"She," Tolin corrected him. "Dar prefers to be known as a woman. You should respect that."

"I don't understand it."

"You don't need to understand it. Simply understand that Yitzak Dar can turn you into a newt if she chooses."

There was another screech from the top of the towers, and Bradlee flinched. Tolin merely grimaced.

"I think Dar conjures the night," Bradlee whispered.

"Sounds like she's screwing the night instead. You stay here, Captain Bradlee. Make sure nobody else enters. I'll see to it."

Bradlee opened his mouth as if he might argue. Then, wisely, he simply nodded and stepped back.

"Cunt," Tolin muttered as he stepped through the gate and headed toward the door of the tower on the right.

A young man in a one-piece gown stood at the entrance. When he saw the general stalking toward him, the acolyte ran. Shaking his head, Tolin shoved the door open and began the long, arduous climb up the circular steps leading to the tower's top chamber. His boot heels echoed hollowly against the stones. He encountered no one else. At one point, Tolin's heel turned on a wet spot, and he put a hand on the stone wall to steady himself. The walls were warm. They should have been damp and cold, but heat coursed through the carved blocks. He frowned, curious, and then continued on his way.

At the top of the stairs, he stepped through a broad, curved arch and into a round room lit by countless candles and a throbbing, pulsating purple light. The purple glow coursed from a figure huddled on the floor. As Tolin strode into the room, the light faded and was gone.

The figure groaned and twitched.

Though her back was to him, Tolin recognized the crouched shape as Yitzak Dar. She wore the same clothes he had seen her in earlier.

Tolin cleared his throat.

"General," Dar croaked, without turning to face him.

"Dar. What ... what's wrong with you?"

"Ah ... come closer."

Scowling, Tolin complied, circling to Dar's front. The wizard knelt in a pool of blood. Tolin's hand crept to the hilt of his sword. As he crept nearer, he spotted a steaming pile of entrails slopped on the floor in front of the wizard.

Tolin grunted. "Reading innards again?"

"That ... and more."

"You ass. For a moment I feared someone had disemboweled you."

"You gave me a task. I complied."

"It took all this to find out the identity of our interloper?"

Dar nodded, eyes closed. Her hands worked, clutching and kneading a glistening length of intestine.

"The lights? Those sound like thunder? That was you as well?"

The wizard opened her eyes. "Aye."

"And what did you learn?"

"He's out there," Dar said.

"Rogan?"

Dar nodded again. "He leads a small but fierce company of fighters. He's joined up with some woman warrior."

Tolin frowned. "Who is she?"

"I cannot quite read her name, General. And her form is not clear. She has red hair."

"Can you read his desire?"

"Beyond wondering if he could survive bedding the woman? No. His intentions are cloudy."

"I see. So, you sit there, wallowing in guts, terrifying the city with your fancy light show ... and yet you know nothing."

"On the contrary!" Dar stood up fast and wobbled on her feet. She dropped the intestines onto the floor and wiped her blood-slicked hands on her robes. "I have dealt with him."

"How so?"

"You think I cry out and use such magicks to see afar? No, the spells I enacted have unleashed a force that will destroy Rogan and all those with him."

"Greater wizards than you have boasted of destroying Rogan. All of them have failed."

Dar grinned. "They didn't have the courage to do what I have done here tonight. They'd never be able to control what I've released."

Tolin's eyes narrowed. "What did you do?"

Saliva ran from Dar's lips. "I have unleashed the hellhounds."

"What hellhounds? We have no hellhounds."

"We do now."

"Dar ..." Tolin's hand crept once again to his sword hilt. "There's a reason that armies don't use hellhounds in battle. They're too indiscriminate. Too unpredictable. They'd slaughter our entire populace in addition to this barbarian."

"These won't," Dar assured him. "I have conjured them in such a way that they are loyal to our lord and master."

Before Tolin could respond, a new series of shouts rose from below. He strode to the window and thrust his head outside. There was no sign of Captain Bradlee, who was meant to be stationed at the tower door, but a group of guards jogged past, armor rustling, heading toward Nosmada's garden. He craned his head out further and heard another cry. It was hard to be certain from this height, but Tolin thought it sounded like Nosmada himself. He whirled again on the wizard.

"What have you done, Dar?"

"I told you." She spread her bloody hands and shrugged. "I summoned a pack of hellhounds. You needn't look so panicked. They are loyal to him whom we serve. I made sure of it."

"We'll talk more later, wizard."

"I look forward to it, General Tolin."

Tolin stalked out of the room, careful not to hurry until he was out of Dar's eyesight and earshot. Then he ran, taking the stairs two at a time.

When he emerged from the tower, Bradlee was still missing.

"I'm surrounded by incompetents."

Cursing, Tolin leaped up onto his horse and galloped across Nodd toward the citadel of Nosmada. When he reached the garden, he found Captain Bradlee along with six other guards. Nosmada knelt next to them, bare-chested, cradling his dog.

Gaping, Tolin reigned his mount to a halt. Charla's mangled corpse appeared as if it had ruptured from within.

"What ... happened?"

Nosmada looked up slowly. Droplets of the dog's blood had dried on his face.

"It was Dar's magick," Bradlee muttered. "A witness said the light flew out of the tower and struck the hound."

"What witness?"

"My men say there was a servant girl."

"Find her," Tolin ordered.

Nosmada waved them off. "There's no need. It was Fallon, and she spoke the truth. The light came down from above like a bolt of lightning and struck poor Charla. She ... had some sort of seizure, and then split open like a ripe melon. Then things crawled out of her. At first, we thought they were snakes, but they changed shape and grew."

"What were they?"

"Dogs," Nosmada said. "Long, lean dogs. A half dozen of them, all told. Black as shadows. They grew to the size of ponies, eyes glowing red. They were hellhounds, Tolin."

"Where are they now?"

Nosmada pointed absently. "They ran off to the east."

"Should we arrest the wizard, my lord?" Bradlee glanced up at the tower and then back to Nosmada. "Perhaps General Tolin could have a company lay siege to the towers?"

"Why would we do that, Captain?"

"Well, begging my pardon, lord, but clearly Yitzak Dar was trying to assassinate you and killed your dog instead."

Nosmada wiped his hands on his trousers and laughed. Bradlee's ears turned red. The other guards stared at the ground or into the sky.

"Yitzak Dar is many things, Bradlee, but unlike you, she is not a fool. No ... that light was meant for Charla. And after all, she was just a dog. A good dog, granted, but I've had many good dogs over the years. What concerns me more is what Dar has conjured up here tonight."

"Damned wizards," Tolin said, and then recounted everything that Dar had told him.

"So, it is Rogan then?" Nosmada nodded thoughtfully. "Interesting. I'll be curious to know his intent."

"If the hellhounds don't kill him," Tolin said.

"You've heard the same stories as I have." Nosmada rolled his eyes. "Do you really believe even that barbarian is a match for them?"

"I've never heard of a man beating a hellhound," Tolin replied.

"Exactly!"

"But I've never heard of a man beating Rogan, either."

CHAPTER 4

HELLHOUNDS ON MY TRAIL

Bonfires dotted the edge of Ellivsulo as the two factions camped for the night. Desultory fighters from both companies had returned from the village's disappointing brothel and retired to their bedrolls or tents. Those who remained awake sat about, drinking and smoking and talking.

Rogan, flanked by Javan and Thaxter, had finished eating and now reclined near the main fire, a skin of local wine in his hand. Across from him sat several warriors from Roan's group—the one-eyed youth, Kenoth; the braggart, Brok Yoshee; and a woman named Angeline.

As Yoshee boasted one purloined tale after another, Thaxter leaned close to Rogan, speaking quietly so that their new comrades would not hear.

"What do you think of these?"

Rogan lowered his wineskin. "The one-eyed kid is just that, a bloodied-up version of Javan. He'd be good in a fight, I'd wager."

Munching some roasted rabbit, Javan whispered, "A formidable force, to be sure, but none of them compare to Captain Xuxan and his crew or to our Kennebeck friends. And that witch, Hyden? I dare say she'd be no match for old Akibeel."

Rogan watched as his nephew's expression darkened. The boy bit off another mouthful of meat.

"You're thinking of Zenata," Rogan mused.

Javan shrugged.

"Well, you're right. Most of this lot don't compare to them. But we shouldn't discount them, either. That gal, Angeline, guards her words, so she has sense at the very least."

"And she probably has more balls than that braying ass, Brok," Thaxter added.

"Indeed." Rogan nodded. "As for the others ... that bloated fighter, Vernon? There's something screwy about that stinking prick. The smell coming off him isn't normal. And the lizard—the one they call Seth? I don't ever trust those things."

Thaxter belched and forgot to whisper. "You afraid of the old snake-people legends?"

Roan's people turned toward them.

"That isn't a legend." Rogan pointed at Seth, attracting further attention. "There's one standing right over there. Wodan says to kill them where we find them. Nothing but trouble."

Angeline's eyes flared. "You obey all the edicts of your god?"

"Sure." Rogan grinned. "At least the ones about drinking and whoring."

Angeline rolled her eyes.

"And killing snakes," he added.

Seth merely stared at them, unblinking. The firelight reflected off the oblong pupils of his eyes.

Roan stepped from the shadows beyond the fire. "The drink is on Rogan, Angeline. Ignore his words, as Seth does."

"My words are sometimes better when I drink," Rogan replied. "Get enough wine in me, and I sound educated like Javan."

"You believe that, do you?"

"This is wisdom I'm putting in my mouth." Rogan brought the wineskin to his lips and tipped it back.

"You've put a thief in your mouth that has already stolen your tongue. In time, it will take your mind and manhood as well."

Rogan reached between his legs. "Nope, still there."

"Wait for it," Roan replied.

Rogan and Thaxter laughed. Javan smiled but remained aloof, staring into the fire. After a moment, Brok began to tell another story—loudly. Rogan and Thaxter glanced at each other. Rogan opened his mouth to interrupt, but before he could speak, Hyden staggered out of the dark, nearly stumbling into the fire.

"Hyden," Roan asked, "what is it?"

She clutched the sides of her head. "Something is coming."

Rogan grabbed his crotch again. "Yes, wait for it ..."

Thaxter brayed laughter, spraying a mouthful of drink. Ignoring them both, Roan jumped to her feet, and Vernon lumbered up after her. Seconds later, Angeline and Kenoth followed their lead. Brok sat between them, blinking. Then, with a groan, he clambered upright.

Arms flailing, Hyden gestured at the open territory beyond them. "Something is out there. Something coming at us ... very fast."

Thaxter cleared his throat. "Is it the judgment of Wodan, coming to sweep us all off the edge of the world?"

Rogan raised his wineskin. "I'll drink to that!"

"You'll drink to anything, Uncle," Javan said. "You'll drink to your ability to pull on your boots."

"Here, here!" Rogan swigged the wine and kicked up his boots.

Roan placed her hands on the witch's scrawny shoulders. "Please, concentrate. Hyden. What is coming?"

Hyden's arms dropped limp at her sides. She stared into the dark and shuddered. "Dogs."

Javan stood. "Dogs?"

"Woof," Thaxter barked.

The witch nodded. "Very bad dogs."

A traumatized shrieking echoed through the night.

Rogan's smile faded. "That didn't sound like a dog. That sounded like a man getting his guts ripped out."

"Shit," Thaxter said. "Where's my ax?"

"Listen," Brok urged them.

Screams broke out from all across the encampment. Soon, the cries were punctuated by an infernal howling.

Angeline shuddered. "What is that?"

"Hellhounds," Hyden whispered. "And they are coming for us...." She turned and pointed at Rogan. "Well, you."

"Me, huh?" Rogan blinked. "Thaxter, give me a hand."

The sounds of panic spread as the big man helped the aged barbarian to his feet. Both Roan and Rogan's forces stumbled from their tents, weapons drawn, glancing about in fear and confusion.

"Sounds like they've broken through the pickets," Kenoth observed.

"Agreed," Javan replied. "And, judging by the directions of the screams, I'd say they are on all sides, working their way toward us."

Rogan belched.

"Stinking drunk." Roan glared at him. "You can barely stand!"

"Maybe," Rogan admitted, "but I can still fight."

The group closed ranks as the sounds drew closer. Hyden hid behind Roan. Javan notched an arrow and planted his feet. Kenoth held a sword in one hand and a small hatchet in the other. Angeline brandished two weapons, as well—a short sword in her left hand and a strange triangle-shaped blade in her right. The massive Vernon and Seth the lizard man stood beside them. Vernon held a mace. The reptilian pulled two thin swords from a sheath on his back.

Thaxter winced, fanning his nose as Vernon passed by him. "You don't need that mace, big man. Your stench is enough to defeat any foe."

"Maybe when this is over," Vernon grumbled, "you and I can put that theory to the test."

"Enough," Roan snapped. "They're coming!"

Six bestial forms appeared in the darkness, looming just beyond the campfire's light. Slowly, they padded forth and then stopped. The creatures growled in unison. Their eyes glowed red, and their bodies exuded an aura of unwholesome light. Each hound was the size of a cow. Their coarse fur was black as coal, and their slavering mouths were red.

"They drool blood!" Brok's voice quavered. His short sword bobbed in his trembling hand as he fumbled to ready his round shield.

"They don't drool blood," Angeline said. "That's the blood of those they've killed already."

Thaxter hefted his ax. "Six of them."

"You're sober enough to count." Rogan unsheathed his sword. "Are you able to fight, as well?"

"Aye. I've heard tales of these things, but never thought I'd see one." Thaxter stared at the beasts in wonder ... and fear.

"Why do they hesitate?" Brok asked.

The monstrous hounds glanced at each other, and then, as if in answer to the question, they leaped forward, bounding at Rogan.

Javan loosed an arrow, drew down, and fired two more times before the dogs had reached the campfire. His arrows found homes, but the beasts disregarded them, unimpeded.

He gasped. "They didn't even flinch!"

"Focus," Rogan cautioned.

Kenoth and Seth attacked simultaneously as the dogs rampaged past them. The snake man's dual blades slashed the hides of two monsters. Roaring, Kenoth swung with both weapons, lopping off a hellhound's leg in mid-leap. The animal tumbled to the ground, snarling. As it turned toward him, Kenoth swiftly planted his hatchet in its rump. The creature yelped but, despite its injuries, didn't lose its ire. It swung about on three legs, hatchet sticking from its backside like an extra tail, and slammed into Brok. The braggart toppled over, belly-flopping in the dirt. He flipped himself over, but before he could rise, the cur hobbled toward him, red saliva dripping from its jaws. Brok threw up both hands and screamed.

Roan jumped into the fray, planted her right foot, and crossed her blades, meaning to behead the wounded hound. Her swords stuck deep in the creature's neck, and it yowled, glaring at her. She roared back at the monster, planted her left boot on the hell-hound's forehead, and pulled back. Her swords ripped free, and she fell backward, landing beside the trembling Brok. Kenoth swung his blade down. The creature's head landed between Yoshee's outstretched legs.

Chaos consumed the camp. Forces on both sides scattered, ducking into ruined tents and staggering over their fallen comrades. Their cries intermingled with the howls of the beasts.

Rogan turned to shout orders at his men, and a hellhound charged.

"Look out," Thaxter warned as the monster crossed the distance between them. Unable to throw himself between the beast and Rogan, Thaxter reared back and struck with his great ax. The heavy blade sunk deep into the creature's back and lodged there, but the monster didn't slow down. Thaxter, refusing to let go of his weapon, was dragged along behind the lunging dog.

"Javan," Thaxter yelled. "A little help!"

"I have you!"

Javan dropped to one knee and fired at Thaxter's unwilling mount. His aim was true, and the arrow struck the hellhound in its side, but the beast only responded with a grunt.

Rogan turned. Bellowing in surprise, he swung his sword, gashing the creature's broad chest. The dog returned the attack, lashing out at him. Its claws raked trenches in his thigh. Still gripping his ax hilt, Thaxter swung off the beast's back and got his feet on the ground. He pulled, trying to keep the thing from reaching his friend. Rogan held his sword like a spear, but before he could deliver the thrust, another hellhound leaped onto his back, crushing him to the ground. His sword flew from his hands.

Pinned to the earth, Rogan wrapped his arms around the crea-ture and clinched it tight, using his armored shoulder to push the slavering, snapping jaws away from his face. Grunting, he twisted with all his might, and the two rolled toward the fire. The hound roared with enraged surprise, but Rogan held on, locking his wrists. They tumbled together to the edge of the crackling flames, and the blast of heat against Rogan's hands distracted the barbarian for just a second—but it was enough to loosen his grip. The monster shook Rogan free, throwing him off. Landing on the other side of the campfire, Rogan sprang up on all fours and spat blood.

"That was fun," he taunted. "Let's do it again."

Growling, the beast circled the fire. Rogan did the same, keeping the flames between them as he frantically glanced around for his sword. In the semidarkness nearby, Thaxter struggled with another of the creatures. The big man's ax was buried deep in the monster's flank, and he held it in place as several stout pikemen from Rogan's mercenary company drove their huge spears into the beast. The hellhound wailed, shuddered, and then slumped to the ground.

Brok appeared, charging through the encampment astride a galloping, terrified horse. To Rogan, it looked as if the man was fleeing the battle. His retreat came to an abrupt and grisly halt as one of the hellhounds bounded toward him and slammed into his mount's rump, slashing through the horse's flank. All three crashed to the ground, but Brok was able to fling himself far enough away that he wasn't pinned beneath the horse. The hellhound ravaged the squealing animal, tearing into it with claws and teeth, and showering Brok's pale face in gore.

Rogan and the hound continued to circle the fire. He snatched up a fallen dagger and tested its weight in his hand. The creature pawed at the dirt. From the corner of his eye, he spotted Angeline and the serpentine Seth facing off against a wounded hellhound. Then Brok came back into sight. The braggart skittered backward through the dirt as Kenoth came to his aid. The one-eyed youth swung at the beast but missed. The dog turned, covered in horse innards, and bared its teeth. Kenoth held his ground.

"Wodan's ball sack, Brok," Rogan shouted. "Get up off your cowering ass and help the lad!"

Taking advantage of his distraction, the hellhound halved the distance around the campfire. Rogan gripped the dagger and spread his feet apart, taking a fighter's stance. Before the beast could lunge at him, however, Javan appeared out of the smoke, arrow quiver and bow strapped to his back, and leaped onto the monster like a child onto a pony. He gripped knives in each fist, and he drove them down simultaneously, stabbing deep. He clutched the hilts like handles as the creature shook, trying to dislodge him. Rogan ran over, dropped to the ground, and slid beneath the beast, gouging open its belly with his dagger. Blood splattered his face, blinding him. He blinked it away as the hellhound howled and trembled. Letting go of his dagger, Rogan drove his fists into the wound. He pulled out loops of guts and wrapped them around the flailing creature's throat. Javan leaped off as it sank to the ground. Rogan took his place, straddling the beast from behind and throttling it with its own intestines. As the fight went out of their opponent, Javan ripped his knives free and plunged them into each eyeball. The hound shuddered and was then still.

Rogan sucked air, trying to assess the situation around them.

Javan grunted. "Back into the fray, sire?"

"The boy, Kenoth …"

"He seems to have assistance."

Roan stood shoulder to shoulder with Kenoth, facing off against the hellhound.

She smiled, seeming to take delight in battling the beast. She swished her two blades as the dog paced back and forth. When it howled, she showed her teeth and let loose with a mock cry of her own.

"She has courage," Javan said.

"Or no fucking brains," Rogan muttered. "She's toying with it like a jester. The two of them ought to try flanking the damned thing instead."

Roan stepped lightly, swaying her hips. The creature scowled in confusion. She stepped forward, backward, and side to side. Then, in a sudden flurry of motion, she leaped to its side and jabbed her sword between its ribs.

"I take it back," Rogan said. "She's not a jester. She's a dancer."

Spotting his sword, Rogan rushed over to the weapon, bent, and retrieved it. Javan hurried alongside him.

"Why are you not using your bow?" Rogan asked.

"My arrows haven't had much impact," Javan explained. "My aim is true, but their hides are too thick."

Rogan nodded at the final hellhound. "Let's just hope our blades will penetrate that."

The dog stood slowly on its hindquarters, snarling as both Roan and Rogan's forces surrounded it. None of the assembled attacked, however. Instead, they gaped in astonishment as the carcasses of the other hellhounds slithered across the ground as if pulled by invisible strings. The carcasses left trails of black, foul-smelling blood in their wake.

Thaxter shook his head. "This isn't good ..."

The dead dogs adhered themselves to the remaining hellhound, wrapping its legs and crawling up its body, increasing its mass. The beast dropped back down to all fours.

Rogan shoved his way through the fighters and stood at Thaxter's side.

The big man elbowed the former king in his ribs. "I think that fucking thing is laughing at us, Rogan."

"Well," Rogan sneered, "maybe we can wipe that smile off its face."

NOSMADA STARED INTO ZILLIAN'S STONE CAULDRON, A MASSIVE oval furnishing made up of dozens of curved bricks. Mist swirled at the edges, but in the center, a series of clear images reflected across the surface.

"The big man with gray hair?" Nosmada pointed at the vision. "That is Rogan?"

Zillian nodded. "Yes, my lord."

"He's older than I thought he'd be."

Schlack leaned forward, peering into the cauldron. "He looks like he can still fight."

"They can all fight, to a degree." Nosmada yawned. "And they're certainly brave. Look how they hold their ground, even as the last hellhound grows in size."

"Good fighters," Schlack agreed.

"Good fighters stem from good leaders."

Zillian gestured. "That redheaded woman with shoulders like a man?"

"I see her," Nosmada replied.

"Her blood screams at me."

"Concentrate. See who she is, if it matters."

They watched as a thuggish man near Rogan swung his ax into the carcass of a hellhound, stopping it from joining the collective. A row of fighters hurled spears at the growing monster, but a handsome, bow-wielding youth near Rogan hollered at them to hold fire, advising that neither their missiles nor his arrows affected the creature. Rogan shouted orders. The tall redheaded woman held up her two blades, joined their hilts together, and spun the weapon as she charged forward.

Both Nosmada and Schlack grunted with admiration.

As her swirling blades struck the beast's enlarged paw, the creature swung its head down and knocked her off balance. The hellhound roared, gloating. The redhead backflipped and landed on her feet. She disengaged her weaponry's hilts and once again brandished a blade in each hand.

A column of pikemen rushed forward, jabbing their long lances into the demonic dog's legs and rump. Taking advantage of the distraction, Rogan charged. His big sword glinted in the firelight. With a yell, he drove the blade into the monster's left forepaw, nailing it to the earth. Abandoning his weapon, the old barbarian dived and rolled, narrowly avoiding a swipe from a set of massive, gore-caked claws.

"A smart play," Nosmada observed. "Rogan must've been impressive... in his youth."

The big man near Rogan swung his ax at the hellhound. He was joined by a man who appeared to be part lizard and a blonde woman who showed no fear. They chopped, sliced, and parried as best they could.

"A snake man," Nosmada observed. "I thought their kind was extinct."

"They live still," Zillian replied. "In places where humanity does not go... and out among the stars. Similar races to their ilk still survive in the oceans and deep beneath the earth. The Dark Ones. The Anunnaki. What this one is doing here perplexes me. I cannot get a read."

"Focus on the redhead," Nosmada reminded her.

The sound of hooves thundered from the cauldron, and a white stallion galloped into the image. The redhead bolted toward it, leaped onto its back, and slapped its rump. The steed barreled into the hellhound, slamming into the massive creature's underside and knocking it backward. The horse struck with its hooves, delivering blow after blow as the monster struggled to recover.

Schlack laughed. "Even the horse fights for them."

"Fights for her," Nosmada corrected. "Impressive. Yitzak Dar has done well, giving us a chance to gather this information. Charla's sacrifice was not in vain."

"Yitzak Dar?" Zillian frowned. "But it is I who enables us to watch and learn."

"Jealousy does not become you," Nosmada replied. "And you've yet to learn about this woman."

The horse reared and moved away from the distressed hellhound as the pikemen attacked again, nailing the creature's other limbs to the bloody soil.

Rogan sprang forward, yanked his sword free, and clambered atop the demonic hulk. He drew in a breath and bellowed, "WODAN!"

Nosmada chuckled. "The old man calls for his old god. If only he knew..."

The three of them watched silently as the barbarian butchered the writing hellhound. Then, Zillian spoke.

"The redhead? She's the daughter of Gorias La Gaul."

Nosmada raised an eyebrow. "How do you surmise that?"

"The saddle of her horse says so."

"Not magic? You guess by her saddle? What if she stole it?"

Zillian shook her head. "The way she fights? With two blades? And how she stands? He taught her that. The men of Thule do that right-foot-forward move."

"I agree, my lord," Schlack murmured. "I watched Gorias fight once when I was young. She has his moves."

"Why is she here?" Nosmada stroked his beard. "And why is she allied with the King of the Bastards?"

In the cauldron, the redhead jumped atop the monster and joined Rogan in hacking it to pieces, punctuating her blows with curses.

"We shall lose the image soon," Zillian noted.

"This is what I'm going to do to him," the redhead shouted as blood splattered across her face. "The coward son of a bitch who hides in my father's armor. I mean to have what is mine!"

The mists swirled across the cauldron, and the image faded.

Schlack frowned. "She spoke of General Tolin?"

"It would seem so," Nosmada agreed. "Very curious."

Zillian coughed.

"Speak your mind freely," Nosmada told her.

"Yitzak Dar and the magicks she makes ..."

"Yes?"

"Dar compromises us... and is loyal to Tolin."

"You fear this girl's animosity toward General Tolin could impact us?"

Zillian nodded.

"I fear nothing from these two," Nosmada said, "nor are my plans threatened. It might be something to see Tolin and the girl in open combat, or Tolin and Rogan, but that would be merely a moment's entertainment for us."

"But what of Dar?" Zillian demanded.

Nosmada shrugged. "What of Dar?"

"Charla and—"

"Just a dog, a mutt, a mangy thing ..." Nosmada's voice trailed off. "I can get another bitch anywhere. And if Dar raises a hand against me, perhaps I will give her the same fate as the one on the tree out in my garden."

TOLIN LA GAUL RECLINED ON A BED IN SPENCE'S INNER chamber, remembering when he'd been a dragon. How long now had his soul been trapped in the body of this man? How long had he worn this thin skin? How long since he'd had scales? He stared across the room, where the armor of Gorias La Gaul was spread out on the madam's dressing table and lounge. That armor, fashioned from the body of a blue wyrmling dragon and near to indestructible, had carried the famed Gorias through centuries of adventures. Gorias had slain the last of the dragons while wearing that armor. Now it served as surrogate scales for the dragon inside Tolin's flesh.

Spence slept curled up next to him, exhausted from their earlier passions. He wished the act would leave him exhausted as well. Attaining sexual release from this human flesh wasn't a bad thing, but the sensation paled in comparison to how it had felt when he was a dragon. He looked down at Spence, his turgid member flaccid against his leg, and then realized something.

She wasn't breathing.

At the same moment, he discovered this, a creak came from the balcony. He turned toward the open shutters as two figures slid over the rail and unslung their crossbows. A rustling came from behind him, and the cold brick fireplace yielded up another hooded figure.

He grabbed Spence's corpse in both hands and was surprised to see her smile at him. Had she been possessed by a Siqqusim or some other demon or spirit with the ability to inhabit the dead? The thought made him once again consider his own predicament of being trapped in this body. With no time to ponder it further, he swung her body in front of him as the two crossbows thrummed. The bolts struck the woman in the back.

Tumbling from the bed, he seized her body again and swung her toward the fireplace as the third assassin fired his weapon. The bolt whizzed through the air and struck the back of her head. Her left eyeball popped out, dangling down her cheek, and the shaft jutted from the bloody socket. She laughed.

A fourth figure dropped out of the fireplace as the two on the balcony reloaded and moved forward into the room.

Tolin tossed the dead woman at the pair on the balcony and raced across the room. He grabbed the dragon skin chest plate and held it up just as the fourth assassin fired, deflecting the missile. Tolin hurled the chest plate at the assassins near the fireplace. Reflexively, one dropped the crossbow and made a fumbling catch. Tolin snatched the helmet—fashioned out of the skull of a baby dragon—off the couch and struck with the helm. He couldn't see the assassin's expression as their faces were hidden beneath black wrap masks, but the sickening crunch of a skull caving in was a familiar sound. The assassin crumpled to the floor.

Tolin spun, ducking, as another round of crossbow bolts soared overhead. He lashed out with the helmet again, smashing the right knee of the other fireplace assassin, who let out a shriek. Tolin stood and punched them in the face with a roundhouse left. The mask wrap fell away, revealing a black-haired woman. She blinked. Tolin drove the helmet down into her head with both hands. Her brains dribbled out.

The remaining two assassins recovered their wits, dropped their crossbows, and pulled out daggers.

Tolin charged the attacker on his right and tossed the helmet at the other. The assassin parried with the dagger blade and sent the helmet careening across the room. The other sidestepped, and Tolin grabbed their wrist, wrenched the dagger from their grip, and pulled them close. His teeth found purchase in the assassin's throat. He bit deep, locked his jaws, and pulled. The killer gurgled a scream.

Turning, Tolin spat the chunk of flesh on the floor and flashed a bloodstained grin at the remaining assassin. "I'd commit suicide if I were you. You're going to wish I killed you soon enough."

Undeterred by his threat, the assassin held their dagger at the ready.

"Tell me," Tolin demanded, "who sent you?"

The assassin glanced at Spence. The dead woman had clambered back to her feet and stood idly, seemingly unaware of what was transpiring.

"You think I can get answers from her?" Tolin chuckled. "Torturing an undead whore won't do me any good. I'd rather work on you."

The assassin still didn't respond.

"What was the plan here?" Tolin spoke quietly. "Given Spence's condition, I'd guess this is the work of a wizard? Was it Dar? Or Zillian?"

Once again, the assassin didn't react.

"Maybe a different wizard?" Tolin frowned. "Fascinating."

Spence tittered with rasping laughter.

"Was Spence killed simply out of spite? Was she supposed to kill me? If so, then why did the four of you attend?"

Neither the corpse nor the assassin answered.

Tolin nodded at the balcony and cocked his head. "Do you hear that? Soldiers are coming. On the double, judging by the sound. Someone raised the alarm. There's no escape for you. I'll peel you like a grape for days. Now give me a name."

After a long pause, the assassin finally spoke. "Tremas."

"The castellan?" Tolin blinked. "The castellan? Why would he want me dead?"

"He lost his family because of you."

"I see. And whose magicks did he deploy for Madam Spence? And for what purpose?"

"She wasn't his doing."

"What say you? That there is double treachery afoot tonight?"

The assassin shrugged and sheathed the dagger. "You were wrong about one thing."

"What's that?"

"There is an escape." The killer ran for the balcony ledge.

"I'll see you again," Tolin promised. "Someday."

The assassin vanished over the side as soldiers began beating on the door.

Tolin turned to Spence. "Damn it, woman. I always liked you. Perhaps that is why they struck at you. But I still don't know why."

She giggled again, an eyeball still dangling.

"Who made you as such? Who's magick was this? Was Tremas involved, or did that assassin speak the truth? Is there another force at work?"

Spence began to shudder and convulse. Another round of laughter gripped her, but it sounded more like choking.

"You can't tell me, can you? Some spell prevents you from speaking their name."

The soldiers burst in the door and glanced about the room in confusion. One of them saluted Tolin, and then the others hurriedly followed suit. Ignoring them, he donned his armor once again, pausing only to grab the corner of a bedsheet and clean the brains and blood splatters from the helm.

"Sir? What happened here?"

"Go arrest Castellan Tremas," Tolin ordered. "You know where to bring him?"

With a fearful expression, the soldier nodded.

"Very good. And do not harm him. Understood?"

"Yes, sir!" The soldier saluted again.

Tolin waved at Spence's still clucking corpse. "And kill that thing. It isn't alive—it's a trick of magick or whatever the fuck. Make sure you destroy the brain and heart."

As the soldiers surrounded her, swords were drawn, Spence finally broke through the malaise that gripped her. She had time to shriek one name before they lopped off her head and impaled her heart. Then they went to work vivisecting her.

"Sir?" One of them lifted her severed head aloft. "What did she mean screaming that name?"

"Who knows?" Tolin shrugged. "Women are mad, in life, in death, and in undeath."

Tolin carried the freshly cleaned helmet with him to the balcony. He looked across the city and beyond the walls, out into the Land of Nodd. Then his gaze returned to the streets below and eventually fell on the garden of Nosmada.

"Huh," he whispered. "Wodan indeed."

CHAPTER 5

THE THRILL IS GONE

Rogan grabbed Roan by the hand and pulled her out of a steaming pile of hellhound guts. She glared at him and gritted her teeth as she struggled to find firm ground with her slippery boots.

"Get up," he growled and steadied her. "Shouting at a dead pile of dogs while standing knee-deep in gore makes you look insane, not strong."

"You dare to lecture me about strength?"

Ignoring her, Rogan raised his arm and motioned. "Thaxter? Get over here and help me. Javan is buried underneath this crap."

The big man trotted toward him. "Are you certain?"

Rogan heaved limbs and innards aside. "I saw it fall on him."

Thaxter reversed his ax and poked through the offal with the pommel. "You don't think...?"

"He's a tough little shit. His father will haunt me forever if I let him die like that."

"Here he is!" Angeline shouted

They turned and saw Javan clambering out of a pile of intestines, glistening and wet, steam rising from his body.

"Are you okay?" Rogan asked.

Coughing, Javan nodded and flashed a thumbs up. He seemed dazed but uninjured. Angeline helped him to his feet.

Rogan elbowed Thaxter. "That girl has bigger balls than the men."

"Aye. And I think your nephew has taken a shine to her."

"Good. He broods too much over Zenata. This girl is fine and has courage and steel." Rogan turned and pointed at Brok. "Unlike you!"

Still on horseback, the man bristled. "Excuse me?"

Rogan sauntered over to him. "You heard me. Where were you during the fight?"

"I was here."

"Only because your horse has more bravery than you. It wanted to stay. Brok Yoshee, the hero of Kreta? Ha! More like Brok Yoshee, the Cunt of Kreta."

Rogan's forces laughed at this, but some among Roan's army did, as well.

"Now you listen to me—"

Rogan crossed the distance between them in two quick strides. He seized the horse's reins in one fist and jabbed a finger at Yoshee.

"Don't say another goddamned word, ass-face."

"Enough," Roan called.

Rogan turned to her. "And you? Who were you yelling about during the battle?"

"La Gaul," she mumbled, looking down at the carnage.

"Huh?"

"General Tolin La Gaul."

Rogan frowned in confusion. "He wasn't here. Did you hallucinate him riding astride those beasts?"

"He wasn't here," Roan confirmed, "but he could hear me, nevertheless. I'd bet your nephew's bowstrings on it."

"This wasn't a military attack," Thaxter said. "I've heard the stories about Tolin. That general doesn't play puppy games with magic, not on the battlefield."

Roan's nostrils flared. "Do you think this is an accident, then? Do you think these hellhounds roam at random? Who did they come for? It wasn't for me or any of my troop. It was for Rogan."

"So, I win the prize." Rogan shrugged. "That's about as useful as tits on a boar."

"But why?" Thaxter asked. "Why would they target Rogan? Who was trying to kill him?"

"People have been trying to kill me since before I was born," he replied.

"It was La Gaul," Roan insisted. "And if he had the sorcery at his disposal to summon a pack of hellhounds, then he had the ability to observe the fight."

"But that still doesn't explain why," Thaxter said.

Roan sighed with impatience. "He knows Rogan is here. He's heard the stories about him."

"I've had to pass crazier tests," Rogan said, dismissing them with a wave of his hand.

"What a damned thing." Thaxter shook his head.

Rogan stepped out of the offal and made his way across the camp. Thaxter hurried along after him. Roan followed a few steps behind. Brok dismounted and trailed behind her, obviously reluctant to be near Rogan. They nodded at Vernon, covered in blood from head to toe but seemingly uninjured. Somehow, Rogan thought, the gore made the mountain of a man smell even worse. Then they passed by the young Kenoth, who sat amidst the still-steaming butchery, his bloodstained hand clapped over his one good eye.

"You fought well," Rogan told him, looking down.

In response, Kenoth sobbed.

"Kenoth?" Brok knelt by the boy. "What is ailing you?"

"I'm blinded, oh the gods take me!"

"Blinded?"

"My other eye," he wailed. "I cannot go on!"

"Wodan," Rogan muttered. "That's a cruel twist of fate."

"Aye," Thaxter agreed, his expression falling.

"Wait!" Suddenly grinning, the youth pulled his hand away, revealing a twinkling and uninjured eye. "I'm sorry. I was just teasing Brok. Thank you for the compliment, Rogan."

"Fuck this," Thaxter said. "These people are a bunch of loonies. We need to take our leave of them."

"For the most part," Rogan replied, "they fought well. He may not be human, but Seth fought like one. And that kid there... Kenoth. And Angeline. And Vernon. You have some respectable warriors, Roan. Too bad you also have some useless pricks." Rogan winked at Brok.

Although clearly seething, instead of responding, the man helped Kenoth to his feet.

Hyden approached them, carrying a length of hellhound intestines in both fists. She stared at the innards intently.

"Is that your supper?" Rogan asked.

She shrugged. "Maybe later. Right now, they whisper to me."

"And what do they tell you? That you should bathe more often?"

Hyden ignored the taunt. "They tell me that my mistress is correct. This was a magical attack."

"No shit," said Rogan. "I thought it a card game."

Thaxter pulled a flask from his belt and unscrewed the top. "I'd go for a round of cards right now."

Hyden sniffed the air. "The hellhounds came from Nodd."

Rogan stepped closer to her. "How can you be sure?"

She thrust the dripping intestines at him, and then closed her eyes. "I can see it in my mind. They came for you."

Rogan looked at Roan. "Did you put her up to this?"

Hands on her hips, Roan rolled her eyes.

"Fuckers," Rogan muttered. "You're all in this crazy shit together."

"Why did they strike at Rogan?" Thaxter asked. "Even if Tolin knew he was here, why would he care? Roan is Gorias's daughter. Seems more likely they'd come for her."

"Supposedly she is," Rogan said.

"Careful, old man." Roan bristled. "Do you doubt me?"

"It doesn't matter to me if you are the daughter of Gorias or of the toothless pole dancer from the brothel at Greenwell. Wodan's sack—does it matter who the hellhounds were sent for? They're dead now."

"You use your god's name freely," Hyden said. "But he doesn't haunt your sleep, barbarian. I'll swap you my dreams someday and see if your bed mat is dry in the morning."

"Enough," Roan yelled. "We need to focus. Nodd sent these beasts. We should be a ways there come morning."

"We?" Rogan shook his head. "My forces aren't for hire."

"But you're mercenaries," Brok said.

"Maybe so, but I'm not about to let my fighters join your happy band of assholes as you charge into the teeth of Nodd. I may be old, but I'm not stupid. I know who rules Nodd. I know who built it and why he built it. And I know what happens to those who try to kill him. As a young man, I might have had a pecker hard enough to tempt fate, but I'm not that fucking senseless. Not anymore. Free whores and all the gold in the world couldn't get me to ride into Nodd."

"Well, this is a surprise." Roan laughed. "I never figured the King of the Bastards to be a coward."

"Call me what you want. That line of crap won't work on me, girl. Not being a coward isn't the same as not riding off a cliff when you know it's there. Whatever hate you harbor for Tolin, that's your own business. I'm weary of all this."

"Suit yourself," she replied. "More bounty for us then."

"What bounty?" Rogan asked. "What are you blathering about now?"

"Before the hellhounds attacked, when we were sitting around the fire, I received word from one of our scouts that a trade caravan bound for Nodd had made camp on the other side of town. Our pickets have kept watch on them and watch them even now. The caravan is resting for the night, and the sounds of our battle seem not to have reached them."

"Easy pickings," Thaxter said.

"Yes, but not for you." Smiling, Roan tossed her mane of hair. "Easy pickings, and my way into Nodd."

"More likely your way to a funeral," Rogan warned.

She looked around and her smile faded. "Where's my horse?"

All of her gathered forces glanced about in confusion.

"Where is Traveler?" she shouted.

Thaxter shrugged. "How can you misplace that big assed white draft horse?"

Rogan placed a hand on the big man's shoulder and squeezed. "The hell with the horse. Where's Javan?"

"He was with the girl ... Angeline."

Both men scanned the encampment, searching the shadows beyond the flickering firelight, but there was no sign of Javan or the girl.

As the moon crept across the sky and the horizon glowed with the first hints of dawn, General Tolin walked down the familiar stone steps—but this time, instead of taking the left-hand path toward his reconstruction project, he turned right. A few moments later, he came to a door. A guard standing watch saluted him.

Tolin nodded. "Is he inside?"

"Yes, sir," the soldier answered.

"Good. Leave us."

"General?"

"Leave your post. I'm giving you permission. Unless you would prefer to stay and listen?"

"By your leave, sir."

The soldier snapped another hasty salute and then hurried off.

Tolin opened the door, which creaked as it swung inward. The inner chamber was well lit by many torches and several candles on a table in the center. Along the far wall was a man trussed up on X-shaped planks. As Tolin closed the door, the man looked up at him and then hung his head. Tolin glanced over at a full-length mirror on the wall, admiring himself all resplendent in the freshly washed dragon skin armor. He removed his helmet, placed it on the table, and patted it. Then he turned his attention back to the prisoner and frowned.

"Castellan Tremas. It grieves me to see you this way. If you wanted my attention, there were other ways you could have gotten it."

Tremas trembled, his breath hitching in his chest. "I suppose so."

"I could be asleep right now, or with my favorite whore. Instead, I am here with you."

"I had other plans as well."

Tolin pulled a pair of gloves from his waist belt. They matched his armor. The knuckles were studded with dragon bones. He stepped in front of Tremas and slowly donned them.

"It is said that Gorias La Gaul seldom wore these. Imagine that. What balls, aye? Wade into battle barehanded when these were available?"

Tremas didn't respond.

"They were fashioned from the paws of a baby dragon. They have a lethal effect."

Tremas sighed. "Just kill me. I don't have anything left."

"That must be true. If you wanted me dead, then you are obviously suicidal. Can I inquire why you wish to die?"

Tremas raised his head, his expression showing no fear. "You took everything from me," he said. "My son died last year in one of your silly raids to find more dragon bones. My wife couldn't live without her baby boy, so she went out and handled snakes until the asps killed her. My daughter then took to the drink and ran off to Irem, where she ended up working as a whore. She was carved up by a cutpurse, her throat slit to match her womanhood. Don't you see? You took everything away from me. My wife, my son, and daughter, everything."

"You have your wealth," Tolin said, "and a colony of concubines."

"You took everything that mattered ... everything that was real. And for what? To fulfill the crazy dream of a madman who thinks himself a dragon?"

"You blame me for the loss of your family. Were our roles reversed, I'd want to kill me, too. I understand that. But your son signed on willingly, I am sure."

"But he was never paid," Tremas argued. "Instead, he was the one who paid ... with his life."

"Is this about money?"

"No!" Tremas spat on the floor. "It's about justice. What need have I for wealth?"

"Obviously. Acquiring assassins wasn't difficult for you. And based on their accents and looks, I'd wager that none of them were from this place or from any land nearby. You must have paid a small fortune to hire killers who weren't afraid of me."

"Afraid ...?" Tremas laughed. "Not everyone is afraid of you, General."

"Their ignorance was their undoing." Tolin held up the clawed gloves. "And your ignorance will be your undoing, as well. But there's still one thing I wish to know. Who did you pay to cast that spell on Spence?"

"Spence?" Tremas almost spat the name. "Did something happen to her?"

"You know very well."

"I know nothing," Tremas insisted. "I had no quarrel with Spence. She was an innocent. If I were to cause harm to her, I'd be no better than you and the strife you caused my family. If one of the assassins struck her down, then I am sorry."

"She wasn't struck down by those swine," Tolin yelled. "She was possessed by an evil spirit ... perhaps a Siqqusim. Who did you pay to do that to her?"

Tremas stared at him, mouth agape.

"Do not feign ignorance." Tolin lowered his voice again. "Just tell me what I want to know. How did it happen? Who reanimated her? I suspect someone beyond your wealth had to be a part of this, as wizards care little for gold, jewels, or pussy."

Tremas looked at Tolin a long time before saying, "Perhaps you don't know as much as you think you do."

"Dar wouldn't betray me, and I cannot see it as the work of Zillian."

"Is it so important you know?"

Tolin gave a single nod. "I'd like to know. I will wring it from you if you don't willingly say it."

"Then we are at an impasse, for I do not know, and you don't seem to believe what I have to say."

"I'd rather kill you fast, Tremas. I'm a soldier, not a torturer."

"Or a dragon? Heh, do you forget to play pretend at times?"

Tolin snapped his arm out. The dragon knuckles smashed the castellan's nose to a pulp. Blood splattered both men. Once Tremas stopped wailing, Tolin folded his arms and stared at him.

"Just ... kill me." His voice was anguished and muddled.

"No. Not yet."

Tremas coughed, face twisting with pain. He spat blood on the floor and then focused on his captor. "Do you pray, Tolin?"

"Of course not."

"Do you believe in God?"

"I know there is a God."

Tremas spat blood again. "There are many gods."

Tolin backhanded Tremas, ripping away the flesh of his right cheek, revealing the wet, glistening musculature beneath.

"You serve another god," Tolin grunted. "Is that it? Has one of the demonic fallen seduced you?"

"He is a god."

The castellan's speech was now slurred, and Tolin struggled to understand him.

"Name him, then. And speak clearly. Who is this god that I might know him?"

"He's more powerful than the fallen. He calls to his children in their dreams. His power thwarts that of the God of Heaven ... and will again when he is freed."

This time, Tolin reached out with a gauntlet and grabbed Tremas's jaw, yanking it up so high that the bones in the castellan's neck audibly creaked.

"Tell me the name," Tolin ordered. "Who was the demon who did this to Spence?"

"I ... told ... you ..."

"You told me you had nothing to do with her fate, and in the next breath you admit to serving a demon."

Tremas smiled. The gesture was garish given the condition of his face.

"I hate puzzles," Tolin said. "Tell me!"

"He's coming for you," Tremas slurred. "He's coming for all of you. His children are nearby, and when they arrive, they will free him, and his vengeance shall be fulfilled."

"Wodan?" Tolin arched an eyebrow.

"Yes." Tremas rasped. "Now go fuck yourself, dragon. I defy you. I spit on you and hate you. All you can do is kill me. Soon, you will be damned with all the rest. Then what shall you do? Concoct a way to escape Hell itself?"

"First things first."

Tolin grabbed the castellan's jaw with both gloved hands, put his knee on his chest, and pulled hard, ripping the man's jaw out of his head, leaving his gullet and throat open. Tremas thrashed against his bonds, gurgling a horrid, anguished cry.

"I would order the guard to put you out of your misery," Tolin said, stepping back to avoid the blood spray, "but I had him leave his post. I'm afraid you'll just have to wait here until you die."

He dropped the jawbone on the floor and exited the room. The castellan's wail faded as he ascended the stairs.

Emerging outside, he breathed deeply, expelling the dungeon's dampness from his lungs. He smelled bread baking, eggs cooking, and meat roasting. The sun now peeked over the horizon. Already, the day was warm. Birds chirped overhead. Hooves echoed on the cobblestones as a cart trundled by. An infant squealed from a nearby building. An elderly person coughed in another.

He ducked through an alley and hurried down an avenue, taking care not to step in the contents of the chamber pots which had been emptied from the windows of the dwellings above. Emerging on the other side, he resolved to find Nosmada and inform him of all that had transpired. As he turned in the direction of Nosmada's garden, a female voice called out to him.

"General Tolin!"

He spotted a short teenaged girl. She looked familiar. He frowned, puzzled, and then remembered that he'd seen her working the stables for Nosmada before.

"Yes," Tolin said. "What is it?"

She took a knee and bowed her head. "I'm sorry, sir, but ..."

"Sorry for what? Stand up and face me, girl. I'm no lord or god and you aren't in the army."

She rose slowly but still did not meet his eye. "I carry a message from Yitzak Dar for you."

"What is your name, girl?"

"Fallon, sir. I serve Lord Nosmada."

"I thought I recognized you. I have seen you in his stables. Yes?"

She nodded.

"If you work for Nosmada, then why do you bring me a message from Dar?"

She paused. "The message was sent to Colonel Shazeal, and ... well ..."

"Yes?"

"He said he wasn't an errand slave for that ... person."

"I bet his language was more colorful."

"Quite, sir."

"Why did Dar ask the colonel to deliver a message to me, I wonder?"

Fallon finally raised her head and met his stare. "Dar said it is a matter of military importance and requests that you please come to the citadel at once."

Tolin was about to pat her on the head, but then he remembered that he was still wearing the gore-encrusted gauntlets.

"I shall go see Dar. Tell your lord I shall be coming to see him next. I assume he will be in his garden?"

"Yes, sir."

"Hurry off, then."

Tolin watched the girl rush away, and then headed to the citadel of Yitzak Dar, where he found the wizard, dressed in shimmering robes and smelling of roses, gazing into a long oval mirror that showed no reflection.

"Is that mirror confused over which version of yourself to show you?"

Dar turned to him, ignoring the taunt. "Ah, General Tolin! How does the morning find you?"

"Fuck the morning, wizard. What is it you want?"

"Having a rough day?"

"And the night before. But you know that. Did your hellhounds work?"

"In so much that we learned a great deal about our new arrivals." Dar gestured at the mirror. "Speaking of which, come have a look."

Tolin edged closer and stared into the polished surface. He saw a young man riding a magnificent white stallion.

"That's not Rogan."

"Correct, General. It is not."

Tolin sighed. "Dar, I have no patience for riddles this morning. I've yet to go to bed. Just get on with it."

"You see before you the key to a quandary in your mind."

"A kid on a white horse?"

"Oh, yes. I found him by chance as the hellhounds did their duty. Now, I have drawn him to us, via a certain enchantment."

"Who is he, and why should I care?"

"He is the means by which we all get what we want."

"I want his horse. I note that it's rather big for his size."

"The horse is another surprise."

Tolin stepped toward the wizard, leaving only an inch between them, and glowered. "Enough. Who is the lad?"

"His name is Javan. He is the nephew of Rogan."

IT SERVES YOU RIGHT TO SUFFER

As both sets of forces prepared breakfast for themselves and recovered from the hellhound assault from the night before, Thaxter approached Rogan, who was packing up his bedroll.

"What do we know, Thaxter?"

"Angeline says she led Javan back to her tent, but he slipped away. Doesn't seem believable to me that your nephew would choose stealing a horse over getting laid, but there are multiple witnesses who saw him leave her tent alone."

"Could she have enchanted him?"

Thaxter shook his head. "I've asked around. The only one in Roan's troop who has that ability is Hyden ... and there's no way Javan would have gone back to that old hag's tent."

"Maybe the spell came from somewhere else." Rogan stroked his beard. "Maybe the same place as those dogs."

"Well, the scouts we sent out can't find him, but they did find the tracks of that big assed stallion. If Javan really stole it, then they're both headed west."

"Toward Nodd ..."

"Yeah. Meanwhile, Ivor and ... uh ..."

"What?"

"I'll tell you later. Speak of the devil. Here comes Roan and Hyden."

Rogan finished stowing his gear as Roan stalked toward them. Her expression was furious. Hyden hurried along behind her, hands working nervously, picking at the rags hanging off her emaciated frame.

Wincing at the aches in his joints, Rogan sat on his knees.

"Good morning," he said, smiling up at them. "Did you ladies come to cook me breakfast?"

Roan glared. "Your nephew stole my horse."

"That seems to be the prevailing opinion. I wonder what that little shit is up to?"

"Stealing horses, obviously."

Rogan chuckled. "That part is rather funny."

"And why?"

"Because it pisses you off."

"Enjoy your laugh, old man. Your nephew has ridden off on Traveler, the mount of Gorias La Gaul. There will be consequences."

"Calm down," Rogan soothed. "There is wizardry afoot. That boy isn't out hunting or looking for girls. Why would he need to? We have food enough, and your Angeline was eager to lay with him. And he's not the type to steal a horse. That's more like something I would do."

"The barbarian is correct, mistress," Hyden agreed. "The boy is under a spell."

Rogan turned to Thaxter. "Before we were interrupted, you were about to tell me something. Was a raven sent to Ivor?"

Hyden gasped at the name. Roan stared at the old woman with a puzzled expression.

"It was," Thaxter replied. "Several, in fact. It's too soon to get a response, of course, but I'm confident Ivor and his wives are on the way."

Roan frowned. "Who is Ivor?"

"The one true Oracle of Wodan," Hyden said.

"He lives in the vicinity," Rogan replied. "We sent for him at sunrise."

Roan arched an eyebrow. "Why?"

"Because," Rogan begrudgingly admitted, "perhaps you lot were right about the hellhounds and their fixation on me. Whatever is going on here, it involves sorcery. I don't do sorcery. So, we sent for someone who does. One of the few who I trust."

Thaxter nodded. "We sent for our best."

Roan gestured at Rogan's group. "Is this Ivor as dirty as the rest of you?"

"He's older than dirt," Rogan replied, "but a lot more powerful."

"Good," Roan said. "Perhaps he can bring back my father's horse."

"Your father is dead," Rogan muttered, struggling to stand. "Quit talking about him as if he were alive. You cheapen your own worth every time you do that. I've seen you fight. You have sand, and your father's blood flows in your veins. But Traveler is your horse now, not his."

Roan stared at him, blinking. Then she turned away and shouted for Brok Yoshee. They waited while the frazzled man hurried across the encampment. He arrived out of breath.

"Yes, mistress?"

"I'll ride your mount for the raid on the caravan."

Brok half bowed. "Very good."

Rogan grinned. "That's okay. That coward would rather stay behind anyway."

"Enough!" Boots squared to Rogan, Brok puffed his chest out. "I have had enough of your insolence, you lowborn swine. The unwashed masses might sing your praises—ignorant fools that they are—but I see the truth of you. Do you know to whom you speak? Can you dream of the men I've killed and the women I've bedded? The monsters I've sent screaming back into the chasm of Hades itself?"

"I don't care." Rogan leaned forward, the tip of his nose

brushing against Brok's, and yawned. "But maybe I'd respect you more if you told me how you killed that Chimera south of Kemet."

Beads of sweat rolled down Brok's forehead. He swallowed and blinked.

"What was its name again?"

"H-hurtzin," Brok stammered.

"And how did you kill it? Tell me the tale."

"I don't need to tell you anything, you ... barbaric braggart!"

"No?" Rogan asked. "Because I know how it died. I'm the one it bled all over."

"You claim my kill to build yourself up?"

Rogan thrust his knee into Brok's unarmored groin and smashed his forehead into the mercenary's nose. Wailing, Brok fell to the ground, writhing in pain and cradling his crotch. Blood poured from both his nostrils.

"Liar!" Rogan reached down, grabbed him by the beard, and pulled his head back. "I killed that Chimera because it was raping the children of Minonk—that village of widows near the coast. I cut off all of its heads, and when I was done, I tracked down the witch who summoned it and fucked her in the ass until she died. I ought to do the same to you. Aye, I am a barbarian, and maybe I started out lowborn, but you are a liar and a thief. You steal the deeds of others because your cowardice keeps you from earning your own."

"Rogan!" Roan stepped forward. "He's learned his lesson. Let him go."

"Choose your men better." Rogan released his grip on Brok's beard. "Your father would have killed him by now."

Shaking her head, Roan stomped away. Brok retreated as well, crawling on all fours and mumbling as blood and saliva dripped from his face.

Thaxter grinned

"What?" Rogan asked.

Thaxter laughed. "Nothing."

"What did he say?"

"Oh, some shit about how you will regret that."

"He'll have to get in line with all the rest. How long do you reckon until Ivor arrives?"

"Hard to say," Thaxter replied. "He dwells not far from here. Perhaps by sundown?"

Hyden gasped. "I must get ready."

Rogan and Thaxter watched her hurry off and then exchanged a look.

Thaxter said, "She looks like a girl with a romantic appointment."

"Aye. Maybe she views Ivor the same way I view Gorias. I always wished I could have met him before his death. Maybe Ivor is her hero?"

"Or maybe he's her former lover."

"Ivor has lots of wives. Who knows? Although I've never known one of his wives to be as homely as she is."

Thaxter picked up his ax. "I always wondered about that. He's the Oracle of Wodan. Why all the wives?"

"Glutton for punishment," Rogan said. "I've always thought that one wife is plenty, but I was much younger last time I was married."

"Maybe you should get a new one," Thaxter teased. "That Roan has a lot of spirit."

"And she can keep it, too. Maybe if I were twenty years younger ..."

"Ah, well, if you're seeking experience, maybe Hyden would do."

Instead of reacting to the jest, Rogan turned and gazed west.

"You're worried about your nephew," Thaxter guessed.

"Not worried," Rogan said. "Javan has been in far worse situations than this. But you and I are fighting men, and he is a fighter as well. He's smarter than both of us. His brain is as broad as your chest. But still ... he relies on his strength, his wits, and his smarts. These forces set against us ... I feel those three things won't do much good against them. That was why I had you send for Ivor. If Javan is bewitched ..."

"We'll get him back."

Rogan gestured angrily. "We should have never come to this place. Things have gone awry since that stop at the whorehouse. We arrived too late for the battle ... a fight we were to be paid for. Then we fall in with this ragtag lot. Then those damned demon dogs. And now Javan."

"You know Ivor. I know only the stories. But from what I've heard, he can set things right."

"The Ivor I remember could, but I have not seen him in decades. Maybe we shouldn't wait for him."

"Why?" Thaxter asked. "Begging your pardon, Rogan, but you said it yourself. We are ill-equipped to go up against wizardry."

"Agreed. We're fighters. But we should start behaving like fighters. We've been reacting instead of acting."

"So ... what do you want to do?"

"We can saddle up and ride that way."

"Toward Nodd?"

Rogan nodded.

Thaxter spoke slowly "I thought ... you didn't care to go in that direction."

"I don't care for goat milk either, but I'll drink it if that's all there is."

"You sound like your mind is already made up. If we were gambling right now, I'd bet you're debating whether to take all of our forces or go it alone."

"I'm thinking go it alone." Rogan shrugged. "I never had an army to search for me when I entered Jericho as a lad."

"But Nodd isn't Jericho, and Javan isn't you. You could give a shit in a saddlebag about the rest of us, Rogan, but Javan? You'd go to the edge of Hell for that boy."

Rogan grimaced. "You know me well."

"Too well," Thaxter agreed. "The problem is ... someone else knows you."

"What are you saying?"

Thaxter pointed west with his ax. "Someone wants you to come to Nodd. Javan is a means to an end—a way to get you there. You are ... hesitant to go it alone."

Rogan bristled. "Are you saying I'm afraid?"

"Calm down!" Thaxter held up one hand, palm out. "I'm not saying that at all. I'm saying your pride is telling you to go alone, but the fighter inside you is saying that you'd do better with an army behind you."

"So, you think I should walk our forces into what is probably a trap?"

"I'd rather carve our way in than walk, Rogan, but yeah, I think we should come with you. And I think you ought to bring Roan's group, as well. She's going to Nodd anyway. Better we have them fighting with us."

"Or use them as arrow fodder," Rogan replied.

"They did okay against the hellhounds."

"I suppose."

"They're mounting a raid on that trade caravan. Maybe we go along, watch them in action, and then you make the proposal afterward?"

Rogan sighed. "Let's go talk to her. The longer we delay, the further ahead Javan gets."

After ordering their troops to prepare for leaving, the two men started off across the encampment. Roan had already departed, taking about half her forces with her. Rogan and Thaxter mounted up and rode off in pursuit.

"I've heard he looks like Wodan," Thaxter said.

"Who?"

"Ivor."

"Piss off. No. Ivor looks nothing like Wodan."

"Then what does Wodan look like?"

"He looks like that blacksmith who helped my father make swords when I was young."

"The wayfaring stranger?"

Slowly, Rogan nodded.

"We heard that tale growing up, how Wodan would visit his people in that form and help them make swords. It was said that he put spirits in the blades."

Rogan gripped the reins in one hand. With his other, he unsheathed his massive broadsword and held the blade aloft. His gaze lingered first on the flat portion and then on the symbol near the handle.

Thaxter leaned across his saddle and peered at the markings. "Ravens, wolves, runes for eternity. Lots of artisans make them that way."

"They do. But not like this."

"You're telling me that sword was forged by your god?"

"My god." Rogan nodded. "And my father."

Thaxter turned his attention ahead again. "When I was a kid, we used to pretend we were your people. We'd make-believe our swords broke open and ghosts came flying out."

"When I was a kid," Rogan replied, "I saw that happen. One of the first battles I was ever in, long before I could even lift a bastard weapon like this, I saw a blade shatter and billowing spirits floating free."

They rode in silence the rest of the way, following Roan's trail. When they reached a hilltop, they stopped, watching from afar.

Roan rode hard and up in front like a field leader. She stood in the stirrups, directing her forces. They didn't scream like a bunch of raiders. They advanced in at her sides with the precise efficiency of a military pincers' movement.

"They've done this before," Rogan observed. "Encircling a target and taking it down."

Thaxter nodded in agreement. "That Yoshee might be a cunt, but like I said, the rest of them know their shit. We could use them on our side, Rogan."

In moments, the caravan—though entrenched and with guards at the ready—was surrounded. Spears and swords were discarded, and arms were raised in surrender.

Thaxter grinned. "You in love yet? Ready for that new wife?"

Rogan shrugged, not taking his attention off the scene.

Roan dismounted, shook her red hair, and stood facing the caravan inhabitants. Slowly, they knelt on the ground, faces down, hands out.

"She is something," Rogan admitted.

Thaxter's laughter echoed across the hills.

"So," a deep voice filled the garden as Nosmada walked toward the big tree. "Shall you set me free today?"

Without responding, Nosmada stopped and dropped a sack at his boots. The bag made a strange sound when it struck the earth.

"Just let me go," the voice continued. "It would be an easy thing for you. Then we can speak, face to face."

Nosmada stared into the bearded visage of the body hanging from the tree, so still and seemingly locked in a rigor of pain. Its sewn lips hadn't moved, but he heard it speak nevertheless. Nosmada closed his eyes and breathed in, held it, and let pressure build in his ears.

"You can hear me today? We both know that is a sign. I grow stronger, and you grow weaker."

Instead of responding, Nosmada continued to hold his breath.

"If you can hear me, so can others. I grow clearer in the minds of many. Soon, assistance will come."

Nosmada bent and opened the sack.

"The time is nigh," the voice continued. "Soon, your end will be upon you. Soon, the general will be ready to fly. Soon, Leviathan will be summoned. Soon, a mighty rain will wash this world away."

Nosmada exhaled, sighing. "That may very well be. And if so, at that moment, you will have outlived your use to me. But not until then."

"Neither of us shall wait very long then."

Nosmada moved forward, grabbed the rope that suspended the

corpse, and maneuvered it until the body was closer to the broad tree trunk. Then he stepped back, admired his handiwork, and bent over, rummaging through the bag. He held up a wooden stake, nearly a foot long and covered in carved runes. Then he reached into the bag again and pulled out a hammer. He waved both in front of the motionless eyes.

"Even if you are regaining your power, influence, or the ability to speak, and even if someone comes to rescue you, you still aren't going anywhere. I'll see to it."

Nosmada knelt, placed the tip of the wooden stake against the figure's right ankle, and then reared back with the hammer and drove the spike through the flesh and deep into the wood. He heard the captive shriek in his mind. Ignoring the sound, he pounded the stake twice more. He then reached over, retrieved another spike, and repeated the grisly procedure with the other ankle. Again, he heard a shriek in his head. Nosmada pulled out a third stake and stood up. He aimed it between the prisoner's legs and drove it into his groin.

This time, the silent scream seemed to echo across the entire garden.

Grinning, Nosmada dropped the hammer. "Nothing to say all of a sudden except for your pitiful wailing?"

He was met with silence.

"For a god, you are very quiet."

Nosmada reached down and turned the spike. The prisoner convulsed, writhing against the bark.

"Tell me something, barbarian god." Nosmada turned the stake again. "Something other than screams or your vacant threats. Prophesy! Tell me something worthwhile."

The figure lowered his head and, for the first time, opened his eyes.

Nosmada shuddered and averted his gaze, glancing down at the wooden stake.

The voice returned, albeit weaker and dripping with agony.

"These spikes are fashioned from the tree in the original garden? You grow desperate."

"I've been desperate for centuries," Nosmada snarled, staring up at the face again. "Why do you think I collect so much blood?"

"Can I tell you a secret, Nosmada?"

"If you can do so without crying like an infant."

"He doesn't care." The prisoner's face contorted and spasmed, slowly forming a smile.

"Won't be long now." Nosmada twisted the stake. "The signs are right. The stars are aligned."

The captive's expression froze again, the smile looking more like a grimace. The voice went quiet. Nosmada was about to taunt him again when he became aware of another presence in the garden.

Several presences.

Nosmada stepped back and picked up his hammer. He gazed into the sky. Nostrils flaring, he sighed loudly.

"So," he called, "are you going to have the balls to attack, or shall I just leave?"

He heard the sound of twine tightening as bowstrings were drawn back. The tall hedge rustled, and four assassins stepped out, flanking his right and left. Each brandished a long spear, the type usually carried by soldiers in the frontlines to strike deeper into the enemy line. Nosmada frowned. The weapons were an odd choice for close-quarters combat. Stranger still, these men wore the uniforms and insignia of the city guards rather than of Tolin's military.

The vegetation rustled again, and Captain Bradlee emerged, carrying a short sword in his right hand. On his left wrist, he sported a diamond-shaped shield, a type used more for fencing and teaching than for real combat. Thus, Nosmada surmised, the captain planned to use it up close.

"So," Nosmada said, "you found some balls at last."

"I always had them," Bradlee replied. "Fear can make a man less of what his father meant him to be."

"And what did your father see for you, Bradlee?"

He hesitated. "My father wanted me to be a fighter, a warrior, or a soldier."

"That's a shame. What a disappointment you must have been. Tell me, did your father have any sons that *didn't* have a vagina?"

Bradlee scowled. "He couldn't be more disappointed in me than your father in you. Certainly, your grandfather, aye?"

"So ..." Now it was Nosmada who hesitated. "You know?"

"I know what is whispered, yes."

"You would slay me and take on the curse?"

"Curse? You mean the tales of the grandson that failed to be a messiah?" Bradlee smirked. "I'll take my chances. If there is a real God above, maybe he'll take mercy on me for slaying you and stopping what you have planned with that abomination below."

Nosmada shrugged and then lunged to the right. Arrows hissed across the garden, missing their target and striking the prisoner crucified to the tree. Still clutching his hammer, Nosmada cartwheeled and landed between the two closest spearmen. He swung hard, denting one of his opponent's helmets. The guard crumpled to the ground, blood pouring from beneath his helm. Nosmada snatched his falling spear. The other spearman raised his weapon, but Nosmada caught the tip beneath his armpit and squeezed, momentarily disabling the thrust. He jabbed with his borrowed weapon, shoving the spearhead through the guard's chainmail and into his chest. The man sputtered, mouth agape, and a bright gout of blood burst from his lips. He sank to his knees as Nosmada pushed down on the shaft.

"Take him," Bradlee ordered. "Pin him to the ground!"

Shouting, the two remaining spearmen charged, weapons raised. Nosmada twirled and shoved the first, sending him crashing into his partner and knocking them both down. While the guards lay sprawled and stunned, Nosmada turned to face Bradlee, but the officer swung his shield, slamming it into Nosmada's jaw. Bradlee yelled in triumph as Nosmada reeled backward.

Wincing, Nosmada struggled to keep his feet. His mouth filled with blood. He spat and then dropped into a crouch as Bradlee swung again. The shield brushed over his head, close enough to ruffle his hair. Nosmada staggered, and the captain pressed his attack, slashing with his sword. The blade sliced through Nosmada's clothing and flesh, leaving a long gash on his abdomen. Heat spread across his stomach. Grunting with pain, he clenched his teeth. He gripped the flat of the sword with one hand, feeling his own blood slicking the blade, and Bradlee's wrist with the other. Grinning, he jerked the captain toward him and head-butted him. Before Bradlee could react, Nosmada tightened his grip on his wrist. His smile grew wider as he felt the man's bones snap. The sword slipped from Bradlee's hand and onto the ground.

"Just like a chicken wing." Nosmada spat blood again.

Wailing, Bradlee stumbled backward, cradling his limp hand. Nosmada stooped, seized his sword, and clubbed the captain over the head with the flat of the blade. Bradlee's eyes rolled white. Convulsing, he flopped onto his back. Not waiting for the seizure to pass, Nosmada drove the sword down, piercing both Bradlee's armor and then his heart.

Captain Bradlee died with a sigh.

Panting, Nosmada wiped the sweat from his brow, and then spat again. His saliva was now clear.

The two spearmen who had clambered to their feet begged for mercy.

"You can live," Nosmada told them. "But you must be witnesses."

He stumbled over to the tree and cupped one palm beneath the captive's bleeding groin. After blood had pooled there, he raised it to his lips and drank. Then he pulled his shredded shirt aside, showing them the wound in his abdomen. The men's eyes widened as the gash began to heal. Within seconds, his flesh was unmarred.

"Go ahead," Nosmada muttered. "Run away. Spread the word to your fellow dissenters. Assassination will not work, and I grow tired of your attempts."

Without a word, they turned and fled for the garden gate.

"Again and again." Nosmada sighed. "When will they learn?"

* * *

"Yitzak Dar tells me that your name is Javan."

The young man, lashed to an X-shaped pair of thick wooden beams, slowly raised his head.

"Yes," he said, licking his dry lips. "That is true."

Tolin nodded. "And from what the guards and Dar say, you've been very forthcoming."

"Indeed. This is all just a terrible misunderstanding. I'll try to be as helpful as possible, sir."

"Sir?"

"Yes, sir?"

"You speak as one used to dealing with authority," Tolin observed, "and yet, your clothing doesn't betray you as a soldier."

"I was actively trained in the slingers and then archers of the Albion military, but I no longer serve in that army."

"Albion? That's far off. You're a long way from home. Were you drummed out?"

"No, sir. When the monarch of our land abdicated the throne in favor of his son, I was selected as one of the men to accompany him on his journeys."

"And you came here with this traveling monarch?"

"No, sir." Javan shifted at the bonds tying his calves and wrists. "We went across the western ocean."

"Indeed? And what did you find there?"

"Lands and peoples neither seen nor written of in this realm."

"But you are here now, back to the cradle of humanity."

"Yes, sir."

Tolin paused, circling Javan. "Do you still serve this king?"

"I do, sir."

"Care to name him?"

"If you know of Albion, sir, then you know his name."

"Rogan the Great." Tolin's tone was tinged with derision.

"Indeed," Javan replied.

"Rogan is here?"

"It's true, sir. I have no reason to lie."

"No, I suppose you don't. But if I were in your position, boy, I would choose a more peaceful monarch to say I served."

"Perhaps, sir. But it is Rogan whom I fight beside."

"Do you know who I am?"

"Judging by your armor, I'd have to guess you are General Tolin La Gaul."

"You recognize this armor?"

"It is similar to the armor of your father, Gorias La Gaul, if not the genuine article."

"It is indeed," Tolin confirmed. "And if you recognize that, then you must recognize his horse, the mythic Traveler—which you just so happened to ride into Nodd."

"Begging your pardon, sir, but I really didn't have any choice in the matter."

"True enough." Tolin nodded. "Dar compelled you here with a spell."

"That would explain why I'm here." Javan sighed. "The last thing I remember was losing consciousness after a fight with a pack of hellhounds. Then I woke up here."

Tolin stepped closer to him. "This Rogan, the aged barbarian of renown, will he come here after you?"

"Absolutely, sir. He's that way."

"What way?"

Javan tried to shrug.

"Loyal?"

Javan wrinkled his nose and looked at the floor, eyes tracing the bricks. "I don't know if that's the word. I'm his nephew and while blood does matter to him, his pride matters more. He will take my compelling ... my abduction ... as a personal affront."

"It will piss him off?"

"Oh, I'd say so, sir. Very much."

Tolin smiled. "He'll kill to get you back?"

"Without pause. He enjoys killing."

"That's a terrible thing."

"Perhaps. But that's who he is. If that wizard wants him, she'll get him. He'll kill himself to see her die."

"Over you?"

"He's killed wizards for far less."

Tolin gave him mock applause. "I believe you."

"Thank you, sir."

"You are an unwitting pawn—bait for your uncle. Dar wants him dead for a slight that occurred decades ago."

"I understand. I'm afraid we run into more enemies than friends on our trips."

"Regardless, Dar is a fool. Even if Rogan comes for you, he'll never get near the interior of this city."

"Well, that's good." Javan grinned. "No one has anything to fear, then."

Tolin glowered at him.

"Of course, General Tolin, I sense you fear no one."

Tolin still stared at him, unblinking.

Javan swallowed. "And I will, of course, inform my uncle that you treated me with hospitality and honor."

"This entire thing is between Dar and Rogan. It has nothing to do with me, my desires, or those of the Lord of Nodd."

"Then, truly, Dar is doomed," Javan said.

"You are such an honest young fellow. You say that like you believe it."

"I do, sir."

"You really think your master can fight his way in here—into the heart of the city—and slay one of the most powerful wizards in all the land?"

Javan blinked. "You're an intelligent man. You certainly understand military tactics and the skill of war."

"What are you getting at?"

"Do you think Rogan would bring a knife to a sword fight?"

"Do not test me, boy. I have heard the tales of your uncle."

"Well," Javan replied, "if he wouldn't bring a knife to a sword fight, then you know he would not bring a sword to kill a wizard. Of course, he might use a sword to kill everyone else who gets in his way."

Tolin shrugged. "I don't care either way who lives or dies in all of it."

"I believe you, sir."

"I don't care if you believe me or not." He grabbed Javan by the jaw and studied him closely. "I don't care who lives and dies in this entire bloody world. You're all just meat to me."

Javan held his breath, not responding.

"Soon," Tolin said, "I shall fly away from all of this."

Javan remained quiet.

Tolin released him. "You are wise for a youth. You know when to shut your mouth."

"Yes, sir," Javan whispered.

"I'll confess something to you, Javan of Albion. I am weary of Dar and of all this fuckery she plays at."

"Does Dar not answer to the ruler of Nodd?"

"Dar is the wizard of Nodd's army. Not something I personally thought we needed, but I am not the lord of this place. If your uncle can put an end to Dar, I wouldn't stand in his way. But the army most certainly will. If Rogan approaches this city with an army and a rival wizard at his back, I cannot give the order to stand down."

"I understand, sir."

Sighing, Tolin undid Javan's bonds. The youth hopped down onto the floor, rubbing his chafed wrists.

"What now, sir?"

Tolin turned to the door and barked for a guard. The door opened, and two men rushed in.

"This young man is not to be harmed, you understand?"

"Yes, sir." The soldier saluted.

Nodding, his companion did the same.

Tolin turned back to Javan. "I cannot let you go free, but I'll be damned if I'll leave you tied up like a sacrificial lamb. You can stay confined to this room."

"And when Rogan arrives?"

"I have bigger targets to slay, Javan. Pray that your uncle and I do not meet."

Javan nodded.

Tolin turned to the guard again. "Get him some water, wine, and food."

"Understood, General. And if the wizard's acolytes should question that?"

"Remind them that he needs to eat. I sincerely doubt Dar wants him dead." Tolin paused and added, "Yet."

Tolin strode across the room, stepped out into the hall, and closed the door behind him. He paused for a moment, listening to their muffled voices.

The guard said, "You are lucky, kid."

"I feel lucky."

"Much luckier than the last man in here."

"I can tell by the dried blood on the floor tiles."

Smiling, Tolin shook his head and walked on down the corridor.

"Rogan the Great," he muttered. "Perhaps it's time I spoke with a god."

CHAPTER 7

THE SKY IS CRYING

The sky broiled over Rogan as he awoke. He blinked, squinting against the glare, and tried to raise a hand to shield his eyes. Surprisingly, he couldn't. He wasn't bound or tied. He was simply weak, but for a man such as he, weakness was its own kind of bondage. His head throbbed, deep and unpleasant—but at least it was still attached to his neck. Rogan closed his eyes and focused on breathing, hoping his strength would soon return. The grainy texture against his back meant he was lying in the sand.

"Getting old," he muttered, licking his heat-chapped lips.

Eyes still closed, he tried to remember what had happened. He and Thaxter had watched Roan and her forces overtake the traders on their way to Nodd—a caravan full of long bones rather than spices or textiles or golds, as it turned out. He'd begrudgingly admired the skill of Roan's group and how fast they'd moved. He remembered agreeing to go along with her plan to infiltrate the city within Nodd. He didn't care about her personal vendetta, but Javan was now a prisoner there. Hyden had confirmed it with a vision. Though he didn't express it, the thought of Javan being held prisoner by a wizard filled Rogan with dread. That was the only reason he'd reluctantly agreed to go along with her plan, but even then, he'd been disdainful of it.

"You'll fight the entire army going after that Tolin," Rogan had warned. "Just to do what? Get your father's armor? Kill his rotten son? Leave me out of your passions for revenge."

"You're a gutless cunt," Roan had taunted him. "You sound like the kind of man you've supposedly hated your entire life, if the songs about you are to be believed. You would let your nephew die, and let that wizard laugh as she eats his heart and giggles over your lack of manhood?"

"No, but I would use caution rather than go charging in. We select a few from your company and mine and disguise them as members of the caravan. We keep a few of the traders who are known at the city gates to talk our way through, in exchange for their lives."

"And once inside?"

Rogan had shrugged. "You go your way, and I will free my nephew."

They had set out on their journey to the city. Rogan had been riding alongside Thaxter, telling a bawdy joke, when a searing pain shot through his head, building in his left temple and then exploding behind his eyes. Crying out, he'd dropped from his saddle and fallen to the sand.

The sky had swirled, blue, red, and gray—and then white. Thaxter and the others vanished. A baritone voice, low and deep like the distant echo of a storm, called his name. He remembered wondering if he was dead, but then he'd felt his heart thud.

"Rise up, my son," the voice intoned. "Take up your sword and walk to me."

Swallowing hard, Rogan had found himself unable to speak. *My father is dead*, he thought.

The voice chuckled. "I gave you life. I gave your father life, as well. You are both my sons."

Who are you? And where are you? Who speaks to me in my mind?

"Don't tell me you do not know who I am."

Some diseased wizard, no doubt. Is this my fate, then? To spend the afterlife with you?

"I am no wizard, Rogan. You seek to deny the things that you fear. How very human of you. Now, grind up your balls like a man and rise up. I gave you and your kindred life. I am the one whose name you invoke. You know who I am."

My father said Wodan appeared in the form of a wayfaring stranger. A blacksmith, a fighter, a simple man in the street who passed by. He never said Wodan was some disembodied voice.

"I have used all those forms at times, but so have others. Amun, the Sleepwalker, for example. These days, I have but one form. You must recognize me in your heart, Rogan."

What is it you want of me?

"I ask for nothing, my son, save for your presence. You will know what to do when you see me."

Where are you?

"You are coming closer to me."

That's helpful. If you are really Wodan, then tell me something I can use.

"I will save Javan in his hour of turmoil. I will give you a path."

A path to what?

"You will know. Be the one you were made to be."

And then Rogan had woken up, feeling old, lying on his back in the sand.

His head still throbbed, but the pain was manageable. Satisfied now that he wasn't dead, Rogan opened his eyes again, squinting. Two forms hovered above him, partially blocking out the intense sun. As his vision cleared, he saw that they were Thaxter and Roan. Grunting, he sat up and shook his mane of hair.

Roan frowned. "You look as if you've seen a ghost."

Rogan shrugged.

"What happened?"

He tapped his temple. "There was a sharp pain ... in my head. Like I'd been shot through with an arrow."

"Old men get those," Roan quipped. "It drops them dead in

their tracks. Or, if they're unlucky, it leaves them paralyzed or feeble."

"I reckon I can still tip you over my knee and spank you, girl."

Thaxter knelt, slapped him on the back, and said, "He's a tough cuss, this bastard. He'll be all right."

They helped him up, and Rogan wobbled a bit on his boots before standing firm on his own, shaking off their grip.

"If I cannot stand alone, I should just die."

Roan smirked. "Then die. I have no use for a legend who cannot fight."

Trembling, Rogan nodded. As Roan's grin grew wider, he turned suddenly and punched her full in the stomach. Eyes wide, she doubled over, gasping for air. Boot behind her shin, Rogan pulled her leg from under her, and she dropped to the ground on her back. Before she could recover, Rogan dropped and straddled her chest. He pulled one of his daggers and held it to her throat.

"Last time I used this dagger," he growled, "it was to gut a fish. What do you think, Thaxter? Should I fish or cut bait?"

Roan grinned. "Cast away, you bastard"

Rogan felt the flat of a blade press against his crotch.

Thaxter sighed. "Will the two of you stop this prick-waving contest? We have shit to do."

Scowling, Rogan clambered to his feet and stepped away from her. Thaxter held out his hand to assist Roan, but she waved him away. Springing up, she sheathed her knife and nodded at Rogan.

"That was a good move, old man."

"I've got more."

"If you're trying to make me horny, keep them coming."

She walked back to her horse and donned the caravan member's cloak again.

Thaxter elbowed Rogan in his ribs. "I think she likes you."

"Shut up."

Roan pulled herself up into the saddle. "Where's Brok?"

Kenoth, also clad in the garb of a hooded trader, replied, "I haven't seen him since you took his horse."

Thaxter drew closer to Rogan as they returned to their horses. "I'd stay away from her, Your Majesty, no matter how hard your cock gets."

"I haven't the inkling to screw her," Rogan muttered. "I could kill her, though."

"I've heard that when a man reaches a certain age, he has to choose that over fucking."

Rogan climbed into his saddle and glowered. "Didn't I tell you to shut up?"

A cry went out among the assemblage. A half dozen riders accompanying a boxy wagon approached from the southwest. The sides of the wagon were etched with a rune.

"I recognize that symbol," Rogan said, squinting. "Ivor."

Roan's forces readied to overtake the new arrivals, but Thaxter called out to them: "It is the Oracle of Wodan!"

Soon, the wagon and riders stopped. When the wraps were removed from their faces, the lead rider was revealed to be an ancient man flanked by two women, one middle-aged with a long face and the other much younger with a smooth complexion.

Roan rode up beside Thaxter and Rogan. "I expected him to be more impressive."

Before either man could respond, an excited squeal rang out. Hyden rushed forward on her gnarled old legs and crossed the distance between the two groups. As the procession dismounted, she knelt before Ivor and put her face to the ground. He reached down, took Hyden's hand, and gently helped her to her feet. Hyden didn't face him until he touched her chin and lifted her face. She then grabbed his hand and started to kiss it.

Thaxter grunted. "They know each other?"

"It looks that way." Roan turned to Rogan. "So, you really sent for him? I'd have wagered you and Thaxter were jesting."

Rogan nodded. "There he is."

"I thought you didn't like wizards?"

"He's more of a warrior than a wizard."

Roan snorted. "A warrior? He's older than you are. Can he even lift a sword?"

"He may be old," Rogan admitted, "but I feel better with him on my side than just that senile old woman you have."

"Pig." Roan spat. "Hyden has served me well."

"Good," Rogan replied. "Let's hope her service continues. We're riding into Nodd. We'll need all the help we can get."

TOLIN ARRIVED AT THE GARDEN GATES AT THE SAME TIME AS three guards. He nodded at the men and gestured at the entrance, but they deferred, insisting that he go first. He did so and found Nosmada standing over the body of Captain Bradlee. The three guards shuffled in behind him, clearly unsettled by the scene.

"It looks like you need to hire better guards," Tolin quipped.

"Can you use him?" Nosmada asked.

Tolin nodded. "I can always use flesh and blood."

"Take Bradlee for your own purposes, then. He's still fresh."

Tolin turned to the soldiers. "Have this taken to my project. I shall be along presently."

Two of them grabbed one each of Bradlee's arms.

"Wrap him up first," Tolin ordered. "No use leaving a trail in the street. That's a waste of tissue."

"Do you have any children, Tolin?" Nosmada asked.

"Children?" Tolin paused, blinking. "I have a son from this flesh that I now wear, but you know that. Why ask rhetorical questions?"

Nosmada chuckled. "You are refreshing in that no one talks to me like that."

"Don't change the subject. What is your point about offspring?"

"Do you miss him? Your son, even in the state you are in?"

Tolin shrugged.

"I recall Maddox very clearly," Nosmada said. "He was a brash but good youngster, a great deal like his grandfather, Gorias. He was more interested in sex than fighting, but he could do both well. Do you miss him?"

Tolin sighed. "Perhaps if I ponder him long enough, I would feel a flutter in my chest where my heart should be. Didn't you originally build this city for your son?"

"You'd be shocked what one will do for a son you adore. One's son should be at your right hand, correct?"

Slowly, Tolin let his left forearm raise and extend, if only a few moments. He looked at his armlet and then back at Nosmada. He pointed at the body hanging from the tree.

"This thing here? That's why I have come to see you."

"Oh?"

"Why have my soldiers rooted out a dozen undead whores in the inner chambers? What is he doing to them? And why Spence?"

"Perhaps some react differently to his calls," Nosmada replied. "Maybe he kills them in their dreams or reanimates them for a lark. Who can say?"

"He can." Tolin stepped closer to the tree, grabbed the spike in the man's groin, and turned it. "Come on now. Tell me a story."

Though the figure contorted, it made no sound.

Nosmada shook his head. "That won't get you any answers."

Eyes ablaze, Tolin turned to face Nosmada. "Why do you keep this thing?"

"You really want to debate habits and desires?"

"No," he said ruefully. He glanced at the figure and then stepped away from the trees. "I foolishly thought any of it might make sense. I have erred coming here."

"The time is nigh," Nosmada said. "Zillian tells me that the stars are correct and all will soon be accomplished."

"The stars are correct? Bah! Like they have any effect on us."

"Oh, but they do."

"If that makes you feel good, then let Zillian roll her bones, read her portents, stick her finger in her ass, face toward Eden and pray. What do I care? I have other things to attend to. The final pieces of my old self are being delivered later today."

"Splendid! I assume you will want to take repossession of your prior self as soon as possible. And what then?"

"I shall leave this place, and you can have your satisfaction ceremony or whatever the hell it is."

"We've gone on this long with our agreement," Nosmada replied. "It's almost over. Let us not be bitter at the end."

They stood in silence as two of the guards returned with a canvas tarp. They watched while the men rolled Bradlee's corpse onto it and wrapped him up. Then they carted him away.

Nosmada turned to the remaining guard. "What is your name?"

"Bernard, my lord."

"Very well, Bernard. You are now captain of the guards."

"V-very good, my lord. I am h-honored."

Nosmada shook his hand and then departed. The newly appointed captain blinked at Tolin.

"Congratulations."

Bernard snapped a salute. "Thank you, General."

"Pray you fare better than your predecessor."

BACK IN HIS TOWER, NOSMADA TOLD HIS SERVANTS TO DRAW HIM a hot bath. Though their faces told a story of how long that might take, none defied him. Instead, they scurried off.

While he waited, the Lord of Nodd looked out across the great city. People moved about like ants on a hill, working, doing business, trading, all sorts of construction, and commerce. He turned his head a little and saw the scribes on the steps that ascended to the university. They read aloud to rows of students arrayed on stone risers. From their tablets, they extolled the basics of knowledge.

Someone cleared their throat behind him. Nosmada turned to see Schlack lurking.

The man bowed and then said, "Pardon, Lord."

"I hope the day finds you well, Schlack."

"Been better, been worse. Just wanted to say that Zillian is making the final preparations."

"Good." Nosmada turned back to the city. "Very good."

Schlack followed his gaze. "I wonder if they tell the children they are lucky to be here and not living out in the wild like a bunch of savages?"

"Perhaps."

"I wonder if they tell them the world is going to end soon?"

"I doubt it."

"Is that still a matter of debate?"

"Oh, in some places, but few give it credence."

Schlack coughed. "Folks still talk of it, accepted or not."

"The angels talk of it, too." Nosmada turned away from the view. "I shall go down to the place to sacrifice and see Zillian's works."

"Very good, my lord. Shall I accompany you?"

"Unless you'd rather stay here and take my place in the bath I ordered."

"No thank you," Schlack replied. "I had one last week."

As they descended the steps in the lower chambers, Nosmada asked, "What is on your mind?"

"Oh, nothing of great importance."

"Indulge me."

After a few moments, Schlack said, "If this all works out, your heart's desire, your life's work ..."

"Yes?"

"Well, if it works out for you ..."

"... or it doesn't?"

Schlack exhaled and they both stopped on the steps. "Well, yeah."

"Yes?"

"What becomes of us?"

Nosmada turned, patted him on the shoulder, and then proceeded down the stairs. "Don't worry."

"I'll try not to."

"Everything will change, for the better."

———

Neither man noticed Fallon as she followed them down the staircase. They were oblivious to her presence as she trailed them through the subterranean corridors. They didn't know she watched from the shadows as they arrived in the place of sacrifice and met Zillian by the door of the great chamber.

The three figures disappeared behind the door. Fallon darted out from her hiding place and peered through the door before it closed entirely.

They became aware of Fallon's presence when she screamed.

———

Anka found Tolin watching the acolytes of Dar attending to the dragon body. The young warrior blanched at the grisly process.

Tolin adjusted his gauntlets and smirked. "I surmised you had a strong stomach, being a fighter and all."

"That isn't typical warfare, sir. I apologize."

"Nothing to be sorry for," Tolin informed him. "It's not natural to see such things when one is a human being."

Anka raised his head and looked into his eyes.

Tolin winked. "Or a dragon."

"Is that ... Bradlee?"

"Aye. It was Bradlee. Now it's just meat. Flesh for the beast. My new skin"

Anka gaped. "They are rolling him into a ball."

Still looking at his armored gloves, Tolin said, "Yes."

"They are putting him near the ... oh damn ..." Anka stepped back, gripped his knees, and gagged.

"What would your father say if he thought you puked on your general's boot?"

Anka stood up straight. "If my pappy saw them turning Bradlee into a dragon testicle, he'd tell me to move over and he's got the other boot."

"I think it's an appropriate fate."

"Before now, I never knew dragons had balls."

"Where do you think baby dragons come from?"

Anka shook his head. "I don't know."

"They are under plates," Tolin informed him. "The balls."

Several of the acolytes exited the chamber, each carrying a tray of spare offal taken from Bradlee's corpse before he became a dragon testicle.

Anka turned away. "Have you ever been to an execution abroad?"

"Why do you ask?"

"There are always a bunch of ghouls who want the body of a hanged or otherwise executed person. If not a worker in magicks, it's some idiot who makes potions or lotions from the bodies."

"At least they are useful."

"Yeah."

"Has the caravan arrived yet?"

"Due any time, sir."

"Have all the undead whores been cleared out?"

"From what I gather, yes."

"Good."

"Sir, I don't understand what is going on."

Tolin sighed. "I'm not sure Nosmada does, either. It is the fault of that thing he keeps imprisoned in his garden."

"Why does he keep it? What is the point? Some control over or prize for the fallen ones?"

"What do you know of such things, Anka?"

"I know a fallen angel or devil needs an earthly body to walk around in. If they can't possess one, then they make one."

"That's not always so. The fallen angels that serve Hell ... yes. They need an earthly body."

"Does that thing on the tree ...? Does Nosmada get power from its body?"

"I don't know what he gains from it, Anka. And soon, it will not matter."

"General?"

"Please go oversee the caravan upon their arrival. Verify the cargo. We will talk more later."

"Yes, sir." Anka saluted and left the chamber.

Tolin walked around the entire body of the dragon, not once making eye contact with Dar's acolytes. Though he loathed the wizard, he needed Dar alive for a little while longer. He stopped at the left side of the dragon and gazed across the body. He noted the sections where flesh still was needed. He also looked longingly at the dragon's head, where a key piece remained absent.

"If that caravan leader is lying," he muttered, "I'll kill all of them and their children."

He walked over to the forearm of the dragon, near where the limb terminated in a claw. He took off his gauntlets and set them on the floor. Tolin then ran his hands over the platelets that covered the wrist of the dragon. His fingers tightened, and he pulled a plate up.

Under the platelet rested a familiar face, embedded in the twisted flesh. Tolin blinked. Jaw out, his shoulders back, he bent down and kissed the forehead of the body.

"We shall fly away soon, Maddox," he said to the face in the flesh and replaced the dragon plate over it. "You will be with me, always."

He picked up his gauntlet and said to the nearest acolyte, "Seal that back. For good this time."

The acolyte bowed, and Tolin stomped out of the chamber.

CHAPTER 8

WHEN THE SUN GOES DOWN

"Bones ..."

Thaxter rubbed his hairy face and gave Rogan a look. "Sorry, what was that? I was lost in thought, watching for trouble as we ride through these interchanges. You should be, too."

"Fuck off then." Rogan turned his head and spat.

Above them, a row of armed guards lined the ramparts of the curtain walls as the caravan slowly moved through. The only sound was the clomping of horse hooves and the creaking wheels of carts.

"Oh, don't get all pissy with me, old man." Thaxter pulled his hooded cloak tighter about his face with a tug. "All these curtain walls and guards ...we are ten kinds of fucked at any moment. My mind's not on ... what was it you said?"

"Bones," Rogan repeated, scanning the towers that rose in the distance. "It's a strange cargo. When Roan's group seized this caravan, I expected dry goods or wares, or maybe even gold or jewels or other riches. But bones ..."

"Dragon bones," Thaxter corrected him. "I guess the wealthy bastard is a collector."

"La Gaul's son? Maybe. In the meantime, it's not our current location you need to be wary of. Those outer rings of earthen works were just the first curtain walls. We'll ride through worse."

Thaxter glanced back at the moat they had crossed. Far back at the end of the procession was Ivor's wagon. He turned back around in his saddle and groaned at the sight of the bridge up ahead and the huge gate beyond it.

"An attacking army would be tired as hell by the time they got to the city," Thaxter said. "What does this ruler guard? All the gold and jewels in the world?"

"Always wondered," Rogan admitted, "but I never tried to find out."

Thaxter frowned. "Not even when you were Javan's age?"

"Some things even a barbarian leaves the fuck alone."

"When was the last time you visited here?"

"A long time ago," Rogan replied.

"Yeah? How'd that go for you?"

Rogan grinned. "I'm the reason there are so many curtain walls around Nodd."

Thaxter laughed. "They didn't put those up after your first visit?"

"I was a kid the first time I came here, but you see those spires over yonder? I remember those. The city has gotten larger and the walls more numerous since then."

"What about the second time? Older?"

Rogan nodded. "Yes."

"And you were probably all about beer and pussy then?"

"Of course." Rogan chuckled. "And about as smart as a tree stump."

"Youth is like that," Thaxter said.

"As opposed to now, when we are bright as the stars, riding into this fortress to get a kid back—a youth who is smarter than both of us combined?"

"Very true," Thaxter conceded. "You realize Roan doesn't give a shit about helping us rescue Javan? She's got another idea in mind."

"She's crazy. Whatever hard-on she has for the son of La Gaul …"

"But you heard what the traders said. These dragon bones are for him."

"Aye."

"So, her band of happy assholes are gonna do what, exactly? Kill the general and take his dragon armor?"

"Simple as that," Rogan said. "She sees it as her birthright."

"She gonna fight his entire army?"

"Would you?"

"Fuck no," Thaxter affirmed.

"I wouldn't either. But she will. She'll be out to find him and get after him."

"And what about us? What's our plan, Rogan?"

Rogan turned in the saddle and looked back at the end of the procession. "That's why we have the Oracle of Wodan along."

"What do you think he's doing inside that wagon?"

"Probably deep in one of those women accompanying him?"

"At his age?"

Rogan snorted. "I hope so. Otherwise, what hope is there for an old man like me?"

"So, that old fucker is how we'll find Javan? He'll keep us safe from the magic of other wizards?"

"That's the plan."

Thaxter shuddered. "Great."

"Ivor is powerful. Trust me."

"I know you hate wizards, so if you vouch for him …"

"He's old, but he's the most powerful of that sort I've ever encountered."

Farther up the caravan, shouts rang out. The procession halted as a few men in robes spoke to those at the front. After a few moments, the caravan started to move again and veered to the left.

"Now what?" Thaxter wondered.

"That Kenoth asshole is heading back our way. Maybe he knows."

"I thought you were impressed with him? He fought good for a one-eyed kid."

"Still an asshole," Rogan whispered, and then smirked as the youth rode up beside them. "What news, Kenoth?"

"They are sending us to set up camp nearer to the Citadel of the Dragon. A representative of the general—a man named Anka—will inspect our cargo soon."

Thaxter grunted and took a snort from his flask. He offered Rogan a drink as Kenoth moved back to the rest of the caravan.

"I'm not drinking after you." Rogan looked at the stone buildings lining the inner wall. They were daunting. Not far off was a huge complex hemmed in by stone brick walls peppered with guard towers. "This will be tricky."

The caravan snaked around to the left and was directed where to stop. Thaxter dismounted, and Rogan, after giving the complex a final lingering glance, followed suit. The procession was composed mostly of long canvas-covered wagons housing the dragon bones, but it had many other carts as well. They had contained varied stock items to sell in the city. Now they were filled by fighters from both Roan and Rogan's groups. Slowly, they clambered out of the wagons and carts and did their best to look occupied with mundane tasks.

Rogan and Thaxter walked to the rear of the group, seeking Ivor. They found his wagon still at the end of the line, with two of his three wives standing beside it, gazing upon the city, and the youngest knitting on the driver's seat. The shuttered wagon squeaked, rocking back and forth on its axles.

Rogan and Thaxter exchanged a look as they approached the three wives.

"Is your master inside?" Thaxter asked.

Rogan grimaced at his question.

The eldest spoke. "Where else would he be?"

Thaxter shuffled his feet, and his ears reddened with embarrassment. "I thought he might be looking for Javan or blocking the spells of this city's wizard to cover our presence here."

"Oh, he is," she affirmed. "He works his magicks even now. You should not disturb him."

"Well, we need to know what he intends as far as Rogan's nephew."

Thaxter walked to the rear of the cart.

"I wouldn't if I were you," Rogan warned, following along.

Ignoring him, the big man pulled both doors open, revealing a stocky old man's bare buttocks thrusting over and over, and a pair of petite legs wrapped about him, smoothing his sides as he grunted. The woman under Ivor's touch convulsed and shouted, gripping his shoulders. Thaxter and Rogan's eyes widened when they realized she was the aged spellcaster Hyden.

"Wodan's sack," Thaxter cursed. "Behold the Oracle of Wodan ..."

Ivor's grunts stopped with a large cough, and he ceased his motions. Hyden trembled and wrapped her legs about him tightly before releasing him. Ivor slid back, his sandaled feet hitting the ground. He pulled his kilt down to cover his manhood and tugged his long suspenders up over his shoulders. Then he coughed again and winked at the two men.

"What do you boys need?"

"Close the doors," Hyden snapped. "I need to compose myself."

"We've already seen everything," Rogan said, closing the doors regardless. He turned to Ivor. "Thaxter is concerned."

"About what?"

"I thought you came to help us find Javan," Thaxter said, "and cover the spells of the wizard of the city."

"I did already." Ivor licked the fingers of his right hand, then wiped them in his long beard and gestured at the citadel complex. "He's in there. They brought us right to him."

Thaxter squinted up at the citadel. "Do they know we are here?"

"No."

"And the wizard?" Rogan asked.

Ivor frowned. "There is more than one wizard in this city, but the one who has a hard-on for you? That one can't tell we are here. I have seen to that."

"I hope so."

"I should warn you both ... there is something even more dire afoot here."

Thaxter frowned. "What?"

Ivor closed his eyes. "I hear it, the voice of my god in my head, heart, and loins."

Thaxter turned to Rogan. "He's as senile as Hyden."

"Shut up and listen," Rogan told him.

Ivor rubbed his temples with his fingertips. "He is here, the god of my life. I know his voice."

"Wodan is here?" Thaxter shook his head. "That's bullshit."

Ivor's eyes opened. "No, I fear not. I must find my master."

Thaxter turned to Rogan. "Do you believe any of this?"

Rogan didn't reply.

Ivor pointed at Rogan. "He's been calling to you, too, boy."

"My ears aren't so good."

"Nonetheless," Ivor said, gazing across the city, "I know where he is. We shall have to seek him out."

"Great plan." Thaxter glared at Rogan. "Were you counting on this?"

"Hell no. I stay away from the gods."

"Well, we better figure this shit out. I doubt they are going to just let us take Javan and ride out."

"No," Ivor agreed. "I'll have to kill that wizard. I'll need you boys with me."

Rogan shook his head. "I am grateful for your help, Ivor, but we are here for Javan."

"I don't want to see our god alone, Rogan."

"And I don't want to see him at all."

Ivor smiled. "You've seen him before. I'll need your help."

"What does he want?" Thaxter asked.

The doors to the complex opened, and a tall, youthful Black man clad only in trousers strolled out, flanked by armored soldiers.

"That must be the representative Kenoth spoke of," Rogan grunted. "Anka."

Ivor patted Thaxter on the shoulder. "Wodan wants what Javan wants. He wants what we all really want."

"Oh, yeah?" Thaxter watched Anka approach the largest of the caravan wagons. "What's that?"

"He wants to be free."

———

Nosmada waited as a slender girl in a black frock whispered to Zillian. She stepped away from the crone, made a slight curtsey to him, and departed.

Zillian watched her go. "That's Martel."

"I know who she is," Nosmada said. "Why is an acolyte of Dar here talking to you?"

The old lady held up a small bone.

Nosmada's eyes narrowed. "I smell a rat. Martel doesn't belong to Dar, does she?"

"Not entirely," Zillian admitted.

They walked together down the hall. "What was that all about?"

"Oh, children and their schemes. She's a very bad girl in her soul, and I don't know if she'll get much older. None of it affects you."

"So you say. She has a lot of gray hair for a girl so young."

Zillian nodded in agreement. "She's seen many an amazing thing. She has brought me something, and I will share it with you." She cleared her throat. "There are a few of the host gathered about, the demons that talk to you and the angels."

"Why?"

"They smell blood in the water. They sense the stars are right and want to watch as it all goes down."

"Whatever. I do not care."

"Perhaps they think if your sacrifice is true and works, there is hope for them?"

"Hope. Don't get me started on hope."

They entered Zillian's inner chamber, and she turned up the oil lamps. The light shone about the room and over her large oval cauldron.

"Well, then," he said with a sigh, "show me."

Zillian held up the small bone and cast it into the cauldron.

The liquid within churned like a substance heavier than molasses and soon swirled with blue and red glowing light. Within a minute, images formed on the surface.

Nosmada squinted into the morass. "Who is that?"

Zillian nodded. "The barbarian king, Rogan and his men. Accompanied by another troop as well."

"They are within the city itself?"

"So it seems."

"I'd kill the captain of the guards if he weren't already fodder for the general's dragon." Nosmada clenched his fists in anger. "Is he here for me?"

Zillian shook her head. "No, for his nephew, Javan, who rode in on the horse of Gorias La Gaul itself. He was compelled here by the magicks of Dar."

"After Dar summoned the hellhounds?"

"Correct. Dar set a trap with his nephew as bait, so the barbarian came after him. You see, there is bad blood between the two."

"So ... that idiot has let one of the greatest killers of all time in through our gates over a personal issue?"

"So it seems."

Nosmada's eyes narrowed. "Why hasn't Dar struck at him?"

"She doesn't know he's here."

"What?"

Zillian waved at the cauldron. Near Rogan stood an old man.

"He carries his own wizard—one who has blocked the eyes and magicks of Dar."

"Who is this wizard?"

"Ivor."

"Ivor?"

"Ivor, the famed Oracle of Wodan."

Nosmada was silent for a moment. When he spoke again, his voice was barely a whisper. "Of whom?"

"You heard me correctly, my lord. Wodan."

"Damn ..." Nosmada cracked his knuckles. "Do you have any more bad news for me? Troubles often come in threes, after all."

"I said there were others with Rogan and Ivor. One of them is ... her."

"The daughter of La Gaul?"

"Yes. And I don't need magic to tell me that she is not here to seek Javan."

"Obviously." Nosmada nodded. "She wants something from Tolin? Perhaps his armor? Or his life?"

Zillian sighed. "If she had taken that before the time ..."

"I doubt she could."

Zillian frowned. "Because she's a woman and he's a dragon?"

"Oh, don't start on that, Zillian. You've seen Tolin fight. You've seen him angry. Even in human form, he's formidable. Whatever her training or grudge, she'll not soon best him in single combat. Rogan, though ... I'd have loved to see those two do battle when the barbarian was a young man."

"You think him weak because of his age? An old man can be dangerous."

He winked at her. "You know it, Zillian. However, as entertaining as their fight is, it's best if Tolin be allowed to leave, to fly away from us and be gone."

She looked to the hallway where they heard the sobbing of a girl. "Fallon, so young, so foolish."

"She will learn. If not, she will die. Such is the world."

"True," Zillian agreed, still looking at the hall. "The sight of the leeches in the chamber almost did her in, truly."

"Leeches. Funny name for them just because they suck and retain blood."

Zillian turned back to him. "My magick created them from bats, leeches, blood, and ground-up bones rejected by General Tolin. Once they serve their purpose, they will fall away and not hinder the other creatures of creation."

Nosmada turned to her and gently took both of her tiny hands in his. "Such power in these hands." He bent over and kissed each hand. "I'm impressed."

Zillian laughed loudly and pulled her hands back. "You need to drink more, my lord."

He smiled and looked at the cauldron. "Perhaps."

GENERAL TOLIN PAUSED AT JAVAN'S CELL AND PEERED THROUGH the bars. The youth reclined on a sparse, simple bunk, hands behind his head. He waved at Tolin, smiling.

"Damned children," Tolin muttered.

"My uncle hasn't arrived yet?"

"You're still alive, right?"

"Last time I checked, sir. I feel good."

"You won't for long." Tolin stepped away from the bars.

"If I am to be truthful, General, I don't care for your wizard."

"Dar isn't my wizard."

"Really? She invokes your name a great deal."

"Dar needs to learn to shut up. She will make the wrong enemy in time."

"I must admit," Javan replied, "I don't comprehend the mind games."

"She taxes your mind? Are you having dreams of your god, too?"

Javan blinked. "Certainly not. My goddess doesn't work in

dreams. No, Dar compelled me to watch something rather frightful—well, frightful to most people."

"There are too many damned gods," Tolin growled. "I don't care how Dar gets her thrills."

Javan lay his head back and thumbed to his left. "Perhaps you should care how your soldiers do. But I will give you your leave, General. I have to rest. Thank you for stopping by to check on my welfare."

Sighing in exasperation, Tolin moved on down the line to where Javan had indicated, past many empty cells. He stopped at the sound of grunting. Eyes rolling, he chose softer steps and approached a cell.

In the moonlight, Tolin saw Anka thrusting against a woman he had pinned with her back against the wall. Her pale legs wrapped around the obsidian warrior. Her hands clawed into his shoulders. Tolin waited for a minute as Anka loudly finished, though the pale woman made no sound. After Anka turned and laid the woman on the bunk, he looked up to see his superior.

"When you are through there ..." Tolin's tone was gruff.

"Sir!" Anka stood at attention and saluted, though his manhood swung limp, a line of semen still connecting him with his partner.

"I really don't care if you screw Dar's prisoners, but ..."

Still saluting, Anka said, "She's no prisoner sir. She ..."

Tolin hadn't focused on the woman until that point. Red-haired, full lips, and huge eyes. "Donnise?" His gaze snapped back to Anka. "All the living sluts in the world and you are down here, hiding like a dog, screwing a zombie whore?" His fist pounded on the bars. "What the fuck is wrong with you?"

His salute fading, Anka lowered his hand and his brazen chest fell some. "I always liked her before, and we got along so well—"

Tolin ripped open the door. "Get dressed. I need you."

Anka nodded, quickly pulled up his kilt, and adjusted his belt.

"Well, at least you can't get her pregnant."

Nodding fast, Anka ran from the cell.

Tolin looked back at Donnise, who sat there naked and docile. "At least I hope not."

As they walked down the hall and started up the stairs, Anka said, "Sorry, sir."

"Don't tell me you are sorry," Tolin shot back. "Go apologize to that Javan kid. I think you almost hurt his feelings."

They stepped out of the citadel and into the late evening air.

"Again, I'm sorry, sir."

"I suggest you take up drinking. I don't care what my soldiers do as long as they kill in battle. However, screwing the undead is ... you understand?"

"Yes, sir."

"Tell me of the caravan," Tolin ordered.

"I surveyed the inventory," Anka replied. "It seems legitimate. Of course, you will know better than I."

The two men stepped outside to where the traders had camped. Tolin looked at the long carts and the dusty travelers that manned them. His face contorted a little.

Anka whispered, "Yes, they stink like the trail, sir."

"You just screwed a zombie, and you want to talk to me of foul scents? Have them uncover their wares. All of it. Aside from what they will sell in the marketplace or barter, the bones are what I want to see."

Anka nodded and barked out the orders.

The traders began to undo their loads.

Tolin walked the length of the caravan and then looked back. "Slow at their jobs and they stink. What a crew."

After several minutes, he waved to the guards nearby, who all rushed over carrying torches. He went to the long carts in the center of the caravan. Tolin swallowed hard and loud as he shucked off his gauntlets. He slapped the gloves into Anka's chest, and then he ran his bare fingers over the long bones.

A dusty old man from the caravan asked, "What you are looking for?"

"Perfection," Tolin said, his voice quaking. "I had not thought it possible to have the wing extension intact. Where were these found?"

"Not far from where the spine was discovered last year. Perhaps that wing was torn off, but it landed unbroken. And look here, what you really wanted."

Tolin walked to the head of the long cart. The old one uncovered a basket. Eyes wide, Tolin reached out and then pulled his hands back. "That is incredible." He looked up at Anka and snatched his gauntlets back. He donned the gloves again and reached into the basket, pulling out an orb nearly the size of a man's head. The orb was dull, but when Tolin held it to his chest, it started to glow red, orange, and then yellow.

Anka gaped.

Tolin smiled. "It knows what I am. If any of you touched it, the orb would stay dull."

"What is it?" Anka asked.

Eyes on the dusty old man, Tolin said, "You know, don't you?"

"Yes," the man admitted. "I'm old enough to remember. I understand from hence power comes. I know the tears of a demon and what they are the trigger for."

Tolin petted the orb and held it close. "You will be well paid."

The trader nodded and stepped back.

"Anka," Tolin whispered. "Bring the bones to the resting place. Give them to Martel. And make sure these people are paid in full." He looked up at the old man. "Enjoy your night in the city."

He then started back toward the lair of the dragon.

Colonel Shazeal stood by the door and saluted.

Absorbed, Tolin didn't return the salute.

"Sir ...? Sir?" Shazeal spoke louder.

Distracted from his gleeful ruminations, Tolin glared at him. "What is it?"

"There's someone here to see you, sir. Someone with important knowledge."

Tolin sighed. "No more mystery. What in the hell is it now?

Some fool to tell me the lower forces are gathering to see if our lord's sacrifice will be good? That was expected."

The colonel shook his head once. "No, sir. This man warns of an enemy far closer."

"Really?"

"Yes. He told me minor details to gain access to you."

"Is it worth my time at a point such as this?"

Shazeal glanced at the tower of Yitzak Dar. "It might prove to be."

"Take me to this person."

They walked into the citadel and Shazeal said, "He claims to be a great warrior of renown, a famed mercenary."

"Another one?" Tolin smirked. "Seems like a lot of that going around."

The two walked into a wide chamber usually used as a meeting room to plot wars. The man waiting for them was studying the chalky sketches on the wall.

"So," Tolin said as he petted his glowing prize. "You are the merc with a message for me?"

"Yes," the big man replied and made a bow. "Brok Yoshee, at your service, General La Gaul."

CHAPTER 9

LAST FAIR DEAL GONE DOWN

Rogan, Ivor, and Thaxter had watched from afar as Tolin and Anka perused the caravan. Rogan was bemused at Roan's body language. She'd glared at the man from beneath a hooded tunic, her frame taught and almost vibrating with repressed rage. Clearly, it was all she could do to keep from attacking him right there. But, Rogan noted with admiration, she knew the folly of such an action and had kept her emotions in check so as not to doom them before they even got inside the citadel.

After Tolin and Anka had withdrawn back into the citadel, Rogan pulled Ivor and Thaxter aside, ducking behind the Oracle of Wodan's wagon.

"We should go now," Rogan said. "I don't intend to let Javan spend another night in this place."

"What do you suggest?" Thaxter asked.

"Roan is distracted with rage, and the rest of her company are gearing themselves up for whatever comes next. We can slip away now without being noticed."

"You think you can," said Kenoth, stepping around the side of the wagon.

Angeline slipped from concealment and stood by his side, arms crossed, scowling.

"Hell's bells," Thaxter murmured. "Are you spying on us?"

"I may only have one eye," Kenoth said, grinning, "but I see all."

Angeline nodded. "If you're going after Javan, then we're coming with you."

Ivor giggled.

Scowling, Rogan elbowed him and then jabbed a finger at the two young warriors. "You're staying here. I'm not a nursemaid."

"We can hold our own."

"Aye," he agreed, "you can. But we're gambling with Javan's life here, and I'll only put it in the hands of those I trust with my own life."

"With respect, Rogan ..." Thaxter paused.

"Spit it out!"

"Well, we need all the help we can get. They're both capable in battle, and fast."

"I just don't want a damned crowd trailing after us while we are trying to blend in and look natural in a city like this."

"And I don't want to have to tell Roan that you snuck off while she was distracted," Angeline countered. "But I will if you don't let us come."

Rogan puffed out his chest. "Are you threatening me, girl?"

"No." Angeline's hand crept to her sword hilt. "I'm promising you."

Before Rogan could respond, Ivor cleared his throat and gestured at a wooden structure near the stone citadel. "If you children are done squabbling," he said, "then focus. Those are the stables. We'll go in through there."

"Why?" Kenoth asked.

"Why not? It will lessen Rogan's concerns about blending in, and ... I sense something roundabouts there anyway."

Rogan frowned. "What? Magick?"

Ivor shrugged. "I'm unsure."

"Unsure?" Thaxter laughed. "You're the fucking Oracle of Wodan! If you're unsure, then what good are you?"

Ivor stared at the stable entrance. "If I told you what I sense and smell, you might piss yourself and run away."

"Unlikely," Thaxter sneered.

Ivor turned, meeting Thaxter's gaze. "Destiny comes for us all. Fate is a fickle bitch, young man. Get ready for her."

After a turn of his ax, Thaxter said, "Lead on."

Rogan surveyed the rest of the caravan.

"Roan's gone," he observed. "Did you two warn her before coming after us?"

Kenoth shook his head. "She has her own business."

"We better get on with this, then, before she gets our tits in a wringer."

"That's the first sensible thing any of you have said," Ivor muttered. "Now follow me and be quick about it."

He led them away from the caravan. Rogan and Thaxter flanked his sides. Angeline and Kenoth kept pace behind them. All wore the hooded cloaks of the traders, concealing their weapons and armor. The group walked to the stables with confidence, and no one impeded them as they entered.

Torches flared on the walls, and dust swirled in the sparse rays of sunlight coming through the barred windows. Water dripped from a crack in the ceiling. The air smelled of manure and hay. Horses, a cow, and a few goats stared at them sullenly, but otherwise, the stables were unoccupied.

"There." Rogan pointed at a wooden door past the long hallway of stalls. "That must connect to the side of the citadel and the cells."

"Are you sure?" Angeline whispered. "Why would the dungeon be near the stable?"

Shrugging, Rogan said, "I've been around the world, and that always seems to be where they are—next to or beneath the stables. No one cares if a few prisoners smell horseshit."

At that moment, the heavy wooden door jiggled, and the lock

clicked. Kenoth and Angeline jumped into an empty stall on the right while Rogan, Thaxter, and Ivor hurried into a stall on the left. A few of the horses whinnied uneasily. The door creaked open, and then footsteps plodded into the stables. Straw rustled underfoot.

Rogan and Thaxter slowly raised their heads and peered through the lattice works separating the stalls. Thaxter glanced back down at Ivor and then elbowed Rogan. He nodded at the older man in concern. Ivor's eyes had rolled white, and his hands trembled, fingers curling and tensed.

"He's okay," Rogan whispered. "Working some kind of magick."

They turned their attention back to the figures that had entered the stables. A thin person dressed in finery stopped in front of an empty stall. A man in the togs of a city guard and another in the dirty clothes of a stable hand flanked her.

Rogan and Thaxter sank back down into the scattered hay.

Still trembling, Ivor said, "That is Yitzak Dar."

Rogan scowled.

"Who?" Thaxter whispered.

"She's an alchemist and wizard," Ivor explained. "I have made sure that she cannot see or hear us, but the strain ..."

Rogan rose to his knees and spied upon the threesome again.

"Gone," Dar shouted, gesturing in anger. "How can he be gone?"

The stableman bowed his head. "I swear by the gods, it was here."

"That was no simple mount," Dar raged. "That was Traveler! Do you know who that is?"

The guard perked up. "The legendary horse of Gorias La Gaul?"

Dar faced him. "Yes, from the bar songs and diaper rhymes."

The guard's eyes widened. "How?"

"I believe it." The stableman smiled. "Every child in Nodd has heard tales of Traveler, but we who groom horses have heard even more. Tales of Gorias range for seven hundred years, and he always had the same horse."

"But stories grow over time," the guard argued. "In truth, it was a series of horses all with the same name. Surely?"

"Traveler was no mere horse." Dar's tone grew testy. "That animal was a gift from the angels. Or the gods. It depends on which legend is being recounted."

The stableman rubbed both his eyes. "He was a beautiful creature, big as a draft horse. And how could he just walk out?"

Dar seized the stableman's tunic in both fists. "Because he didn't, you ass. He's gone."

The stableman gulped.

"How can I sacrifice that horse if he is gone?" Dar asked.

"I'm sorry!"

Dar released the man and turned toward Rogan. He ducked back down into the stall and held a finger to his lips.

"I told you," Ivor repeated, "she can neither see nor hear us right now."

"There's something else," Dar murmured.

"What?" the guard asked.

"I'm uncertain," Dar replied. "I can sense something at work here, but I don't know what it is. Something isn't right. Let us go and see if Javan is still there. And increase the guards."

"Very good," the guard said. "Shall I call out a search for the horse as well?"

"No, do not raise an alarm. Not yet. I'd hate to get excited over a childish prank."

Dar hurried from the stables followed by the two men. When the door slammed shut and the lock clicked into place, Ivor exhaled and relaxed.

"That was ... difficult."

Grimacing at the pain in his joints, Rogan clambered to his feet. He offered Ivor a hand, but the oracle waved him away.

"Do you need a moment?" Rogan asked.

"I'm fine." Panting, Ivor stood slowly. "But she's strong, that one."

Kenoth and Angeline crept out of the opposite stall and joined them.

"I thought we were caught for sure," Kenoth said.

"Still time for you both to turn around and go back," Rogan grumbled.

"You first." Angeline gestured back the way they'd come. "Age before beauty."

Rogan scowled. "I can see why Javan likes you."

"Enough," Thaxter snapped. "What do we do now? They locked that door behind them."

"Sneaking through a series of locked doors doesn't seem like a good plan," Kenoth said.

"Aye," Rogan agreed, "but smashing through them does."

"No," Ivor panted, weaving on his feet. "I know where we must go. I know where he is."

Thaxter frowned. "Javan?"

Instead of answering, the old man jogged out of the stables. The group exchanged puzzled looks before following him. They rushed past Roan's decoy caravan, but Ivor slowed to a hurried walk as they went around the opposite side of the citadel and started through the streets of the city.

"I thought we wanted to avoid the streets," Thaxter said. "Where are we going?"

"I know where he is," Ivor promised.

He led them deeper into the city. Rogan and Thaxter followed. Angeline and Kenoth trailed them.

"Stay together," Rogan warned. "Try to appear natural but be ready for anything."

They heard laughter and the sounds of a crowd ahead. They passed the small granary that serviced the stables and then a blacksmith and a tannery. Then the dirt alley gave way to an irregular cobblestone street, which led into a broader thoroughfare lined with rustic taverns, brothels, and a tattoo parlor. The street was packed with laborers and lower-class citizens carousing in drunken revelry.

"My kind of place," Thaxter said.

"Focus." Rogan's jaw tightened. "Maybe we can stop back here after we free Javan."

They rounded a corner and walked past a brothel that bordered a dark alleyway.

"Through there," Ivor indicated.

They followed him, and the sounds of the crowd faded behind them. The narrow passage reeked of urine and feces.

"Watch your step," Ivor cautioned. "They empty the chamber pots here."

Halfway down the alley was a red-curtained doorway—a service entrance to the brothel. As they approached, four guards emerged from the opening, grumbling to one another.

"I don't want to wait an hour," one said. "Let's just go to a different whorehouse."

"Nodd has no shortage of women," another agreed.

A third guard spotted Angeline and grinned. "It certainly doesn't."

Ivor, Rogan, and Thaxter walked around the guards, heads down.

The fourth soldier grabbed Angeline's arm as she passed by. "Where are you in such a hurry to get to? My friends and I have need of you."

Kenoth started toward him, but the third guard intervened.

"Don't worry, lad. We'll bring her back in good condition. We just—"

Rogan slipped up behind him and slit his throat before the others could even act. Blood pumped from the wound, splattering Kenoth and Angeline's tunics. The other guards went for their weapons, but Thaxter, Angeline, and Kenoth sprang into action, killing them before they could even cry out. Rogan stood over the still bleeding corpses and glanced around hurriedly.

"We weren't seen. Get those uniforms off them."

Thaxter playfully slapped Angeline's back. "Good job luring them like that. Now we've got better disguises."

Angeline scowled at him.

Ivor laughed. "Too bad there weren't five of them."

"I could kill Thaxter," Angeline suggested. "Then there would be enough uniforms for each of us."

Thaxter's grin vanished. "Rogan's right. I can see why Javan likes you."

Ignoring the banter, Rogan stripped off his tunic and grabbed a guard's uniform. The others quickly followed suit.

Shuffling footsteps stopped at the mouth of the alley. A tall soldier wavered on his feet, belching in his drunken state. "What are you doing?"

Ivor faked a limp, waddling over to him. "Impromptu orgy. Want to watch? They are all well hung, and I'll be inspired to paint some beautiful nudes from the scene."

The soldier stumbled toward them, deeper into the alley. "Paint?"

"Yes," Ivor said. "Would you like to be immortalized on canvas?"

"Huh?" The soldier gaped at him.

"Never mind," Ivor replied, and then sneezed in his face.

The man stumbled, went to his knees, and cried out. Spasming, he began to rip at his face. His fingernails dug ragged furrows into the flesh of his cheeks and forehead.

"Die quietly," Ivor said.

As if in compliance, the soldier stuck his tongue out and bit down savagely, grinding his teeth together until it was severed. Blood poured from his ruined mouth and face as he thrashed about like a dying snake. He kicked his feet against the cobblestones, jittering, and mewling. Then he gouged his own eyes out and lay still.

Kenoth and Angeline gaped.

Thaxter tried to make the undersized tunic of the dead guard fit on his big body. "That's a hell of a cold you've got there, Oracle."

Ivor winked at him and started to undress the soldier. "I've had it for years. I caught it on the plains of Thule while waiting for my master ..."

"Shut the fuck up," Rogan said. "Get dressed."

"Next time," Thaxter said, "let's kill some who are our size."

When they were dressed, Rogan and Thaxter dragged the bodies deeper into the shadows.

Rogan then pointed at their discarded tunics.

"Bring those with us," he ordered. "If somebody finds them with the corpses, all of Nodd will be on the caravan."

Angeline pointed at the insignia on her uniform. "Looks like I'm the leader."

They gave her a mock round of applause, and she bowed, then grabbed her crotch and spat.

Ivor pulled up the soldier's togs and said, "Onward!"

Kenoth wrinkled his nose. "What about the blood splatters on us?"

"This is Nodd," Rogan reminded him. "People here are used to blood. We'd stand out more if we weren't stained with it."

They walked several blocks until they reached one of the biggest buildings in the city. It stretched upward, seeming to touch the clouds. The steep sides were adorned with sculptures and ornate frescos. Thaxter, Kenoth, and Angeline marveled at it, but Rogan and Ivor simply moved on. They skirted the edge of the tower, keeping to the shadows, and circled to the rear. There, the area opened up into a large flat spot, about an acre in size. It was fenced by stacks of clay bricks overshadowed by a forbidding hedge. The only visible entrance was a set of sturdy bronze gates, which were attached to stone pillars carved into the shapes of winged men.

"What is that?" Kenoth asked. "A walled garden?"

Angeline nodded. "Yes. It's huge."

"He's inside," Ivor said, stepping forward.

Rogan frowned. "Javan?"

Ivor stopped and looked back at them. "No. Hades, no."

"With respect, Oracle," Rogan growled, "we are here to free my nephew from captivity. Choose your next words carefully. If Javan is not in there, then who is?"

"God," Ivor replied. "God is in there, Rogan."

Nosmada sat near the edge of Zillian's cauldron, peering intently at the mists. Zillian waved her thin hands over the surface, and the contents swirled within.

"Quite a troop of them," she said.

"So stealthy," Nosmada remarked. "But why are they here if they don't seek me? What are they after?"

Zillian shrugged. "Ivor is among them. He's so old and yet he still moves like a cat."

"Good for him."

"For him, perhaps. Not so good for all. He's a master."

"Then why doesn't he sense you?"

"He does," Zillian replied with confidence. "But he's apparently more concerned about blocking Dar."

"I see. Regardless, that is Rogan. Of that I am certain. He is older but still looks formidable."

Zillian chuckled. "It is good the barbarians can't live a thousand years like some. He's caused enough trouble as it is, frankly."

"That he has."

"Should they be allowed to roam, or shall we have them captured?"

"Notify Bernard but tell him to hold off. Simply watch them for now. I wish to see what they are about."

As the mists continued to swirl, Zillian trembled and struck the edge of the cauldron with her walking staff.

Nosmada turned toward her. "What?"

"They are here. Outside this building!"

Nosmada jumped to his feet. "What? I thought they didn't seek me?"

"Look! They are at the garden gates, attacking the guards!"

The two watched as Rogan moved first, dropping to his knee as if injured then swiping out with a long sword. The thick blade sliced through the knee of the first guard and stuck in his other knee. The victim screamed, but before he could strike back, Rogan rose and yanked him forward. He stomped on the still stuck blade, ripping it out and leaving the second leg dangling by a strand of gristle.

The second guard struck at one of Rogan's companions—a bigger, younger man wielding a huge double-headed ax. The guard's attack was true, but the upswing of the ax blocked the blade and shattered it in half. As the big barbarian handled his weapon's backswing, he put a boot in the groin of the guard, doubling the man over. The great ax fell, splitting the guard's head in a diagonal angle. Once this body fell, the big man set his feet and smiled at Rogan ... then raised the ax again and dropped it on the head of the legless guard at Rogan's feet.

The one Zillian had indicated as Ivor stepped between the two bigger men and shoved Rogan's companion. This led the axman to push the wizard backward until he collided with Rogan. The three quarreled for a moment before stopping to stare at the gates. Their other two companions stood apart from them, their expressions confused.

"They've slain the guards," Zillian said

"So they have." Nosmada's hands curled into fists as he stared into the images. "You have a knack for pointing out the obvious."

"They fight well, even among themselves."

"They are barbarians."

"True."

"If you don't mind my saying, Lord Nosmada, you are taking this exceedingly well."

"They won't gain access. The gate is locked."

"They will try," she noted. "See there? They are considering whether they can climb the hedge."

"Not unless they burn it down."

In the mists, the ax man and the two younger companions

examined parts of the hedge while Ivor stood back. Rogan, meanwhile, pulled out a slim dagger and began working at the locked gate.

Nosmada fists clenched even tighter. "They won't get in that way."

Zillian rasped in a deep breath. "But they will this way. Look again. Fallon has the key and is letting them inside."

When he turned to the section of the cauldron where she pointed, his brow furrowed in rage. "Damn. Curse my mercy."

"You should have killed her, my lord."

"Children and dogs, my weaknesses."

"Better if it were liquor and women."

Nosmada scowled. "Yes, I was kind. I won't make that error again. I suspect my prisoner has toyed with her mind. Influenced her. He probably calls to the barbarians, as well. I have been a fool."

Zillian did not reply.

He turned away from the cauldron and shouted, "Schlack!"

The door banged open. "Yes, sir?"

"Get Bernard. Tell him we have company in the garden. Meet me there with men. And send word to Tolin, as well. Tell him it is Rogan."

Schlack's eyes widened. "Right away, my lord."

"And Schlack?"

"Yes, sir?"

"Tell him I want Fallon and Rogan captured alive. The rest may be slain."

"It will be a tricky thing, taking him alive, my lord. He is a great warrior."

Nosmada nodded. "Did I ever tell you about my son, Enoch?"

"Yes, sir, many times."

"Enoch dreamed of being a great warrior. He saw the angels and the fallen kindred fight, and was inspired by them. Such glorious battles, eternal wars, heroes, devils, monsters wrought by the curses of sin. But like those angels ... even great warriors can fall."

"SLAYER OF THE CHIMERA, AYE?" TOLIN RAISED HIS CUP AND toasted Brok Yoshee. "That is some resume in itself."

"Just one of my exploits, really." Grinning, Brok returned the gesture. "This is excellent wine, by the way. I now see why Nodd's vineyards are so renowned."

The two men sat at opposite ends of a polished wood table, which had been set with bowls of fruit and a bottle of wine. Subtle incense smoked in a brazier, and torches flickered from alcoves in the walls. Shazeal and Anka, positioned near the doorway, watched silently as Tolin conversed with the traitor.

"Please," Tolin said, "help yourself to more."

"Thank you." Brok reached for the bottle. "I shall."

"Fascinating facts you have for me, mercenary." Tolin set his cup down on the table and picked up a glowing orb. "So, the barbarian king and his men slipped into the city as part of the caravan?"

"That was their plan," Brok confirmed, staring at the orb. "They hoped to infiltrate the citadel and remove Rogan's nephew."

"Interesting. How many accompany him?"

"I cannot say for sure. My employer did not want any of her company going with them. I would wager a guess that it is just Rogan and his second in command, a brute named Thaxter. Not all of Rogan's warriors came along with the caravan. Most of them remained behind in Ellivsulo. The forces outside are mostly my employer's."

"I'm not concerned about a few hundred bastards outside the walls. Those who travel inside, though ..." Tolin turned to Shazeal. "They walked right in."

Shazeal nodded. "Under the nose of the wizard."

"And Dar was looking for him," Tolin noted. "Dar knew he was coming. How in the hell did Rogan do that? I've never heard tell of him working magicks. He works weapons ... and blood."

Brok took another drink of wine. "They talked among themselves about a great oracle of his god who was set to arrive."

"That would be Ivor," Shazeal said.

"Yes," Brok confirmed. "That was the name they used."

Tolin stopped stroking the orb. "But you departed from them before all of this was set in motion?"

"Correct. I knew a military man would appreciate this information."

"Certainly." Tolin glanced at Shazeal and noticed that the colonel was biting his lip. Then he turned back to Brok. "As a warrior for hire, you didn't care for the idea of entering the Land of Nodd, unto the city our lord built for his fallen son, and fighting your way out?"

Brok grinned. "I'm a fighter for hire, but I'm not a fool."

"So you say," said Tolin.

Anka laughed.

Brok turned to him, and then to Shazeal, and back to Tolin.

"So," Tolin said, scooting back his chair and rising from the table, "in true mercenary fashion, what will this information you have already given cost me?"

Brok set down his cup, cradled his hands behind his head, and stared up at the high-arched ceiling. "Obviously, this information is worth something. I've given you the barbarian—a former king—as he assails your walls. Not to mention I've given you the object of your wizard's craving."

"Ah, but we'd already heard he was coming."

"But you did not know the hour," Brok countered, "nor the means. I have given you that."

Tolin began to pace around the table, clutching the orb in one hand. "That is indeed a good thing. Perhaps worthy of your life. Would that suffice as payment? That we allow you to leave this place with your life?"

"I can give you more," Brok said.

"Really? Such as?"

"Something I think you will find worthy of financial compensation." Brok stared at the glowing orb. "Something that will save *your* life."

Again, Anka laughed. This time Shazeal and Tolin joined him. After a moment's hesitation, Brok did the same, eyes darting about nervously.

Tolin's expression grew serious again. "Do I look afraid for my life? Who would want it?"

"Someone else is here that wants it," Brok replied. "She wants it badly."

"She?"

Brok nodded. "My employer. She who is hidden among the caravan, along with the strongest and best among her company. I rode with her hereunto this land. She intends to get something of yours, even if it takes your very life to attain it."

"Speak plainly and stop humping my leg. Who is this mysterious employer?"

"Roan La Gaul."

Tolin blinked.

"I see that I have your attention," Brok continued. "When Rogan's nephew, that kid Javan, rode in on Gorias's horse, Traveler, I thought you might be curious."

"Am I supposed to be concerned?"

"She is quite a warrior," Brok replied. "She was trained by the old man himself before he vanished into the land of Shynar."

"He didn't vanish," Tolin said. "He is dead."

"She blames you for that."

"I didn't slay him, though. I'd never lay claim to mighty deeds that I didn't perform. Such vainglorious lauds are beneath me."

Now it was Brok's turn to blink.

There was a knock at the door. Anka opened it to reveal a nervous soldier. The man bustled in, saluted both Tolin and Shazeal, and then whispered something into the colonel's ear.

Shazeal frowned, and then nodded at the man. The soldier hurried off, and Anka closed the door again.

"No," Tolin continued, "he died fighting the Draco-lich, an undead dragon."

"That's what the songs say," Brok agreed.

"An undead dragon, can you imagine such a thing?" Tolin asked, petting the orb again.

"The bards have quite the imaginations." Brok drained his cup and reached for the bottle.

Shazeal and Anka stood off to the side, speaking in hushed tones. Tolin glanced at them, and then walked around the table and placed a hand on Brok's shoulder.

"Never let it be said that I'm ungrateful. I'll compensate you for this information truly. Shazeal, see to it that the guards overseeing Javan are tripled."

The colonel nodded. His expression was troubled.

Tolin turned back to Brok. "Tell us, Yoshee, how will we know this Roan?"

"She is a tall woman, full-figured, with hair like fire. And she's deadly in a fight."

"So, if I see a red-haired warrior woman coming for me ..."

"For you, and for that armor you wear."

Tolin frowned. "Then I shall be ready."

Anka cleared his throat. "Um, sir?"

"Anka? You and Shazeal care to tell me what has you both so agitated?"

Anka nodded. "The horse Javan arrived on disappeared from the stables tonight."

"Did it now?" Tolin wondered. "Isn't that something? Stolen, I assume. Perhaps Rogan and the others intended to free it, as well."

Anka shrugged noncommittally.

"Dar is apparently livid," Shazeal added. "She had plans for that steed."

"Isn't that something?" Tolin repeated. He looked at Brok. "Could this be the work of your former employer?"

"Perhaps," Brok admitted. "Traveler has served as Roan's mount for many years. She loves that horse more than she loves people."

"Well, we had best be on the alert then. Come along with us. I have work to do, but you will be compensated."

"Should I retrieve my weapons and gear first?"

"Your property shall be returned, of course. But I wish to show you something first."

As Brok stood and bowed, Tolin started for the door. His men stood to one side and let Brok follow him before falling in line behind. They trekked along a series of long halls until they turned to a short stairway that led down to a wide series of stone steps. On this landing stood Yitzak Dar.

"I've just come from your cells," Dar informed Tolin as he stopped.

"Any reason for that?"

Fists clenched, Dar snapped back, "I wanted to see if the prisoner Javan was still there."

"And is he?"

Her face flushed violet. "Yes, he is."

"Then what is the problem?"

"Something is wrong! I can feel it but cannot see it."

"Go cast more spells," Tolin said and started to head down the steps. "I have work to do. My time is nearly here."

"I see," replied Dar. "Then maybe I should rest for the coming ceremony."

"Do as you like."

Tolin descended the stairs, followed by the line of men.

After another series of steps, Brok asked, "Why didn't you tell her what I told you?"

"I have my reasons," Tolin said. "Keep your mind on your reward and out of our personal affairs, yes?"

"Yes," Brok agreed. "I live to serve."

"Excellent. Spoken like a true soldier of fortune. You will find good service for me."

They descended into a large chamber, and Brok stumbled at the sight: a dragon's corpse covered in a patchwork of mismatched flesh with bones peeking through the hide. Robed acolytes scurried around the construct, chanting and casting.

"My word," Brok gasped.

"Impressive, isn't it?" Tolin stroked the orb. "Few living folk today have ever seen a real dragon."

"Much less this," Brok rasped, trying to find his bearings, looking up at the ceiling. "Is that a tent?"

"There are rafters to move, but yes. It's a series of canvas covers." Tolin walked up to the dragon's gaping maw. He stood next to an acolyte sporting short hair and a youthful face. "Here, Martel."

He handed her the orb. Her eyes wide, she nodded and accepted it. The object changed color in her hands.

"Thank you, my lord," she murmured. "Once the final bones are installed ..."

"Yes," Tolin agreed. "Later on tonight."

Smiling, Martel gazed into the orb. Then she stepped into the dragon's mouth and squeezed into its throat, vanishing from sight.

"Magnificent," Brok exclaimed. "I'm glad I lived long enough to see such a thing. That's really amazing. This is why you collect the bones. What a project. What a construct!"

"Look closer," Tolin urged.

Brok frowned. "What do you mean?"

"Is this just a collection of bones?"

"Well, no, it ..."

"Has flesh on it?" Tolin laughed. "Since there are no dragons left alive, I had to substitute what I could find."

"Horseflesh?" Brok guessed.

"Not a one. It is the flesh of the many who have served me. And that orb? That was the final piece I needed. Soon, I will fly away from this wretched place."

He pointed to a section of the dragon's underbelly that held a crude humanoid shape, empty.

"What is that for?" Brok asked.

"That will be made clear to you very soon. You'll have a great view of it."

Brok smiled. "I'm afraid I don't understand?"

Tolin folded his hands in front of himself. "You said that you live to serve. The dragon needs two balls, after all."

Brok had little time to act as the acolytes surrounded him. He reached for his sword, and his face registered panic when he realized he was unarmed. Hands pulled at him. He danced and whirled, trying to avoid their grasp. Shouting, he pushed past the swarm, but Anka and Shazeal rushed forward and seized him, holding him in place.

"Such an outcry," Tolin scolded. "Rejoice, mercenary. Finally, you will have a tale worth telling."

Eyes wide, Brok Yoshee screamed.

CHAPTER 10

BORN UNDER A BAD SIGN

"I have known you since I was a lad," Rogan warned Ivor, "but oracle or no, I have had enough. We are here to free my nephew. I don't care about the gods. Now ... take us to Javan, or by Wodan, I will leave you here and find him myself."

Without responding, Ivor pushed between Rogan and Thaxter and stomped through the open gates and into the garden.

"He seems to know where he's going," Thaxter said.

As the ax man turned to follow, Rogan glanced to their right. The girl who had let them in was whispering to Angeline, who knelt beside her. Kenoth glanced at them, then at Rogan, and then jogged ahead to catch up with Thaxter and Ivor. Shaking his head, Rogan walked over to Angeline and the child. The girl's eyes went wide as he approached, staring at his bloody sword. Scowling, Rogan stared down at them.

"You're scaring her," Angeline scolded. "She's called Fallon."

"So, she's not a moron," Rogan said. "Why did she let us in? Does she know what lies within?"

The girl clutched Angeline's shoulder.

"Her tongue stuck?"

The girl backed away from Angeline and ran away into the night.

"We ought to kill her," he grumbled, "before she alerts the guard."

Angeline leaped to her feet and put her hand on her sword hilt.

"Relax," Rogan said. "I'm not going to kill her. She's already out of sight. What did she tell you?"

"She told me to set him free."

"Who?"

"She didn't say. Somebody in the garden. Javan perhaps?"

Ivor suddenly cried out from within the garden. Startled, Angeline drew her weapon.

"I've never heard the old cuss make that sound," Rogan said as he brought his blade to bear. "Careful now. Let's approach with caution."

As the two crept into the garden, Angeline glanced at the statues of the angels by the gate. "He sounded afraid."

"No, that sounds different."

"I don't like this. That girl was afraid of more than you."

"I used to be afraid when I was small."

She gazed up at him as they walked between the plants. "You haven't been small in years."

"Quite a few."

"No crime to be afraid," she muttered.

They spotted Ivor, Thaxter, and Kenoth next to some tall trees that dominated the center of the garden. None of them seemed in danger, and there were no threats or foes in sight. Ivor was on his knees, facing one of the trees. As they drew closer, they saw a body nailed to the trunk. Rogan's eyes narrowed as he peered closer. After a moment, he shuddered.

"Angeline?"

"What?"

"I'm afraid," Rogan confessed, his tone hushed.

"Me too," she whispered.

"No, I'm just fucking with you." He laughed. "I've seen men crucified before."

"Asshole ..."

Striding forward, Rogan slapped Thaxter on the shoulder. "What's wrong with you?"

Thaxter stood still, mouth agape. "Can't you hear him?"

Glancing up at the prisoner, Rogan shrugged. "A voice crying out to be free, full of foreboding?"

Thaxter gave a slight nod.

"No, I don't."

Groaning, Ivor rose to his feet. "How can you not?"

"He looks like the figure in my dreams," Rogan admitted. "But I can't hear anything except maybe the piss running down his leg."

"It's not piss," Ivor said. "Look. He cries."

Shaking his head with contempt, Rogan snorted with laughter.

Ivor's eyes narrowed. "Do not laugh at this, boy. As you said, I've known you since you were a child, and we've laughed many times. But this is not the time for laughter. Show some damned reverence!"

"Very well, Ivor." Rogan held up his hands in mock surrender and stepped closer to the crucified form. "Out of respect, I will humor you this last time. But then I am going after Javan, whether you—"

"You see?" Thaxter whispered.

Rogan stood gaping. Like Kenoth, the prisoner only had one eye, but both his right eye and his empty left socket flowed with a steady stream of tears. Rogan peered closer, studying the face.

"It can't be," he murmured.

"It is," Angeline said. "The girl wanted us to free him. That's why she helped us."

Kenoth nodded. "We have to."

Ivor reached up and grabbed the wooden spike piercing the man's feet. "Someone has held him here. Tortured him. Blasphemy …."

Ivor twisted and pulled the spike, grunting. Thaxter joined the effort and, with their combined might, yanked the spike loose. As the oracle staggered backward, holding the implement up for all to see, Thaxter went to work on the second one sticking from the victim's groin.

"You see?" Ivor thrust the spike in Rogan's face. "You see what is there?"

Rogan nodded. The shaft was dotted with glowing green runes. As he watched, the glowing figures slowly faded.

"What are they?" Kenoth asked.

Behind them, Thaxter worked the second spike free.

"They sap his power," Ivor explained. "They keep him in check. Keep him weak. We need to get the ones in his hands out."

"I can't reach that high." Thaxter turned to Angeline. "I'll hold you up, all right?"

She blinked. "I can try, but I don't know that I possess the strength."

"Rogan," Thaxter said, "you hold up Kenoth. The two of them can work together."

Rogan did not answer. He simply stared, wide-eyed, at the figure on the tree.

Suddenly, a new voice shouted, "Fire!"

A series of heavy mesh netting fell on them. Before they could react, uniformed figures rushed from the shadows and forced them to the ground, holding them in place. Four archers emerged from the darkness and trained their bows on them, arrows notched and ready. A man wearing the rank of an officer stepped forward.

"Barbarians," he said, "you may wear the insignia of this city on those pilfered garments, but your stink gives you away. I am Bernard, captain of the guards."

"Why should we care?" Thaxter taunted.

"Because," Bernard replied, "before you die, I want you to know who beat you."

He stepped forward and spat at the net. Another guard did the same. Soon, all of the guards laughed and spat.

"Go on," Bernard sneered. "Call out in anger to your heathen gods now."

Taking a deep breath, Rogan shook with rage as he bellowed, "WODAN!"

He staggered to his feet, the net rising with him, and managed to free his sword. Before the assembled guards could react, he'd slit the netting open and sprang free. He ducked instinctively, expecting the archers to fire. Instead, they stood transfixed, staring behind him at the tree.

As his compatriots clambered to their feet, Rogan cast a glance back, wondering what had captured his opponents' attention.

The figure on the tree had somehow freed itself of the last two spikes. As Rogan watched, he slipped off the trunk and landed on his feet beside Bernard. The prisoner boxed the officer's ears, and Bernard's head exploded in a shower of blood and skull fragments. The other guards cried out in fear and disgust, backing away, as Bernard's brains dribbled down their uniforms.

"Wodan!" Thaxter echoed Rogan's shout, shrugging free of the net.

Turning away from the tree, Rogan swung his sword, lopping the head from a frightened guard. Another guard fell as Thaxter lashed out.

On his knees still, looking up at the figure from the tree, Ivor whispered, "Wodan ..."

As more guards clamored into the garden, the figure from the tree stalked forward, unsteady but determined. He stepped over Ivor and gazed down at him. The oracle raised his hands and lowered his head.

"Ivor," Rogan shouted, "get off your knees and help us. We are overrun!"

Thaxter grabbed a fistful of Rogan's hair and yanked him backward, out of the way of a sword strike. Nodding his thanks, Rogan disemboweled the attacker. The two waded into the horde, slashing and hitting, while Kenoth and Angeline struggled to free themselves from the net.

"Ivor," Rogan yelled again. He was about to curse the oracle, but the words died in his throat. The figure standing over the old man disappeared.

Rogan roared as more nets landed over him and Thaxter. Both men were pummeled down by the guards. Ivor was ensnared, as well. Though stunned and near to unconsciousness, Rogan noticed something odd. The tree's trunk still held the impression of the figure that had been nailed to it. Then he realized something else: Thaxter didn't seem to be breathing.

"Thaxter," he said. "Wake up!"

"Take them to the cells," one of their captors commanded. "The sun rises, and our lord will deal with them soon."

"I thought Bradlee was in charge?" another guard wondered. "Who are you to give us orders?"

"Bradlee is dead. I'm assuming command until this is all sorted. Unless you would rather speak with the Lord of Nodd?"

"Curse you," Rogan grunted at Ivor. "Why did you lead us to this place? Our mission was to get Javan."

"We'll see him soon enough," Ivor promised. "But be of good cheer, Rogan. Our mission was successful."

"The old man has doomed us," Angeline said. "Thaxter is dead."

Ivor smiled as the guards yanked them to their feet. "No. He is something else."

<hr>

"Thank you for returning her, Schlack." Nosmada poured water from a pitcher. "Did they injure her?"

Schlack strapped the unconscious Fallon to one of two slabs in the center of the room. "No, my lord. She gave them access to your garden. I captured her afterward and gave her a sedative to make things easier for Zillian's workings."

"Very good." Nosmada gestured at a long window along the wall. "Perhaps the thing we have put inside of her will appreciate that her form was not harmed."

"Indeed, sir."

"Open the shutters, Schlack. Let the light in."

Schlack's boots echoed as he walked across the room. The latch snapped as he worked it, and the shutters swung open. Though they faced south, sunshine could be seen washing across the buildings.

Schlack turned back to Nosmada, slumped in a cushioned chair. Zillian lay on a reclining bench to his far right. The elderly woman snored. He then glanced at the two slabs in the center of the room. Fallon lay still on one. The other was occupied by a monstrous pile of greasy flesh. Shuddering, Schlack closed his eyes.

"Don't weaken on me now, old friend," Nosmada said. "Today is the day I've looked forward to for centuries. I am glad for your and Zillian's company. I only wish Charla was here at my side to celebrate as well."

Schlack's lips parted. and he opened his eyes.

"Zillian is so strong," Nosmada mused. "She has such power and knowledge, yet she can only do so much. Perhaps I should have had her bring Charla back. Animals are such good company and wonderful friends. Well, dogs are. Cats? You can have those independent little bastards. I'm such a fool for sentiment, no? The dark Lord of Nodd misses his dog." His laughter echoed.

Schlack remained silent.

"They can kiss my ass," Nosmada said. "All of them. Every damn last one in the world. This isn't about them. It's about me. My life, my soul, my sacrifice. Soon it will all be over, and I'll see if this has been a life worth living. All of this petty nonsense and fighting means little in the scheme of the universe."

Zillian snorted loudly in her sleep, and Nosmada's smile faded. "For all of her power, for all of her ways and abilities, Zillian can't bring my dog back. And she can't bring my son, Enoch, back either. Oh, she could make him stand up and walk, move around and speak, but he's gone, long gone away from here. What good would having his flesh be? A bitter reminder of my failings as a father? Of the Siqqusim wanting human flesh to walk about in?"

Schlack's eyes were drawn again to the huge figure on the slab.

"No," Nosmada continued. "No, my son is gone to where the real heroes go. Enoch loved to watch the spirits fight, to see angels and demons clash in the sky and the ground. He thought it amusing when the fallen took on different personalities when tainted with the commonality of this planet—the flesh and shapes of creatures they crossbred with, like great birds, tusked jungle beasts, or, in the case of Pergamus, saurian reptiles. The dragons spawned from those unions were so amazing."

Sweat rolled from Schlack's brow.

"My son, taken with the epic tales of warriors fighting dragons and devils, trained so he could become a grand warrior." Nosmada gestured at the slab. "And look what it got him. Not so heroic in his repose, aye? He is dead, yet his flesh does not rot."

Shifting from boot to boot, Schlack glanced out the window.

"Enoch fell victim to the lies, the venom that dripped from the tongues of wizards, witches, and warlocks. They who sell their pitiful souls to the demons for greater glory in their finite lives. Putrid bastards all of them. The demons need flesh to walk about on this world, and Enoch, being a huge warrior with an appetite for glory, didn't realize what he'd fallen into ... or what was going to fall upon him. That damned demon latched onto him and they became one, out warring and whoring, inspiring countless barbarian fools to see him not just as a chief or king but as a god."

Schlack's eyes strayed from the buildings and returned to Fallon's still form.

"But I'm no fool," Nosmada ranted. "I have learned much in this long life. I have learned how to trap them, the hosts that think themselves better than common men."

Schlack took a deep breath. "Had it been one of the Siqqusim who possessed your son ..."

"Aye, but it wasn't. It was one of the fallen. And so when magick didn't work, I captured gods—the little gods—and forced them to help me. But they couldn't help either. I held that bastard prisoner for ages in my garden out of spite. Alas, I finally understood that Enoch could not come back. His soul had fled. But that didn't mean I'd let that denizen bound for the pit go free. No, I kept him, too. I never quite knew what to do with him in the end, but since he held tight to Enoch's flesh, I couldn't just let him go."

Nosmada stood, and Schlack tensed.

"At ease." Nosmada walked to the slab that held the body of his son and blinked. "I've cried so many tears for him over the years, and now that he is free of the spirit, now that he will begin to decay at last, I can't shed a single one. Amazing, no?"

Schlack nodded.

Nosmada turned to Fallon and stroked the girl's hair. "Have we done the right thing, Schlack? Casting the demon from Enoch's form into this girl? And how will the demon react when it awakes?"

"I do not know, my lord."

"Has my wrath this day dried up my tears? Has this last small act of vengeance made my soul so coarse, or is it just time to put that all away? Wodan freed, Enoch's tormentor freed, my enemies within the city walls, the dragon ready to fly. Think about everything we have done in our arrangement with Tolin. All the blood we collected for him. Is it time to move on, old friend, and leave it all behind?"

"Yes, sir," Schlack replied. "I think it is."

"I think so, too." Nosmada put his hands to his face. "I'm very tired, but soon it will be time to rest at last."

"Yes, sir."

Nosmada walked over to the window. "I see the trails in the sky. Those bastards are here to see it happen. Usually, they won't crawl out from under their rocks or mounds of baby skulls in case one of the angelic hosts sees them and drags them down to the pit."

"Perhaps you give them something, some hope for ..."

"Redemption? For them?"

Schlack shrugged.

"Bah." Nosmada spat out the window. "They are fucked, every last one of them. Let them dream and jack off into eternity. I'm not like them. I still have life, I still have breath, and I have a soul. And besides, God loves me."

Fallon twitched, but her eyes remained shut.

"That really has to be terrible," Nosmada said, "to be hated by the one that made you, no?"

"Yes."

"Schlack, your father was a soldier, if I recall."

"Yes, my lord."

Nosmada nodded. "You got along with him well?"

"Well enough. He was a tough man, but fair."

"He loved you?"

Schlack shrugged. "He wasn't the kind to say so, but he never let me go hungry, and he made me strong."

"See? There you are. That's love." He turned back to the city and then the sky. "We shall see what love is by the end of this day."

"And then ..." Schlack faltered.

"Oh, go on, say what you wonder."

"What happens tomorrow?"

"Sleep."

*   *   *

"It's morning," said Tolin as he opened the door and approached his other body.

The acolytes all looked up from their labors. Martel, seated atop the dragon's head, smiled and nodded.

"We wouldn't know," she said. "We have been here, finishing."

Tolin's eyes widened. "Is it in place?"

Martel climbed down off her perch, grabbed two of the longer incisor teeth, and scaled the tongue. "After some difficulty, yes."

Trembling, Tolin balled his fists tight. "Very good."

Her short legs swinging down, Martel dropped over the side of the dragon and righted her kilt. "We are ready, General."

"Good."

She approached him, wiping blood from her hands on a flour sack. "Are you ready?"

Tolin turned away from the dragon and faced her. "What?"

"Are you ready, General?"

"Quite. Anka will be here with the harem soon."

"Let's hope they can waddle on over," Martel quipped, throwing the bloodstained sack onto the floor. "It is finished."

"He is finished," Tolin corrected her and again looked the dragon over. "Almost."

"Very true, General," Martel agreed. "*He* lacks something. *He* lacks soul."

"Not for long." Tolin smiled.

Martel called out, "Ready yourselves. The time is at hand."

The acolytes all stood up and silently shed their cloaks. Then they filed through an open archway and disappeared. Soon, the chamber echoed with the sound of splashing water.

Tolin frowned. "Once they are finished re-baptizing themselves ..."

"You want this done correctly or half-assed?" Martel undid the clasp by her neck and let her garments slip to the floor. Then she walked through the archway as well.

Teeth grinding in agitation, Tolin turned to the door. "Where in Hades is Anka and the harem?"

Just then, a tall figure filled the doorway. It wasn't Anka or one of his soldiers or a member of the guards.

"At last," the figure said. Her voice was female.

"Who are you," Tolin demanded, "and how did you get access to this chamber?"

The figure dropped her cloak, revealing a towering, muscular frame. Her eyes were as green as emeralds. She sported a mane of red hair tied back in a ponytail and brandished two gleaming short swords.

"Another assassin?" Tolin rolled his eyes. "No ... you're the one Brok warned me about. Roan La Gaul, daughter of Gorias."

"Brok?" Her eyes widened in surprise. "Yes, Gorias was my father. And I am the niece to Tolin La Gaul, whose body you stole."

"You came all this way and penetrated our city just to try and fight me?"

"How arrogant you are, but what can I expect of a dragon?"

"Daddy tell you all about dragons?"

"He slew the last of them."

"He thought so."

Roan stalked forward. "Gorias instructed and trained me well. I shall finish his work."

"You will fail."

She nodded at the reconstructed corpse. "Been busy, I see."

"One needs a hobby," Tolin deadpanned. "I have the bones shipped here. The lord of this city provides the blood, under arrangement. And the flesh ... well, there's no shortage of that."

Roan's eyes scanned the chamber, the torches, the station, the altars all around, and the tiny troughs that led to the basin where the dragon's body lay.

"Impressive, no?"

"No," she replied.

"Can you fathom my dreams?" he asked.

"I have an idea," Roan replied. "Thirteen troughs. I suppose they will run with blood. But you just said you can get blood from elsewhere, so my guess is it's some sort of ritual. Probably one involving that harem you mentioned. What if I told you I slew those thirteen bitches on the way here?"

Tolin's body tensed, but then he relaxed. "If you knew my intent, you may have, but you didn't. Like most women, you don't lie very well."

"Most women can't reach down your gullet and pull your balls out."

Tolin laughed. "I believe you can. Still, this is my moment, and your timing is quite bad. Those swords ... they belong to the old man, don't they?"

"Ripped from the back of an angel."

"I had them for a time, but they were stolen from me."

She smirked. "Careless of you."

"I tire of you," he sighed. "Martel?"

A ball of green light erupted out of the alcove the acolyte had vanished into. It flew at Roan La Gaul, but the tall fighter swiped at it. The twin blades shredded the orb-like water. More lighted objects flew out of the opening. Some resembled scorpions and others snakes. Each time, her blades shattered them.

Roan smiled. "You'll have to do better than that."

Instead of responding, Tolin glanced past her. "Where are my guards?"

"All dead, every last one," promised Roan. "Tell me, you son of a bitch ... do I lie?"

Tolin hesitated. "What is my business to you? I'm not your father, nor did I kill him. And you never knew your uncle. What is your feud with me?"

"I have none. But you have what I want."

"What in the hell is that?"

"My father's armor."

Tolin patted his dragon skin chest plate. "This?"

"Yes."

"Are you sentimental or a collector?"

"I'd feel better wearing it when I go to slay the Lord of Nodd."

"Oh," Tolin nodded. "Is that all?"

Grinning, he took off the right gauntlet and dropped it on the floor with a loud clang. Then he did the same with the left. He reached behind his back and touched his sides, undoing the clasps. The chest plate thudded onto the stones.

"Take it." He gestured. "The helmet is outside."

Her eyes narrowed. "This is a trick."

"I assure you, it is not. I don't need this armor anymore. In another few moments, I will have my own."

Roan glanced at the armor and then back up to him. She shifted her feet. Her expression was confused.

Tolin stripped off his undergarments. "I'd wish you good fortune in slaying Nosmada, but I don't give a shit about that either. I hope you both kill each other."

He stepped away from the armor and turned toward the dragon corpse. He glanced back when he heard the acolytes emerging from the archway. Roan knelt and gathered up the pieces as the acolytes entered the room. Martel glared at her, but Tolin shook his head and waved his hand. Roan stripped off her leathers and chain mail and donned the dragon skin armor. As she did, Anka burst into the room, followed by the thirteen women, all heavily pregnant.

Anka's eyes flared as he turned to Tolin. "Sir?"

Tolin shook his head. "Let her go."

"But you should see the slaughter outside! The guards ..."

"You will join them if you fight her." Tolin turned back to Roan as she pulled up the leggings. "It fits?"

"Close," she responded, struggling to get the chest plate in place.

"Gorias La Gaul sired no dwarves. Go on, then. My time is here."

Roan bolted past the assemblage and out the door.

"Now," Tolin said to them all. "Places, everyone!"

CHAPTER 11

KILLING FLOOR

Rogan glared through the bars of his cell and across the corridor. Javan waved at him.

"You're making it easy for me to hate you and myself right now," Rogan said.

"I am happy to see you, too, sire."

Rogan glanced at his cellmates, Ivor and Thaxter. The big man lay on the single bunk, breathing hard, and sweating badly, though it remained cool in the room. The old wizard knelt by Thaxter, muttering and chanting low, never taking his gaze from the prone man.

Javan said, "I knew you'd return for me."

"Yeah," Rogan snarled. "That is the idea, that it was a trap."

"I wonder why the trap hasn't sprung," Javan said gently, looking at Angeline and Kenoth in the cell next to Rogan's.

"If that wizard wants me, what would stop her getting at me now?" He looked at Ivor. "Even if his spells blocked her out, she would know we are imprisoned, right?"

Javan shrugged. "I would think, sire. It makes one wonder."

"Speaking of wonder," Kenoth said, "are we not going to talk about what we saw in the garden?"

"What did you see?" Javan asked.

"Wodan." Kenoth's voice was filled with awe. "He was imprisoned—crucified to a tree. But we saved him."

Javan's eyes widened. "Is this true, uncle?"

Rogan shrugged. His expression contorted.

"Tell him," Kenoth urged. "This is the god you worship. Why do you deny it? What are you afraid of?"

"Mind your tongue," Rogan snarled, "or I'll rip out your other eye."

"It was Wodan," Kenoth insisted. "Ask Thaxter."

"Thaxter's not saying much right now," Rogan replied.

Javan frowned. "What happened to him?"

Rogan peered down at the big man again. "That's the question, ain't it? I can't tell if he's dead or not, and I've some experience in determining that."

They all fell silent for a moment. Then, Angeline spoke.

"So, do we sit here and wait for our deaths? Is that the plan? We rescued Wodan, and he can't give his oracle the power to return the favor?"

"Quiet," Kenoth cautioned her.

Angeline persisted. "What good is that old man if he can't get us free of a few bars?"

Rogan observed Ivor, half entranced. "He seems kinda busy at the moment. I'll kick him in the ass in a minute. I don't care for this waiting around crap."

They fell silent again, and Rogan brooded. The man on the tree had looked like Wodan, certainly. But Wodan would have never allowed himself to be imprisoned like that. Wodan was not weak. He wouldn't have needed rescue. The barbarian's brow creased with worry and confusion.

His ruminations were interrupted by the sound of keys jingling. He looked up and noticed that Javan was grinning.

"Who the hell is this, nephew?"

A short woman glided between the cells, keys rattling in her right hand. Her hair bobbed about as she looked at Rogan and then Javan. She smiled, her lips red and her face freshly painted, and unlocked the door to Javan's cell. He stepped out, and she handed him the keys.

"You going to introduce us?" Rogan asked.

Javan opened Rogan's cell door. "That's Donnise."

"Friend of yours?" He stepped into the corridor.

"Not really," Javan confessed, looking at Ivor and Thaxter for a moment and then moving on to Kenoth and Angeline's cell.

"Why not?"

"Well, first of all, I have had my mind on someone else." Javan nodded at Angeline as he said this. The girl smiled in return and slipped from her cell. "And also," Javan continued, "you should know that Donnise is dead."

"What?" Rogan stared closer at their savior and realized that she wasn't breathing.

"She's a byproduct of some spell," Javan explained. "I don't understand all of it. There are too many doings in this city—too much subterfuge, too many plots—and I cannot keep track of it all. She was once one of the concubines here. Now ... she's this. Nice girl, though."

Angeline's nose wrinkled. "A zombie whore?"

Rogan grunted. "She freed us. I don't care what she is. Can she understand us?"

"Yes, sire."

"Unlock the cell with our weapons," Rogan told her.

Donnise stepped to the next cell, where the guards had tossed the weapons on a bunk and unlocked the door. She stepped to one side and curtseyed to Rogan.

Angeline retrieved her sword and handed Kenoth his weapons.

"They sure dropped these in a hurry," she said.

"Aye," Rogan agreed, glancing around suspiciously, and then retrieved his sword. "Something is wrong here—something bigger than us."

Javan stood at the open cell door. "No sign of my bow or quiver, I suppose?"

"We'll find you one." Rogan returned to his cell. "Ho! Thaxter.

Ivor. You fuckers coming along or are you going to stay here and take your turns with the zombie whore?"

"Rise," Ivor said to Thaxter, and then stood himself.

Thaxter sat up, eyes closed. He swung his legs off the bunk and turned his face toward the door. Then he opened his eyes.

Javan stepped back. "By the goddess!"

Rogan gaped. "What happened to his left eye? It's gone!"

Ivor moved out into the corridor as Thaxter stood. "I fear our friend Thaxter is no more. He who remains is more than I could have dreamed."

"Speak it plain," Rogan told him, glancing down the hall again. "The time for ballads and yarns is at an end."

Thaxter's voice thundered. "If not for ballads and yarns, some of us might never be immortal. Isn't that what you fear, my son?"

"I'm not your son." Rogan frowned.

"But you all are, all my children from the lands of ice and snow."

Angeline and Kenoth joined Javan behind Rogan.

"Is he possessed?" Angeline asked.

"That's Wodan's voice," Kenoth whispered.

"Bullshit," Rogan argued. "Thaxter isn't right in the head. That's all."

Ivor shook his head. "Search your mind, Rogan. Search your heart. You know who he is. My master was imprisoned there on the tree for quite some time. He heard our prayers and entreaties, but he could not answer them. It was only when I got close to this place that he had the strength to call to me. Now he walks the earth again, unencumbered by the reeds of Eden, free from the shackles of the grandson of the Creator. Here is the one who talks to us in our dreams, the one who inspires us to war, but cares little for our paths."

"No ..." Rogan's voice trembled. "It's a spell."

"Is it? He knows your feelings, your doubts on age and life, yet he doesn't judge you for them. He just is. He gave us life, and it is my hope he can give us a pathway out of this shithole and into life again."

Thaxter stepped forward, and all drew back ...

... even Rogan.

"I do not expect lauds or honors," the entity inside Thaxter said, "but I want to be free of these foul folk as much as you do."

"Wodan." Rogan coughed and cleared his throat. "You expect me to accept that you are my god?"

"I don't care if you do. I have known you since you were born, Rogan. I know you better than you know yourself. If you were to suddenly turn religious, I'd doubt your motivations."

"Why are you inside Thaxter?"

"My form was weakened ... my flesh dying. This was the only way I could live again."

"And my friend? Where is he?"

"In a place where his goblet never runs dry and there is always a woman to laugh with him."

"That sounds nice," Javan murmured.

"It is," Wodan agreed. "Now, let us be gone from this cell block. I sense a great ceremony nearby, one we shouldn't miss."

As Wodan walked out of the cell, Rogan turned to Javan.

"Yes, sire. The guards nip at the flasks and tell tales of two great happenings. One was that General Tolin La Gaul is rebuilding a dragon body out of flesh and bones. Today is the day it is complete, and he thinks he can make it arise again and put his soul into it."

"A dragon's spirit inhabits Tolin's body," Wodan agreed. "But I understand his desire for a new form."

Ivor's brow furrowed. "What we're talking about would require magick on a scale unheard of. What could he sacrifice to gain such power? It would have to be practically angelic."

"I've heard whispers," Javan said, "that there is some mass sacrifice to be readied, one they won't speak of."

Rogan shrugged. "I don't give a damn if they kill everyone in the city. We need to get out of here."

He started down the corridor, followed by Angeline and Kenoth, but Ivor, Javan, and Wodan stayed.

"But where shall you go?" Wodan asked. "Glorious as it would be, we cannot just fight our way out. There are thousands of troops and hundreds of guards."

Rogan stopped and turned. "Then what would you suggest?"

Wodan pointed with Thaxter's ax at the doorway on the opposite end of the corridor. "This is the way."

Rogan frowned. "That leads deeper into the complex."

"Truly so," Wodan agreed. "Probably to where the dragon lies."

"You want to go deeper into this mess?" Rogan looked to Ivor. "If you want to follow him, go ahead. I've got what I came for."

"I'm going with them, Uncle," Javan said.

"Why?"

"Because it is the right thing to do."

Rogan sighed, and then motioned to Wodan. "Well, if you truly are god incarnate, lead on. I reckon if I have to die in a fool scheme, it might as well be while fighting at your side."

Wodan smiled. "We shall be magnificent this day."

***

Nosmada emerged from his bathing pool and toweled off. He spied Zillian and Schlack waiting by the door. After he was dry, he walked toward them, naked.

"Thank you for letting me sleep," Zillian said. "Transferring a demon from one host to another is taxing business."

"I'm glad you are rested," Nosmada said softly. "My final jest is afoot. Shall we go to the place of sacrifice and be done with it all?"

Both stood to one side and let the towering man pass between them.

As they walked, Nosmada asked, "Are the spirits all around?"

"Quite a few," Zillian replied, favoring her long cane on the stone passageway. "The harem is gone and at the lair of the dragon."

Nosmada frowned. "No one cared to look after the harem?"

"No."

"Curious. You would think the spirits would have looked after them, at least."

"Demons, devils ..." Zillian spat. "Though I know them, they are but petty bastards. We mean little to them, even ones carrying their offspring inside. Still ... they are gathering."

"Is he here?"

"Who?"

Nosmada sighed. "Saying his name won't make him appear. Bismillah."

"Not as such, but I can feel him." Zillian shuddered. "He watches with a thousand eyes."

They walked down into the depths of the castle, through many bolted doors where no guards were allowed. Upon reaching the place of sacrifice, Schlack unbarred the final door and faced Nosmada, who gripped him by the shoulders.

"Seal it once I enter, just as we rehearsed."

Schlack nodded with vigor. "Fare you well, my lord. It has been an honor."

"No, old friend. The honor was mine." Nosmada turned to Zillian. "Ascend and release when it is time."

Without a word, she slowly started up a series of winding steps.

Nosmada entered the massive funnel-shaped chamber, and Schlack closed the door behind him. The bolt clanged in the darkness. Nosmada gazed up into the shadows and heard the gentle chittering of the thousands of leeches on the walls. They hung there, bloated, full of blood, waiting.

Then came a new sound—a loud grating noise. Stone sliding across stone. The roof began to move. The leeches fell silent. In a few minutes, the opening at the top of the funnel cleared and sunlight poured down. Nosmada saw wispy clouds overhead.

"I can see straight unto heaven."

Trembling, he knelt in a large circular depression in the center of the chamber. The sloping walls formed a bowl, and the stone floor was cold against his bare flesh.

"Soon, I will be forgiven. With this sacrifice, I will gain his favor."

When he heard the lock clang again behind him, Nosmada turned, confused and aghast. The door flew open, and someone tossed an object into the chamber. It soared through the air, landed in the bowl, and rolled to a stop beneath him. Nosmada gaped.

Schlack's decapitated head did the same, staring up at him, and blinking twice.

Then a woman barged into the room. Surprisingly, she wore Gorias La Gaul's dragon skin armor. The leeches grew agitated at the commotion.

"What are you about?" Nosmada rose to his feet. "Why are you here?"

"I am Roan La Gaul!"

Nosmada waved impatiently. "I know who you are. What are you doing here at such a time?"

She raised her twin swords. "I'm here for your life, curse or no curse. I'm not afraid."

"You should be." He kicked Schlack's head out of the way. "And your timing is bad."

Her eyes narrowed. She looked up at the walls, beholding the thousands of leeches. "What say you?"

"I've spent my entire life getting ready for this moment." Nosmada nodded at the head of Schlack. "He was a good man."

"Not good enough, obviously."

"There was no reason for him to die," Nosmada whispered. "He deserved better."

"We all have to die, be it in battle, in a bed, or murdered."

"Speak to me not of murder." Nosmada's voice rose in anger. "I invented murder."

"Then I hope to improve upon it." She leered at him through the crossed blades.

"I have worked toward this for centuries. I won't have it spoiled by a big girl with daddy trauma."

She smiled. "There is no trauma."

Nosmada nodded. "Your father taught you not to talk too much. I can tell because you want to. You want to tell me how killing me will validate you, make you a warrior as good or as feared as Gorias La Gaul."

"Did it hurt when you got that mark on your forehead?" Roan asked. "I wonder if you'll scream louder when I carve the rest of you?"

Nosmada clapped his hands in a mocking gesture. "Your father knew when to fish or cut bait."

"Rogan said the same thing about him. And my father would have beaten you."

Nosmada slowly walked toward the edge of the bowl. "Dressed in that armor, carrying his swords, his training ringing in your ears, you feel good enough to best me?"

"Yes," she admitted, her gaze darting again to the leeches on the walls.

"I stand at the greatest moment in my life, and you piss on my leg." He sighed, hands to his hips. He then dropped his arms to his sides. "Go on, then. Go ahead. I am unarmed and unarmored. Kill me if you can."

Roan blinked, hesitating.

"Come along now," Nosmada held out his arms as if to embrace her. "You couldn't ask for an easier target. Kill me and claim the greatest mantle of all. Kill the killer."

Roan took a single step.

Nosmada stood still, arms spread out.

She pounced, jumping downward, the points of both blades seeking his heart at alternate angles.

Nosmada's arms came together with blinding speed, as he slapped the flats of the blades together and pressed them tight, an inch from the skin over his chest. Then he swiped away the swords, pulling them from her hands and throwing the weapons to the floor.

The leeches squealed and hissed.

The two combatants' eyes met for barely a moment. Then Roan pounced again. Her heavy gauntlets gripped Nosmada by the shoulders and her boots stomped atop his bare feet. Instead of crying out in surprise or pain, he merely grinned. She slammed her forehead into his nose. Blood erupted from his nostrils, and Roan howled, stooping lower and trying to pull him off his feet. Instead, Nosmada clutched her armored forearms and reversed the action, flinging her over his head and backward to the floor. She landed just short of the wall of leeches, flat on her back. She immediately flipped onto all fours. For a second, she eyed her fallen weapons, but Nosmada kicked them further away. Shouting, Roan sprang forward. Before she could tackle him, two clubbing blows from Nosmada's fists dropped her back to all fours again. Grunting, Roan grabbed his knees as he struck her again.

"I tire of you, little girl."

Her body shook, and she sank lower.

Fists high, he paused. "Finished already? Good. I've tarried with you long en—"

Nosmada screamed in agony as Roan turned her armlet sideways and raked the dragon's dewclaw across his bare thigh.

"Finished? I'm just getting started, old man."

Nosmada screamed again as Roan hamstrung him.

TOLIN STOOD BETWEEN THE LEGS OF THE GREAT DRAGON AND nodded to Martel. The girl touched a plate in the center of the dragon's underside and lifted it, revealing red and gray innards. Amidst the gore was the indented shape of a large humanoid form.

"You do great work." Tolin smiled at Martel.

She smiled back. "The final piece of the puzzle, General, is of course you. Once we commence the sacrifice and the spell unravels, you will enter unto your new form just as planned."

"What would I do without you?"

Martel's smile creased a little. "Best not to think on that, General."

He stepped back and looked at the harem in their places around the chamber. "This is a great day for you, as well, Martel. You will be the survivor. All of your servants will follow and laud you, and your power will increase."

"Let us carry on, then. The time is nigh."

At the door of the chamber stood Anka. He called out, "Dar is approaching!"

Tolin looked at Martel. "Ready for your first test?"

Jaw firm, Martel clenched her fists, which started to glow an emerald hue. She stood behind Tolin as he moved toward the door.

Anka stepped aside as Yitzak Dar filled the opening.

"You weren't leaving without saying goodbye, were you Tolin?" Her voice was light and full of humor, but her tone and expression changed as she looked at the assemblage. "What is going on here? I didn't authorize this? And Martel? What are you—?"

Martel thrust both fists forward. Green energy erupted from them, forming the shape of an emerald dog. Eyes wide, Dar scrambled backward, but Anka blocked her way. The conjured cur fell on her, knocking Dar to the ground. Her frightened cries became muffled as the creature's jaws clamped around her throat.

Anka moved to one side as blood sprayed in an arc across the doorway.

The acolytes watched, their expressions impassive.

"See?" Tolin gestured. "Already, they serve a new master."

Dar's arms and legs flailed. She gurgled once, and then the dog tore her throat out. It stood over her, holding her flesh in its jaws, and then evaporated. Dar convulsed and then lay still, bleeding out onto the floor.

"Why a dog?" Tolin asked.

Martel's hands ceased to glow. She lowered her arms. "Charla."

"Nosmada's dog? But you had no connection to it ... or to him."

"I didn't need to." The girl shrugged. "I like dogs, and what Dar did ... this seemed apt."

Tolin threw back his head and laughed. "You will go far, Martel."

She curtsied. "Thank you. And you will fly far."

"Indeed. Let's get on with it."

Nodding once, Martel turned back to the dragon and the assemblage. She ordered her acolytes to give the harem girls their drinks.

In turn, all thirteen sipped from the small cups offered by the acolytes. They then lay down on the stone slabs at each point in the dragon's lair. Each stone bench was set an equal distance from its neighbor. The harem girls, their bellies huge with child, were stripped of their gowns by the acolytes. None resisted.

"Anka," Tolin called. "Have the overhead planks been removed?"

Anka nodded.

"Then at last," Tolin said, voice thick with emotion, "let it begin."

Martel raised her arms over her head. "The thirteen wives of the fallen have partaken of the wine prepared. The journey to goddess-hood is nearly complete."

Tolin licked his lips. "Birth the Nephilim."

Martel threw open her gown. Her right hand went to a sheath hanging on a leather belt about her waist. Following her lead, the other acolytes did the same, gripping the hilts of their daggers.

"Now," Martel proclaimed. "Birth."

The thirteen knives rose and descended, slicing into the bellies of the pregnant harem. Not all cuts and slices were perfect, and not each victim slept perfectly. While Martel's girl only opened her eyes wide, the one next to her flailed her arms, grabbing the shoulders of the acolyte who wrenched the dagger about her stomach. After they made their final cuts, each acolyte reached in and scooped with their left hand, pulling out the monstrous child within. Every newborn had six fingers and six toes. Some sported nubs of horns, wings, or a tiny tail. They moved their blood-slicked limbs like swimmers, flexing in the air. A few squawked and croaked.

The acolytes moved quickly, holding each struggling babe aloft. They placed the thrashing babies into the small troughs beside the slabs and cut the umbilical cords. Instead of blood, a red glow seeped from the severed cords. The glowing substance flowed down the troughs in lines and joined together like a rope. All connected, the hue increased and spread out over the dragon.

Tolin inhaled deeply.

The dragon's nostrils flared.

UP JUMPED THE DEVIL

Rogan and Wodan cut a bloody swathe as they stormed through the complex. The two moved side-by-side, slashing and hitting and pulverizing anyone who got in their way. Blood, innards, and severed appendages flew through the air and splattered across the walls. Javan, Angeline, Kenoth, and Ivor followed along behind, gingerly avoiding the gore on the floors. They trailed the two berserkers, stepping over the butchered guards, soldiers, and others who had fallen under the savage duo's assault. The four didn't speak. It would have been pointless, given the volume of Rogan and Wodan's battle cries.

Javan knelt briefly, nimbly snatching a bow from the grasp of a severed arm. After a few more corridors, he found a quiver full of arrows.

Finally, they paused. Rogan's broad chest heaved from exertion, but Wodan stood serenely. Both men were drenched in the blood of others.

"Where in Hades are we going?" Rogan panted.

Javan quipped, "I hope to a place with a better escape plan."

"Very soon, my child," Wodan said.

"Knock that shit off," Rogan growled. "I know who Javan's parents were ... and they weren't you."

They began to move again. The god led them down a twisting series of unoccupied corridors. The silence was unsettling.

"You still cannot accept me for who I am, Rogan?"

"Not really," Rogan responded. "It's all too screwy for me to follow. You look and sound like my friend, but you fight like no man I've ever seen before ... except for maybe myself."

Wodan laughed at this. The sound echoed through the empty hall.

They ascended a series of steps and came to an open room lit only by the sunlight creeping through the cracks of the shuttered windows. Chains hung from the walls and ceiling.

Kenoth scrambled about. "What is this? An interrogation room?"

Rogan nodded.

Wodan led them through another door at the far end of the room. The light increased as they hurried through a short hall and into an open courtyard.

Ivor nudged Rogan. "There, see? This small alcove runs parallel to that place with the tented roof."

"And why are we going there again?" Rogan asked. "This is a bullshit idea."

"Because," a voice said from above them, "that is where destiny lies."

"Javan," Rogan murmured.

"I'm on it, sire." The youth raised his bow, arrow already notched.

The slight man, who wore white trousers and a sleeveless white tunic, was perched between two stone gargoyles. His black hair, slicked back with oil, gleamed in the sun, as did his perfectly trimmed mustache. He gave them a friendly wave.

"Who the hell are you?" Rogan shouted.

"You can tell your boy to fire upon me if you wish, but it will be a waste of an arrow."

"He's not my boy," Rogan replied. "He's my nephew, and a man. What is it you want?"

"To see."

"See Javan's arrow then, as it spears your eye."

Ivor reached out and stayed Javan's hand. "He's not tangible."

"A trick of the wizards?" Rogan wondered.

Ivor shook his head. "No, a demon."

The smile spread under the mustache of the figure. His teeth shone like polished ivory.

"I know you," Wodan said.

"You should, brother." The smile faded.

"I am not your brother ... Bismillah."

Ivor jumped as if startled.

"Well, fuck me running," Rogan muttered.

Javan whispered, "Shall I shoot him, sire?"

"I'll fuckin' shoot you in a second," Rogan said. "Stand down. Ivor is right. Your arrows won't do anything against this one.

"You're Rogan, the barbarian king?" Bismillah asked. "I'm an admirer."

"Ignore him," Ivor said. "He speaks lies."

Bismillah feigned offense. "Me? I'm not the liar here. What did he tell you? That he is your god? The mighty Wodan, imprisoned by the master of Nodd? Suffering and needing to be set free? What kind of a god is that?"

"I am Wodan."

"What's truly in a name?" Bismillah cooed. "Well, maybe a great deal, but I digress. You can call yourself whatever you wish, dream whatever you want of yourself, but you are still one of us."

Wodan pointed Thaxter's ax at the demon. "Liar. You are nothing more than one of the fallen hosts, deluded, thinking your-self a god and appearing as such to foolish men. You steal the flesh of a human and act like a god!"

"As I said, you are one of us. You accuse me of this while you yourself are wearing stolen flesh."

Wodan turned to Rogan, Ivor, and the others. All but Rogan took a step back from him.

"It's not true," he pleaded. "I come from the north, born on the icy winds ..."

"Well, someone did," Bismillah explained. "But it wasn't you. You are a shadow of someone, Wodan, but mistaken as to who you are. You have lived this lie for so long, you've come to believe it yourself. Even the lord of this city believed your lie. And look at how you suffered for it."

"But, I dreamed," Wodan argued. "My power ... I reanimated the dead girls, sent them out. I called to my children in their dreams. I called to my oracle."

"And good show, too," Bismillah agreed. "And yet, this is what you are, another of us devils."

Ivor looked up at the demon. "Why do you tell us this?"

"Because," Bismillah's smile returned. "I'm a real bastard."

"Perhaps you test our faith," Ivor said.

The demon shrugged. "I don't care about your faith. But I'd hate to see you walking about so confused. And it's time for me to collect this pretender. Join us, brother. Quit playing games and join us as we go to see what the grandson of God has in store. Forget these little dolls. Yes, Rogan may be fun to watch, but he is doomed like all the rest. The army of Nosmada is now on full alert. He has thousands of warriors. They are but a handful of barbarians."

Wodan's shoulders slumped. He looked as if he might weep.

"Thaxter—Wodan ..." Rogan clapped his shoulder. "Whatever you want to call yourself. Do you really want to go with that pretty prick for any reason?"

"No. No, I don't. I enjoyed fighting at your side. I felt alive when we were killing."

"Then let's go kill some more. Let's kill them all. You had something in mind before we saw him. What was it?"

He looked at the end of the open hall leading toward the building with the tented roof. "Follow me."

"I will," Rogan replied, "but I'm calling you Thaxter."

"I would like that."

As the others fell in behind the big man, Ivor hesitated.

Thaxter smiled at him. "One last time, my good and faithful servant?"

Ivor sighed. "Might as well. If I'm going to die in this city, I'd rather not do it alone."

Bismillah giggled and waved as they fled. "See you in eternity."

Rogan paused and cast a glance over his shoulder. "Tell me, demon. When I get to hell, will you be there?"

"Most certainly," Bismillah promised.

"Good," Rogan said. "I'll kill you then. See you in eternity."

They headed out of the courtyard and into another building. As they made their way down a long hall, they encountered several slain guards, beheaded, stabbed, dismembered, or disemboweled.

"Are we retracing our steps?" Kenoth asked, confused.

"No," Rogan replied. "Someone else killed this lot."

Footsteps pounded down the corridor from somewhere ahead.

"Soldiers," Ivor whispered.

"Javan," Rogan growled as they all hugged the walls.

The young archer took a knee and, as the three soldiers rounded the corner down the hall, fired four times. The group stepped over the still jittering bodies and continued on their way.

"Here," Thaxter shouted. He pulled open a broad door, moved back to avoid the swipe of a short sword, and drove the pommel of his ax forward—and then released it, spearing the handle into the heart of a muscled black trooper.

As they entered the chamber, Ivor kicked another body: an androgynous figure whose throat had been torn out.

"Yitzak Dar," Javan informed them. "This was the one who set the hellhounds upon us."

Rogan stepped over the impaled soldier and the mauled wizard and gaped. Thirteen butchered women lay flayed open at thirteen stations. Robed supplicants stood next to the bodies. Beyond them towered an obscene homunculus of dragon bones and patch-work flesh. Beneath the beast stood Tolin La Gaul, naked and glistening, and a young woman. Rogan's silver hair stood up on his arms and neck. The power crackling through the room was immense.

"Do you feel that?" he asked Javan.

"I do, uncle. It feels like lightning striking over and over."

Angeline agreed, drawing back. "Like the air is afire."

"Well, it should feel that way." Rogan pointed. "That's a dragon."

The girl next to Tolin pointed at them and screeched.

"The King of the Bastards," Tolin shouted. "You're too late."

"For what?"

Before Tolin could answer, Thaxter marched across the chamber. Tolin watched him, his expression registering surprise. Before the general could react, Thaxter drew his right hand back and slapped him across the face. Tolin tumbled to the floor.

Rogan laughed while Javan, Angeline, and Kenoth gaped in confusion and astonishment.

"Hello, father," the girl called out, suddenly smiling.

"Martel," Ivor said. "Is daddy's girl a good girl?"

"Oh, I've been very bad." She cackled as Tolin got to his feet, shaking. "Very bad indeed."

Thaxter looked back at Ivor and undid the clasp of his cover. He then shed his belt and armor and took down his trousers.

"What is going on?" Tolin balled his fists. "You wish to fight me naked?"

"Not particularly."

"Then what is this?" Tolin demanded.

"It's the end." Thaxter removed his boots and clambered up onto the torso of the dragon, climbing toward the open plate at its belly.

Nosmada screamed again as Roan ripped the dragon's dewclaw out of his thigh. She swept her left leg, trying to knock him off balance, but he gripped a handful of her hair and steadied himself. As he took a breath, she balled up her gauntlet-clad fist and punched him in the testicles. His grip faltered and she rolled away, then tumbled in a somersault over to where the swords lay.

Doubled over, Nosmada roared. Above them, the leeches chittered in response.

Roan raised her swords just as Nosmada attacked anew. She struck, blades flashing, but as before he batted the flats of the weapons away with such force that Roan dropped them.

Snarling, he grabbed the sides of her head. "I'm going to squeeze your brains through your ears until your head pops like an overripe melon."

Roan grimaced. "Speaking of overripe fruit ..."

She clutched Nosmada's manhood with both hands, pulled him toward the wall, and smashed his head against it. Nosmada let go and lurched backward. The mark on his forehead flushed with blood and he struggled to stand up, favoring his wounded leg.

Roan picked up her swords and set her boots. Nosmada wobbled toward the door, breathing heavily. She joined the blades at the handles and spun the weapon fast. Nosmada tried to ward her off and shrieked as the fan of blades sliced the fingertips off his left hand.

Emboldened, Roan moved forward.

Nosmada jabbed his uninjured hand forward into the spinning handles. The blades caved at the pommels, creating an opening and stopping Roan's assault. He kicked at her. Roan threw a punch and missed. Nosmada countered with one of his own, landing on her jaw. He seized her mane again and smashed his knee into her crotch. The dragon codpiece fell away, and he kneed her again. Groaning, Roan collapsed to her knees. A follow-up blow to her head dropped her flat.

"Damned girl." Nosmada glanced again at Schlack's decapitated head. "How can I close myself in ...?"

"I have done it," Zillian's voice echoed from far above.

Grinning, Nosmada wiped sweat from his brow with the back of his hand. Then he spat on Roan.

"Cut your hair. Any foe can get an edge on you with that mane flopping around."

He limped back to the center of the room. "Zillian! Do it!"

A sound like thunder rolled through the chamber.

Nosmada turned his face to the sky. "Now, Lord. Tell me if this sacrifice is worthy!"

Above him came a loud creak, like the turning of a rusty hinge. Then Zillian dropped something ... something afire, like a small star. The object landed in front of Nosmada and erupted into a giant geyser of red flame. In response, the leeches released all the blood from their bodies. A flood of crimson spewed from their mouths and rectums, washing over Nosmada, baptizing him. As it pooled around him, Nosmada struggled to his feet and raised both arms. The tide rose to his knees, stinging his wounded leg.

"Not for my glory, but for yours!"

The blood tide rose over his waist and up to his belly. The leeches hung limp on the walls, silent and still. Nosmada sucked in air as the blood rose to his chest.

A loud tone rang through the chamber, like a gong under water. The air began to thrum as the torrent reached his neck. Beneath the surface, the flaming object still burned. Now, it began to rise. The blood bubbled and boiled. Another deafening tone rang out and the blood flushed past his ears. Nosmada closed his eyes and then ...

... the blood was gone. He stood alone in a dry chamber. The leeches hung, as desiccated as mummies found in old tombs.

"Where are you," he rasped. Then he called out stronger, "Where are you?"

He took a breath and waited for a voice from above, but the only response was silence.

"Are you there, Lord?" He took a deep breath. "Zillian?"

Again, he heard nothing.

Falling to his knees, hands to his scarred forehead, Nosmada wept.

"Stop," Tolin roared, hurriedly trying to climb the crotch of the dragon as the big man with the ax squeezed his form inside. "That is for me! That is mine!"

Martel raised her arms and a great wind rushed through the chamber. It staggered Rogan and the other interlopers, but it also caused Tolin to slip back down to the floor. The man's ax clanged on the floor, and the open plate on the dragon's belly slammed shut. As Martel and the acolytes began to chant, the dragon took on a reddish hue.

"Cease this at once!" Tolin's voice broke with rage. Again, he tried to scale the dragon, and again, Martel knocked him backward with a flick of her wrist. "You betray me? You filthy bitch!"

Powerful hands seized Tolin's bare arms from behind and threw him to the floor.

"Is that any way to talk to a young lady?"

Tolin rolled over and stared up at the old man Martel had called father. Next to him stood Rogan. Before Tolin could move, the barbarian pressed the point of his long sword over Tolin's heart. Ignoring the weapon, Tolin focused on Ivor.

"You ..." Tolin spat.

The old man bowed. "Ivor, until recently the Oracle of Wodan."

"If you're done exchanging pleasantries," Rogan grunted, "I'm going to kill him. We need to get away."

Ivor studied Tolin. "I don't think he can do much now."

"It's not Tolin I'm worried about." Rogan's gaze rose to the dragon. "Javan, Kenoth, Angeline, fall back!"

Tolin slapped Rogan's sword aside and sprang to his feet, once again leaping onto the dragon and scurrying up its hindquarters. He gripped the sealed plate and pulled hard, but to no avail. Straining, he tried again and succeeded in opening it a crack. Peering inside, he saw the big man nestled among the innards, congealing into the bands of muscle and membranes.

Tolin released the plate and it snapped shut. The red corona about the dragon surged and singed his palms. He quickly slid back down to the floor, intending to take his fury out on the barbarian, but Rogan was already halfway across the room, helping the old man retreat.

The thirteen stations burst into flame, spewing a white light. Like the thrum of a thousand bowstrings, a deafening chord struck. Tolin clasped his hands over his ears and saw the invaders do the same. The loud pulse stopped and then struck again, over and over—the beat of a colossal heart.

Tolin shrieked with rage.

The dragon moved, twitching its huge claws.

"The eyes are opening," Martel exclaimed. She turned and set about undoing a long rope lashed to a metal outcropping. As she ran to a second rope, the dragon's feet uncurled and flexed.

Tolin scrambled backward, and the beast's tail flicked. Tears streamed down Tolin's cheeks as the giant shuddered. He shook his head, over and over, and glanced again at the intruders. They were gathered in the open doorway, staring in astonishment ... and fear. All except for Rogan. Tolin's eyes narrowed.

Martel untied the final rope, and a canvas roof peeled back. Sunshine poured into the chamber.

The dragon's head rose slowly, and the eyes—striped like a serpent's—blinked, scanning first the light overhead and then those huddled by the door. It then turned its attention on the acolytes. The dragon shifted its weight into a crouching position. Its head swayed side to side atop the long neck, and its wings unfurled.

"By the goddess," Javan uttered.

"No goddess there," Ivor promised. Smiling, the old man fell to his knees and raised his arms in praise. "WODAN!"

The dragon's mouth opened, displaying rows of spiked teeth. It drew in a rush of air. For a moment, all was still, but then it issued a concussive roar that knocked them all off their feet.

The dragon stood on its hind legs and flapped its wings, testing them. Slowly, it rose into the air. The beast gazed down at them, then drew up higher. The neck swung about as if noting the city before the wings flapped strong. It hovered in the sky above the city before looking north and flying away.

"You fucking bitch!" Tolin grabbed the pommel of the thief's ax. "You took it all away!"

Tolin charged, crashing into the clustered acolytes, who still stared skyward. He swung, cleaving and hacking. The weapon split one between the shoulder blades. Another was halved down to their kidneys. Others were beheaded or disemboweled. Drenched in blood, he stomped through the gore, focused on Martel.

Smiling, the girl grabbed one of the ropes that had tethered the roof covers. She leaped over the side before Tolin could reach her.

Ranting unintelligibly, Tolin scrambled back down the steps. By the time he had reached the bottom, Martel was already hiding behind Ivor and the others. Rogan stood before them all, sword at the ready, glaring.

"I could have lived forever," Tolin yelled.

"Why should you be so different," Rogan challenged. "Why are you so special?"

The two charged at each other, weapons raised. Tolin reared back and swung the great ax. Rogan parried with his long sword, deflecting the blow. He quickly followed by kicking Tolin in the balls, causing him to backpedal and lower the ax.

"Tell me, General," Rogan panted. "Why should any man or woman shed a tear for you? What makes you so special? Because you house the soul of a dragon in that body? You were the victim of a wizard's plot ages ago that screwed La Gaul's son out of his soul?"

"You ... don't understand ..." Tolin gasped, holding his testicles. "I'm the last dragon on this world—on any world. Once I am gone, there is no more of my kind."

"I used to think about that too," Rogan told him. "Being the last of my kind. I fathered children to replace me, and some of them were disappointing, so I still lamented."

Tolin winced. "Burn in hell."

Rogan stepped forward, and Tolin receded a step.

"I used to care only about myself," Rogan continued. "Such was the arrogance of the life I lived. How would I be remembered? Indeed, would any remember me at all? Would my bloodline carry on or only be known through bastards? Would statues be built in my memory, or would I only be a song in a tavern or a joke badly told?"

Tolin's reply was a choked sob.

Smiling, Rogan raised his sword. "But I won't be remembered as the one crying and clutching my balls at the moment of my death."

Trembling, Tolin fell to his knees, closed his eyes, and let the ax slip from his hands.

"No," Rogan said. "I'll be remembered for being the one who slew the last dragon."

Tolin lowered his head and shuddered.

"Speak your name!" Rogan plunged the sword downward, skewering Tolin's breastbone and his guts, cracking his pelvis, until the blade emerged from his groin.

"Stregoicavar ..." Tolin choked

Rogan twisted the blade but it didn't move. He put his boot on Tolin's thigh and tore the blade free.

Javan crept up behind him. "Stregoicavar?"

Rogan nodded. "I've heard that name before."

"As have I," Ivor said. "It's a dragon name—an old one. A water dragon, I think."

Rogan stared down at the corpse. "Not anymore."

CHAPTER 13

CROSSROADS

Taking Martel with them, the group fled the lair of the dragon and made their way through the city streets, out into the open area where the caravan had encamped. Curiously, they encountered no soldiers or guardsmen but had to struggle through a horde of civilians. Nodd was in chaos, and panic ruled over all. When they reached the carts and horses of the faux caravan, Hyden and Seth rushed toward them. Seth offered up a skin of water.

"What news?" Rogan asked. He drank deep and then passed the skin to Javan.

"Do you not have eyes and ears?" Hyden gestured. "The city is gripped by fear. There are spirits in the sky!"

"Bah," he waved the blade, dismissing her. "You mean the dragon ..."

"No. I mean the demons from the pit. Nosmada has performed his abominable blood sacrifice to appease his God. That is what the demons are in a frenzy over."

"I don't care," Rogan said. "Where is Roan?"

The old woman and the lizard man exchanged a glance.

Rogan grabbed them both by the arm. "Answer me."

Hyden bowed her head. "She went to slay Nosmada."

"Damn it," Rogan cursed. "What was she thinking?"

Hyden shrugged. "With Nosmada's head, perhaps we could get free of this place. I fear though that if he performed his ritual and set the devils alight, then she has failed."

Seth hissed.

"What's he saying?" Rogan asked.

"The army has fallen out in between the curtain walls," Kenoth translated. "We are ringed in and surrounded by the military, and the guards are in full alert."

"Beautiful," said Rogan. "That explains why we didn't see any of them on our way here. I wonder if Nosmada's head could buy us a ticket past all that?"

"Sire," Javan said gently. "It won't take them long to figure this out. The chaos of the city, the dragon, and whatever is going on with their lord, they will see our part in it soon."

"So much for blending in and escaping." Angeline sighed.

Rogan wheeled on Ivor and Martel. "Well, do you magick fuckers have any ideas?"

The two didn't respond. Indeed, they didn't seem to have heard him at all. Glowering, Rogan grabbed Ivor's shoulders and shook him.

"This isn't the time to go all quiet and maudlin on me, you old prick. If that really was Wodan and not a pretender like the demon said he was, then he flew away. He never gave two fucks about us. And why should he? That was always our lore."

Ivor's eyes still scanned the skies.

Rogan's tone grew harsher still. "When we get free of this place, you're going to explain to me what your daughter was up to. And then we can fucking discuss theology and religion through the night if you want. Javan will like that. But first, we have to actually escape."

Ivor finally met his eye. "Arrogant though he is, Nosmada would have an escape hatch, a murder hole, a tunnel leading out of the city. We gather our forces and go to his abode. If we can't find it, it will be as good a place as any to die."

"If I can slay Nosmada," Rogan said, "maybe that will buy us freedom."

"That's a slim chance," Ivor replied. "Roan already tried and failed."

"Maybe we can all give it a try," Rogan replied. "As Javan is fond of pointing out, I ain't as young as I used to be. Maybe the rest of you can each get a piece of glory."

Ivor shook his head. "Rogan, you know the tales. Nosmada cannot die. The curse ..."

"Is nothing more than a story," Rogan interrupted. "That's all it is. A tale they tell. Same as the tales they tell about me. Same as the ones they told about Gorias La Gaul. Let's go together and give them all a new tale to tell."

The group exchanged glances.

Javan shrugged. "I'd be happy with telling the tale in the next town."

There was a commotion to their flank, and Roan's forces parted as a white horse moved through their midst. The animal stopped and snorted at Rogan.

"It is Traveler," Hyden said. "Roan's mount."

Rogan frowned. "I know who the fuck Traveler is. How did you get him back?"

"He came to us this morning." She reached out to take the dangling reins. Her diminutive stature made Hyden appear child-like as she walked under the giant horse's head and offered the reins to Rogan. "He might even let you ride him."

Rogan took the reins and looked the horse over. "He came to you all saddled up and ready?"

Hyden shrugged and smiled.

"So go the legends," Rogan muttered. "I never rode a magical horse before."

"I have," Javan said. "Give it a go, sire."

"If we get out of here, lad, you are walking home."

Rogan grabbed the saddle and climbed up onto the huge animal. Traveler turned and danced, facing Nosmada's citadel.

Rogan gave the horse a gentle prod, and they set off, with Roan's group following.

A half dozen guards soon crossed their path but were quick to flee down an alley when they saw the force.

"We just might have a chance after all," Angeline said.

Traveler's hooves clomped on the cobblestones as Rogan led them forward. The chaos continued to spread through the streets. Smoke rose from varied buildings.

"This is more of a general panic than a riot," Javan observed, jogging alongside the horse.

"Reading my mind?" Rogan wondered.

"For years now, sire."

Rogan gazed down at him. "Now what am I thinking?"

"Either wondering about the nature of these fires or the three-breasted whores of Irem."

"Not even close."

"The smoke seems minimal," Javan said, "so I don't think they are burning the place down."

Ivor's nostrils flared, but he kept scanning the skies.

"They smell almost sweet," Martel said, "like roasting."

Reaching the citadel, they entered the courtyard. Rogan climbed down from Traveler, drew his sword, and glanced around warily. "I expected resistance. Even with the trap waiting for us between the rings, you would expect guards here in this place."

Javan held his notched bow at the ready. "Agreed."

Angeline studied the shadows. "Maybe they are abandoning their master at his moment of glory?"

Two guards emerged from behind a pillar. One shoved Kenoth and the other went after Angeline, smashing a baton into the left side of her head. Kenoth staggered but swung his sword, slashing his attacker's thigh. The guard cried out, his leg hindered. With two quick strokes, Kenoth plunged his sword into the man's chest and kidneys.

The second guard faltered, realizing he was outnumbered.

"You've slain her!" Kenoth shouted, pointing at Angeline. He lunged, but before he could strike, an arrow buried itself in the guard's eye. The man toppled over, driving the shaft further into his skull. Kenoth turned to see Javan cast aside his bow, and they both rushed to Angeline's side.

"She's okay," Javan said, gently cradling her head. "Just stunned, thank the goddess."

"One of you will have to carry her." Rogan turned his attention back to the courtyard.

"Let us go up to the tower and see what transpires. I wonder if there are any more guards or just these two?"

"No," said Ivor quietly as he pointed at the funnel-shaped object protruding from the earth near the rear of the citadel. "Perhaps they left at the sight of the dragon, but ..."

Rogan gripped Ivor's shoulder. "What is it?"

"See that figure there, near the spout?"

They all strained to look.

"It's an old wizard woman," Ivor said. "One I haven't seen in centuries."

"Zillian," Martel confirmed. "She's the mage of Nosmada."

"I have heard of her," Hyden murmured.

"What is she doing?" Rogan asked.

Martel squinted. "It looks like she's weeping."

Rogan studied the group and surmised their number. Then he turned to Kenoth. "Ask the snake man if this is everybody?"

Kenoth translated the question. Seth nodded at Rogan and then hissed.

"He says this is everyone, except for a lone rider that Roan sent back to advise the rest of our forces we left in the village with your company of mercenaries."

"Okay. I've taken fortresses with less than this. Pull up the bridge over the moat. Secure the gates and walls here. Hell, they left the doors open. If we get attacked, it'll at least take them a while to get in."

As Roan's forces scurried off to enact his commands, Rogan patted Traveler's flank. Javan approached.

"How's Angeline?"

"Conscious. She will be fine."

"Good. She's handy in a fight. We can use her."

"Sire?"

"Yeah?"

"Now what?"

"Aren't you my advisor, Javan? What would you suggest?"

"Well ..." He hesitated. "Perhaps we ought to go up into the tower and see what is happening."

Ivor gestured toward the funnel. "We should also see what transpired there."

Rogan looked at both structures and then turned back to Ivor and Javan. "The two of you check the tower. I'll take the funnel. Have the others finish securing this place like I said."

"I'm too old for this," Ivor sighed.

Rogan gripped his sword. "I never wanted to get old. And yet here I am."

WHEN NOSMADA GAINED CONSCIOUSNESS, HIS EYELIDS WERE stuck fast with blood. He finally pried them open and blinked. Sunlight streamed down through the top of the funnel, alighting on the dead, fibrous leeches. When he moved again, the congealed blood covering him split apart. He emerged from the crimson husk, but when he looked down at his body, he had not transformed. His right hand went to his forehead, and a quick exploration confirmed that the mark—and the curse—remained.

As he attempted to stand, pain shot through his thigh. "My leg didn't even heal. What a grand joke. And what happened to Roan? If she drowned, then where is her body?"

Behind him, the door banged open.

"I rescued her because it amused me to do so," a soft female voice cooed. "She's just outside, waking up now."

Nosmada spun about, slipping in the gore. Fallon stood in the doorway.

"So, you got free," he said. "Enjoying your new body?"

The demon inside the girl ignored the question. "Was this grand gesture of blood all for your own glory?"

"I did it to offer a great sacrifice, one that He would accept."

"Really?" Fallon's voice rang cold. "Did you really think overstating your brother's simple sacrifice would appease God? You really thought this great scheme would be met with approval? That you would be forgiven?"

"Go away. I gave you that human form. Go out and enjoy it."

Fallon persisted. "What did you expect? For the Creator to change his mind, to whimper and say that you were right all along?"

"Shut up."

"It was never about blood, Cain. It was about respect. Honor. Love."

"I told you to go away. And don't call me by that name again. I rid myself of that name long ago. My name is Nosmada!"

"You didn't do this for the Creator. You did it for you."

"I said leave me."

"The first time you made a blood sacrifice? You didn't do it for Him. You did it for yourself, to show off the works of your hands. Pride. It was always about your pride. And so was this."

"Go away."

Fallon persisted. "All of those lives, all of those souls, all of that blood gathered here to do this. You loved your own son enough to keep his carcass alive, with me replacing his soul. What of all those other sons and daughters who died for your pride?"

"If that kept me up at night," Nosmada replied, "then I'd not have been able to do it."

"I understand. I just wondered if it ever occurred to you."

He nodded. "Of course. But tell me, demon, if you're so wise to the mind of God ... what does he want? If not this, then what?"

"What does any father want? Love. Love Him, the way you love yourself."

"That simple?"

"Like you loved your son."

Sighing, Nosmada got to his knees and clasped his hands together. He turned away from Fallon and looked up at the sky. Then he bowed his head and took a breath. Before he could speak, something punched him in the back. He opened his eyes and glanced down. A sword tip stuck out of his chest. Not blinking, he gaped. Then the pain rushed in. He gasped for air and choked on own blood.

The blade withdrew, and Nosmada fell to his side. He flopped over onto his back and looked up at the tall man standing over him. His eyes widened in recognition. Mouth open, he fought for words.

"Y-you ..."

"No one will ever know I stabbed you in the back," Rogan told him. "We are alone."

Nosmada realized that Fallon had disappeared.

"C-coward ..." Nosmada coughed.

"Why? Because I stabbed you in the back?" Shrugging, Rogan raised his sword high. "So I did. I don't have time to fuck around. I'm tired, Cain. I want to get out of here. And I'm too old to get caught up in some prideful fight to the death with you."

"Not ... Cain. I am ... Nosmada."

Rogan shrugged again. "Any last words?"

Nosmada turned away from Rogan and looked at the sky. "I ... love you."

Rogan drove the sword down.

***

"Where is the exit?" Kenoth yelled at the old woman.

They were clustered together in an open-air room near the top of the tower.

"Have a care," Ivor admonished him. "She's ancient, Kenoth. Older than me."

Seth, who held the end of a knotted rope that bound the crone's hands behind her back, hissed at Ivor.

"She was raising her hands to conjure," Kenoth explained.

Nodding, Ivor leaned close. "Zillian, tell us where the murder hole is. I'm certain your master has one."

"You have nothing I want," she replied. "Let the devils take you all when the barriers break."

"Very well." Ivor sighed. "You two lads kill her. But be quick about it. Lop her head off when you are done, and her hands. Scatter them so that they cannot be rejoined."

"Are you sure, Oracle?"

Ivor nodded. "She will never tell us."

He walked away as Kenoth and Seth closed in on their prisoner. She gave one squawk and was then silent. Ivor did not turn to see. Instead, he started down a staircase. Soon, he heard footsteps and found Javan hurrying up the stairs to him.

"With the tower cleared," the youth suggested, "perhaps we should see how my uncle fares in the funnel?"

"There is no need."

Ivor pointed as Rogan and Roan ascended from below. Roan was dressed in bloodstained dragon skin armor, and Rogan held aloft the severed head of the Lord of Nodd. Curiously, the cursed mark that had always marred the flesh of his forehead was gone.

"You slew him," Javan gasped.

"Your grasp of the obvious is perfect as usual, nephew."

"But the curse ...?"

"Not the first time I've beaten one."

Rogan weaved past them on the staircase. Kenoth and Seth gaped in astonishment when they saw his grisly prize.

"Zillian dead, too?" Rogan asked.

Kenoth nodded.

"Good."

Rogan walked out onto the balcony. Javan, Roan, and Ivor joined him.

"More fires down below," Rogan observed.

"Altars," Ivor explained. "Both official and impromptu. The people of this city have been the victims of so many different horrors today, and of so much conflicting subterfuge, that they are confused and panicked … driven by fear. They are sacrificing to any god they can think of in their terror."

"They'll come for us soon," Javan said. "The soldiers will check this place when they don't receive new orders."

"Then let me give them a scare."

Rogan took a deep breath and bellowed. His cry boomed over the city. Below, the people stopped scurrying and fighting and turned their attention upward. Clutching it by the hair, Rogan raised Nosmada's head high. For a long time, the people stared. A few raised field scopes to confirm what Rogan held. Then, the shouts began. They didn't flee in terror, nor did they cry out in jubilation.

Kenoth peered over the balcony. "I think you made things worse."

Rogan lowered the head. "Can't please everyone."

"Sire," Javan said, "perhaps the lord of this city was better loved than we thought."

"What happens to them now?" Ivor asked. "A city with no leader, a realm with no lord."

"Like an oracle without a god," Rogan teased.

"You revered Wodan as well," Ivor reminded him.

"I don't know what I believe anymore. At my age, after all I've seen and done, you would think I'd have insight, but I don't. You want to know what I think, Ivor? We know what a selfish prick Wodan is. I think all this time, we've been worshipping one of the fallen—a demon who reinvented himself as Wodan. And our people were stupid enough to fall for it. I think this entire thing was a way for him to get free. The dragon thing, well, that was gravy. I reckon he planned to walk out of here in Thaxter's body, or, hell, maybe in my own."

"As much as I love a good theological debate," Javan reminded them, "the crowd are growing more restless."

"He's right," Roan said. "You two stand around bickering like old women while the mob begins to move on us."

"No escape route found?" Rogan asked, and was met with silence. "Well, fuck me sideways."

"We could go to the bowels of this place," Roan suggested, "and try to find a way out."

Rogan watched the masses grow in the streets below. "We will die like rats in a tunnel if we do."

She gaped at him. "Then how?"

"We go down and make our stand. We can't live forever. Nobody can."

Trumpets rang out below.

Javan notched an arrow. "Are we ready?"

"Yeah." Rogan smiled. "I am. Roan, you fight better than most. And you lead better than most. Get on your daddy's horse and lead your forces into battle."

"I don't need your approval, barbarian."

"I'm not the barbarian," Rogan replied. "The barbarians are at the gate. Let us go meet them."

CHAPTER 14

GOD'S GONNA CUT YOU DOWN

Their forces gathered in the courtyard and watched as Rogan walked toward the gate. None of them spoke. The clamor of the crowd outside would have drowned them out if they had. Horns and trumpets signaled, and soldiers and civilians howled for blood.

Rogan reached the metal gate and stared out across the moat. A platoon of soldiers on horseback arrived, forcing their way forward. In the distance, he saw a company of troops marching on their location.

"Yeah," he whispered. "This is truly where I die."

He checked the sun and saw that it wasn't yet noon. Then his gaze sought out and found Javan. His nephew winked at him. Stiffening, Rogan paused for a moment. Then he saluted the young man.

"Are we going to die?" Kenoth asked.

Rogan turned to the assemblage and raised his voice so that he could be heard over the mob. "Yes, you are going to die. But you all had that on your schedule since the day you were born. Every day is a step closer to death, and this is the final one. But how shall you die? Will you go out like Nosmada, crying and scared? Or will you die like Goria La Gaul, whose daughter leads you now, determined and unafraid? Decide now, because death is here."

Rogan turned his back to them and strode to the guard booth. He threw a lever, and the drawbridge started to lower to the baying crowd across the way.

"I know how I shall die," Rogan shouted over the cacophony. "I shall die first!"

The bridge touched down, but the crowd drew back from it.

Rogan unlocked the gates and shoved them open. He tensed.

Still, the mob did not charge.

"You see?" he gestured. "They lack the balls to take a step."

Then Rogan realized that the crowd was pointing to the sky. A great collective gasp echoed among them and was repeated by Roan's forces. A huge shadow fell over them all, blocking out the sun.

The dragon roared.

Rogan answered in kind. "*WODAN!*"

Sword upraised, he ran forward through the gates and out onto the bridge. Roan, resplendent in her armor, galloped after him astride Traveler. Angeline, Kenoth, Javan, Seth, Ivor, Martel, and the others charged along in their wake.

The dragon descended to a few yards above the throng of citizens and soldiery. Each flap of its wings knocked the shingles from rooftops. It opened its maw and belched a burst of blinding yellow flame. Its long neck snaked back and forth, and the fiery stream grew more robust as it bathed the crowd. The fire flowed across the populace like lava, coating them and melting them onto the stone streets in boiling, waxen globs.

When the barbarians struck the confused masses outside the moat in a wedge, their chaotic line broke. Too concerned with the dragon setting the population afire behind them, the masses panicked, scrambling as the bloodthirsty force slammed into their midst. Few had the will to fight back as Rogan and Roan and their forces cut through them.

The dragon rotated in the sky and unleashed another rain of fire on the towers and spires of the city.

The group fought on, but the resistance had peeled away. They made it to the first of the inner walls to where the long gates made of solid metal were closed.

Kenoth slammed into the gates, fumbling with the bar clasp across the handles. Rogan grabbed the youth and pulled him out of the way. He swung his blade in an overhand arc, smashing through the restraining bar. The blade stuck in the slight gap between the gates. Boot on the gate, Rogan roared as he pulled the weapon free. As he staggered back, Ivor stepped up and flung the gates open.

The dragon spun downward and unleashed another volley of flame, consuming the people outside the gate. The backwash knocked Ivor backward. Angeline and Martel ran to him, patting his smoking clothing. Ivor waved them away and got to his feet.

"You gonna make it, you old prick?"

Ivor winked at Rogan. "The smell of those people cooking ..."

"Yeah?"

"I'm hungry."

Rogan smiled. "Then let's press on."

Angeline peered through the opening. "The dragon has burned all of them out!"

Roan pulled her helmet off. "Damn ... the stench."

They walked through the gates and stepped over the still sizzling corpses. All around them, the fires crackled. Buildings collapsed in billowing clouds of dust. People screamed. The smoke rose and formed a haze over the city.

Hyden pointed into the air. "The spirits flee this place."

"Demons aren't stupid," Roan replied. "Even they know to run away from a dragon."

The dragon spun about and roared again—one word. Its name. Then it turned away and flew north.

Weeping, Ivor fell to his knees and held up his arms in praise.

Angeline said, "That expression on the dragon's face ..."

"He didn't do any of this for us," Rogan argued. "He did it for himself."

"Of course he did." Ivor got to his feet again. "He doesn't care about us."

Javan shook his head. "That's some god."

Rogan looked north, watching as Wodan disappeared. "Yeah."

The group moved through the city but was met with no further resistance. Though fearing the worst, they were surprised to find the caravan wagons and steeds intact and unburned.

As Kenoth and Seth liberated more mounts from the stables, Rogan elbowed Javan. "I'm glad we have horses," he said. "I'd hate to have to take Traveler from Roan."

Roan leered at him. "You're welcome to try, old man."

"I'm too tired," Rogan groaned and then turned serious. "What will you do now?"

"I shall gather what remains of my forces and strike west," she replied. "There are kings and queens that need fighting folk."

"I don't really care," Rogan told her. "I was just asking because Javan tells me I should try to be more polite and civilized. Ride up the devil's asshole and like it."

Roan smiled. "I'd have let you all die to get this armor back and see Nosmada punished. But I'm glad you are alive."

Nodding, Rogan waved. "Thanks. Now fuck off. I never want to see you again."

Roan reeled Traveler about. "Pray that you do not."

"Be a long time before I pray again."

While Kenoth, Seth, and the others followed their leader, Angeline lingered. She reigned her horse next to Rogan and Javan.

"What is it?" Rogan wondered.

"It was great fighting beside you." She saluted.

"You as well, young lady," he replied, smiling. "Watch your ass following her."

"Actually," Angeline said, "I was hoping to come with you all. Javan told me I should ask."

Rogan smirked. He looked at her for a long time. "Won't that break Kenoth's heart?"

"It's going to get broken someday anyhow. Besides, without Thaxter, who will fill the void as your right-hand man?"

"There are a lot of piss poor prospects." Rogan playfully punched Javan's shoulder. "Yeah, I have no problem with it, and I don't care to hear Javan lamenting if I don't let you come. But I don't know what's next."

"I don't care. Wherever it is, I'm happy to accompany you."

"Good. But I'm a feeble old man. It might take longer to get there."

Angeline laughed. "Then so be it."

Ivor and his wives rattled by in the oracle's cart. Martel sat beside her father

"Speaking of feeble old men," Rogan called out, "back to home, I take it?"

Ivor nodded, grimacing with pain.

"Getting too old for battle?" Rogan teased.

"I am." His tone was serious. "I want to spend time with my wives and my daughter. My work is done."

"Fare you well, Ivor."

"Till we meet again."

Rogan smiled and they shook right hands. "We'll see."

Javan led Rogan's horse over to him and offered the reins. "Too bad you couldn't have had Traveler."

"Helluva horse, mystical or no."

"Indeed, sire."

Back in the saddle, Rogan sighed and looked over the city.

"Too bad the rest of our forces are still back in Gorias La Gaul's home village. We could have looted the place."

"We still can, uncle."

"Perhaps. But first I need some sleep."

EPILOGUE

Now I'm Here

Rogan walked out of the abode of Gorias La Gaul. For two nights, he'd slept in the legend's bed. He sat on the porch and waved to Javan as he walked up.

"Good morning, sire. Where to now?"

Rogan gazed out at the sky and ruins of the town. "Ever been to the east?"

"No, sire."

"It's a warm place, but not too bad. They have women there who can make you spill your seed just by looking at you."

Javan pondered this. "That must make for a messy marketplace, sire."

"I went there years ago."

"I thought ..."

"What?"

Javan shrugged. "That you were looking for a place to ... retire?"

"Nodd wasn't the sword with my name on it. Even Gorias couldn't sit on his porch forever. He met his fate in Larak, the story goes, and he wasn't retired. So, no. I'm not retiring."

"Very well."

"But Javan ... you don't have to come with me."

"Where else would I go, uncle?"

"I don't know. I just figured you might have something better to do than follow an old bastard like me around."

"Perhaps, someday, but not at the moment. And where I go, Angeline goes."

Rogan smiled and rubbed his beard. "All right. Then we shall leave on the morrow. Tonight, we will eat, drink, and tell good yarns."

"Always come evening, that happens," Javan smiled. "I'll see you then, sire."

Rogan sat back in the chair of the legend in a place that might be mistaken for his own someday. "It will be a good life, Javan. For however long I have left."

"Sire?"

Rogan smiled. "Good enough."

No dreams for me, just roaming free ...
Red wine and battles roar;
I'll breast the gales and ride the trails ...
'til I can ride ... no more.

— ROBERT E. HOWARD

ACKNOWLEDGMENTS

Our thanks to Paul Goblirsch and Thunderstorm Books; Jason Sizemore, Lesley Conner, and Apex Book Company; Charles Rutledge; Mark Sylva, Tod Clark, and Stephen McDornell.

Steven: Thank you to my family. Also, to Stephen Zimmer, Joe R. Lansdale, Brady Allen, Bob Freeman, Peter Welmerink, Angie Hawkes Fulbright, John Skipp, Kristin Staggs, David Barnett, Julie Lauth, Christine Whitehead, and Cody Goodfellow.

Brian: Thanks to Steven, Mary SanGiovanni, Cassandra Burnham, Dave Thomas, Mike Lombardo, and Stephen Kozeniewski.

ABOUT THE AUTHORS

STEVEN L. SHREWSBURY lives, works, and writes in rural Illinois. Over three hundred and sixty of his short stories have been published in print or electronically, along with over one hundred poems. His novels include *Godforsaken, Overkill, Thrall, Bedlam Unleashed, Hawg, Tormentor, Stronger Than Death, Hell Billy, Bag Magick*, and many more—all running the gamut from sword and sorcery to historical fantasy to horror. A husband and father, he loves books, British television programs, guns, movies, politics, sports, and hanging out with his family. He looks for brightness wherever it may hide.

BRIAN KEENE writes novels, comic books, short fiction, and occasional journalism for money. He is the author of over fifty books, mostly in the horror, crime, and dark fantasy genres. His 2003 novel, *The Rising*, is often credited with inspiring pop culture's current interest in zombies. He has won numerous awards and honors, including the 2014 World Horror Grandmaster Award, 2001 Bram Stoker Award for Nonfiction, 2003 Bram Stoker Award for First Novel, 2004 Shocker Award for Book of the Year, and Honors from United States Army International Security Assistance Force in Afghanistan and Whiteman A.F.B. (home of the B-2 Stealth Bomber) 509th Logistics Fuels Flight. The father of two sons, Keene lives in rural Pennsylvania.

THE COMPLETE ROGAN SAGA